FORGIVING BERNADETTE

Charlotte Ashby

GW00374464

For Jimmy, Jude & Leila

1

Nothing makes us so lonely as our secrets.
Paul Tournier

It's funny how courage is often portrayed. An epic struggle, bloodshed and battle, running blindly through a spray of bullets. But sometimes the bravest thing of all, is the simple act of getting out of bed.

You get up, put on the kettle, pick up the dirty underwear from behind the door, scrape the ice off the windscreen, prepare to submit to life's tedious routines. And then one day you can't.

***

The police had taped off a large holding area to keep the watching crowd at bay. There was quite a festival atmosphere, blue lights flashing, splashes of colourful wet weather gear and the throb of the helicopter blades above. News travels fast in a town like Lower Hinton, especially bad news.

If it hadn't been for the commotion at the foot of the hill, you might not even have noticed two very distant matchstick figures. A couple of tiny, brightly coloured specks, suspended half way up a rocky promontory, with no obvious sign how they had got there. You couldn't miss them now though, a searchlight trained on them in the fading light and the massed ranks of emergency services camped out below: three ambulances, five TV crews, four police cars, about 150 'passers by' and an RAF Search & Rescue helicopter.

Standing next to the red and white tape, a TV reporter blotted her nose with a tissue and reapplied blood red lipstick. It was starting to rain again and tiny droplets formed on her stiffly lacquered blonde hair.

She adjusted her expression, a slight frown for a fraction more sincerity as she stared intently into the camera. This was a really big chance for her. The studio counted her in.

…three, two, one, you're live on air…

Good Evening Declan, we're getting reports now that a woman in her late 40s and a teenage girl appear to be clinging on to a rocky outcrop suspended 300 feet above the town and known locally as Devil's Chimney. They were spotted about two hours ago by a group of walkers. It appears that torrential rain has caused the cliff to literally collapse under them, leaving the pair trapped on a shallow ledge about 200 feet above the ground, with nothing but a sheer drop beneath them.

Pausing for dramatic effect.

Declan they are literally holding on for their lives and the weather is deteriorating rapidly. As you can see behind me, ambulances have started to arrive, RAF search and rescue are attempting to reach the pair, so far unsuccessfully…

Thanks Katy, can you tell us anything about the two people involved….

We don't know what they were doing up here. As far as we know the pair are unrelated. The older woman appears to be wearing some sort of animal print fancy dress, possibly a leopard outfit and the younger woman is wearing a bright yellow, lace party dress. Whether this is some sort of dare or protest gone wrong, it's unclear at this stage. We've had unconfirmed reports that the older woman is Bernadette Spicer known locally as Bo. Earlier I spoke to some of her neighbours...

A ruddy faced couple in their 50s appeared on screen. They stood very close to each other, wearing identical hi-vis jackets and cycling helmets. It appeared the husband had been nominated to do the talking, while wife nodded vigorously in agreement.

She's very quiet, you know, we don't know much about her. Doesn't really mix much with the rest of the village, now that her son has left home.

And that appeared to be it, until the wife, evidently feeling that her husband had missed something important, leant forwards towards the camera.

We did hear that her husband has been... seeing another woman... quite a lot younger apparently...

The TV reporter raised an eyebrow before turning to face the camera...sincere expression again...

Why on the wettest day since records began, did these two women choose to climb one of the highest peaks in the area in what appear to be party outfits? Is this a protest, did they intend to attract public attention or could this be some sort of bizarre suicide pact, we just don't know Declan. The light is failing and rescue teams are working against the clock to reach them before nightfall. A search light has been trained on the stricken pair, but the cliff is extremely unstable and as the weather worsens, the outcome remains far from certain. Declan.

Thank you, Katy. That was Katy Partridge reporting from Lower Hinton, Dewsbury, where two women are stranded on a cliff face after heavy rainfall caused a local landmark to give way. We'll keep you updated throughout the programme on the dramatic events unfolding in the small town of Lower Hinton in Wiltshire. As flood alerts are issued across the UK, here's Liam with the latest weather report.

The crowd gasped as a large piece of rock dislodged itself just above the stranded pair, missing them by inches and shattering on the cliff a few feet below. The relentless rain had transformed this once benign beauty spot. A craggy outlook favoured by walkers for its unbroken views across the Wiltshire downs was now a sheer, greasy precipice, lashed continually by the heavy downpour.

The tiny figures appeared to be clamped on, spread eagled on the rockface, one slightly higher than the other.

A local newspaper cameraman trained his lens on the face of the older woman, who turned her head very slightly and glanced tentatively down to see where the rock had shattered. As she leant over, her leg missed its footing and he could just see her mouthing the words 'Fucking hell' as she struggled to right herself.

'Oh my God we're going to die, oh my God, we're going to die, oh my God we're going to…'

'Just shut up will you!' The older woman mouthed at the girl. 'If you get hysterical you'll kill us both.'

'You said you didn't care about living.'

'Maybe I don't, but I'm sure as hell not going to die like this, not now, in a nylon onesie, two stone over weight, with all of them watching. Can you see how many people are down there? I haven't got my contacts in. It just looks like a blur to me.'

'At least a hundred people and police and oh my God, TV. And two ambulances.'

They both went quiet for a minute at the thought of the two ambulances, just the sound of their heavy breath, then the helicopter throbbing overhead as it swooped in above them once again.

The older woman squinted. 'Do you think they can reach us?'

The vibration of the blades caused a few more rocks to dislodge and crash down beside them. The younger woman began to cry. 'This is all my fault. You didn't even know me. If you hadn't looked out of your window, you'd still be in bed watching telly.'

'Yes well, there was nothing on.' They both started to laugh slightly hysterically.

The two of them looked up as the helicopter tried to descend again, sending more stones flying. Neither woman saw the large chunk of rock break off from the top of the cliff and hurtle down until the second it hit them. Smacking the younger woman on the back of the neck and sending them both flying down the cliff edge, flailing limbs, screaming for their lives. Seconds away from impact, the older woman grabbed a branch and locked her arms around it. She looked down to see the younger woman who was caught, wedged between her legs, a piece of her torn yellow dress was hooked onto a thin branch offering some support, but the rest of her weight was between her knees, dragging her down and threatening to send them both plummeting to their deaths.

The younger woman was no longer conscious, blood dripping from a cut on the back of her neck.

Oh please God, I want to live so much. If I can just hold on, keep my knees together, don't move. Oh please God, don't let me die now. The pain in her arms was excruciating, her face pressed right against the branch. She looked down to see the lifeless body, hanging off the branch, head and shoulders gripped between her thighs like some bizarre birth scene. The helicopter swooped down and she could just make out the blur of a man leaning out of the door. 'Listen to me love! I'm going to throw you a harness. But you're going to have to let go of her.' Bo let out a scream.

He shouted again above the noise of the blades. 'Let her go love! She's gone, let her go!'

The helicopter swooped off and back again. She could see his blurred face again. 'When I count to 3, I want you to let her go.'

Bo took a deep breath and shouted back at the blurred figure. 'I will not.'

'She's gone love. I can clip you on in a few seconds. You can't hold on much longer. Just let go!'

'I said I will not'. Bo didn't recognize her own voice as she spoke. The helicopter moved again and the man disappeared. She was left alone, waiting quietly for the inevitable moment when her arms and thighs could no longer take the pain. She looked down at the body beneath her. 'I won't let you go.' She began to weep and tears and rain ran off her nose and chin.

The blurred man had gone and she had missed her chance at life. The body she was propping up between her knees was drained of blood, a bluey white pall, but she was unable to let go, like a mother clinging to her dead baby. She could see her own mother's face.

The throbbing blades again. She couldn't look up, but this time, the blurred man was suspended a few feet from her by a harness. A miracle, from nowhere, he was right there next to her, fitting a harness around the lifeless girl and shouting again. 'I will be two minutes. Two minutes and I'm coming back for you. Can you hang on for that long? Nod if you understand.' She nodded wordlessly as he clipped the harness to his own and released the body from under her. She couldn't even look up as they hovered overhead. Two minutes to live, two minutes. Her arms no longer felt any pain, there was no muscle, she could feel nothing, two minutes. She began to count...

120, 119, 118, 117, 116, 115, 114, 113

2

4 hours earlier...

You get up, put on the kettle, pick up the dirty underwear from behind the door, scrape the ice off the windscreen, prepare to submit to life's tedious routines. And then one day you can't.

I can't do this anymore. The courage to get out of bed had finally eluded her.

She looked at the pizza box, two empty bottles of Pinot Grigio and the half eaten packet of Jaffa cakes on her bedside table. She couldn't remember when she'd started to fantasize about killing Neil. Lately it had become something of a hobby.

She watched expressionless as a fly landed on the jaffa cakes. She brushed it off and ate it anyway. It's strange to feel absolutely nothing, except a dull nagging anxiety sitting in its usual place just above her belly button, only lately it had begun to feel more like terror. Through her velour onesie, she stared unblinking at the fold of flesh spilling out over her knickers. The hairs on her legs formed a fringe under the elasticated ankles, a centimetre long at least, chipped purple nail varnish on the ends of her toes.

She wanted to turn the TV channel over to get this annoying, chirpy wildlife presenter off the screen, but that would have required her getting out of bed.

The telephone rang.

Bernadette will you pick up the phone, just pick up will you. I phoned your work and they said you're off sick. Are you actually sick or are you having another one of your turns? Have you been reading that bloody letter again? Look, will you just pick up and put down for feck's sake, just so I know you're alive. Bernadette Maloney!

It was her cousin Lois. She never used Bo's married name, on account of her contempt for Neil. She would go away eventually but it made Bo feel bad to listen to her pleading. And she was right of course, she had read the letter, taken it from the back of the drawer under the bed, in the box where Neil wouldn't find it. It was there with the death certificate, in the shoe box where she had kept it now for 21 years. She knew it always brought it all back, opening up that box, but she couldn't help herself. Right now all she wanted was to be left alone, for everyone to just piss off.

How do you know if you are having a nervous breakdown anyway. She had googled it. Loss of interest in sex – tick, loss of interest in hobbies and work – tick, feeling that even the smallest task is too difficult to attempt – tick, feeling guilty or pathetic – tick, loss of interest in food – unfortunately not. What might she add…inability to stop watching the Jeremy Kyle show, even though it promotes feelings of shame and low self worth - tick. Wearing a leopard print onesie that is clearly intended for a size 8 teenager - tick, telling your boss that you are menopausal and won't be coming in for a while - tick, and yes, fantasizing about how you would dispose of your husband's body having dispatched him with a fatal quantity of pesticide, … 200 milligrams of highly concentrated organophosphate. She had googled it, God forgive her…

Neil was away at a sales conference, at least that's what he had said. She didn't actually care enough to check.

I hate myself. But it was more accurate to say that she just didn't care any more about anyone or anything – *I'm dead inside* – she said it out loud and instantly felt like an idiot.

Neil Spicer. Formerly my saviour, love of my life. And ironically she hadn't even liked him at college, thought he was a terrible show off. She had studied History and Economics at University and look at her now. He was at the local poly doing business studies. He had been the one doing the chasing. And now here she was, a spent sack of flesh, asexual, sapped, wasted and lifeless, a husk. Bernadette and Neil, such a fun couple. She had given birth to his child, picked his pants up off the floor, worried about his vegetable intake, monitored his cholesterol levels, made him tea, sent his mother flowers on her birthday and now the life was entirely sucked out of her. And they always say the wife is the last to know.

She burped and surprised herself at the force of it, a faint waft of stale white wine and Jaffa orange. Dear God what had become of her!

But she wasn't really the last to know was she, because it was obvious if she'd cared to think about it. And if she had never seen the note pushed under her door, she might not have had to confront the truth of it, but somebody had decided to tell her. Some busy body had scrawled the bare facts on a little scrap of paper and shoved it under her kitchen door 'Mandy Edwards is screwing your husband.' There it was, on a little torn off piece of lined paper, now scrunched up in an angry ball in her handbag.

Was it more shocking that somebody had decided to involve themselves in her business, creep around to the back of her house and push this under the door. Or perhaps it was the fact that the note declared that her husband of 21 years was having sex with their former babysitter, 20 years his junior. Mandy Edwards. She tried to work it out. Mandy could only have been 16 the last time she had babysat Liam. Please God say he wasn't shagging her then. 'I'm just going to walk Mandy home.' Oh God no! 'Did you know Mandy speaks fluent Spanish.' Really!

And there was that time he had come bounding up the stairs like an overexcited puppy. 'Did you know Mandy can do the splits!' 'Well, good for her.' Thinking about it now, she felt a wave of nausea and her upper body flushed bright pink.

Her iPad flashed up a message. You have 8 Facebook notifications. What? She didn't even post on Facebook. Scrolling down the newsfeed she scanned through the usual smug updates.

Talia Grossman is in the British Airways First Class Lounge
7 hours ago

18 comments

Where are you going sweetie?
Maldives! Absolute bliss!
Have a fab time hun!
Heavenly…
Lucky lady!

Bernadette Spicer commented
Thanks for sharing Talia, wow first class. Good luck on the flight, let's hope it's not an Airbus 320! *6 likes*

Congratulations Holly Edwards Distinction on your Grade 6 violin, proud mumma! #lovemykids

7 hours ago

7 comments

You go girl!
Awesome!
So proud!
Well done Hols!

Bernadette Spicer commented
Let's hear it for the most competitive mother in Wiltshire! Smiley face, LOL!!!!!

Jane Ann Harvey sent you a friend request

6 hours ago

Bernadette Spicer commented
I'd love to be your friend but I don't actually know who you are.

Janey Hicks shared a link

6 hours ago

Animals do the funniest things – 'This house is maintained entirely for the comfort and convenience of the dog!' *26 likes*

Bernadette Spicer commented
Ha ha hilarious, that's so funny I think I just wet myself, NOT! *1 like*

Debs Martin shared a link

6 hours ago

Friendships are the foundation of a fulfilled life. Amazing restaurant, fab food, wonderful friends #feelingblessed *14 likes*

Bernadette Spicer commented

Can someone tell me how I unsubscribe from this smug shite please!!!!

Debs Martin

Hi Bernadette, I'm sorry you feel that way. It's simple enough to unfollow or block if you don't wish to receive my posts *56 likes*

Davina Edgerton-Davis has changed her profile picture

5 hours ago

13 likes   8 comments

Stunning!
Amazing, gorgeous girl!
Love, love, love you hun!

Bernadette Spicer commented

Wot ANOTHER profile picture - you spoil us Davina! GORGE!! Gush, puke…smiley face!

There was a definite change in tone at 3am, probably around the time she'd finished off the second bottle of Pinot.

Ali Watson - Arrived in Verbier this morning - absolute dump last night! Perfect powder, wonderful friends, mountain top restaurant, vin chaud on order – bring it on!!!!

3 hours ago

Bernadette Spicer commented:
I had a dump last night. No one cares Ali.

Scrolling desperately down, she counted 26 Facebook friends she had abused between the hours of midnight and 3.20am.

She put her head in her hands. Dear God, what was she going to do. The only saving grace was that none of them were actually her friends. She was sweating profusely inside the viscose lining. Just close your eyes, control your breathing, go to sleep and let it all drift away.

She reached for the interiors magazine on her bedside table, knowing it would offer little solace. 25 homes that are nicer than yours: smug looking housewives talking about their perfect country kitchen, with their bloody breakfast bars and perfectly placed pendant lights. Did it make you a misfit if you didn't really care about breakfast bars? *Five things to do with driftwood.* She'd give them five feckin things to do with driftwood. *Jamie and Samantha were desperate for more storage space. Lucy and David wanted to bring the outside in.* Bloody hell. Bloody people with their bloody scented candles. *Be inspired by Deborah's coastal look!* A house littered with lighthouse cushions and wooden fish. This wasn't helping at all.

The only thing about lying in bed, eating Jaffa cakes and drinking a litre of diet coke in a state of torpid self pity, is that it does require frequent trips to the lavatory.

The urge became too pressing and she swung her legs over the side of the bed and shuffled down the corridor. The house was in an appalling state. Discarded underwear, odd shoes and wet towels lay scattered over the floor, a thick layer of dust on every surface and cobwebs hung from the hallway light fitting. Their son Liam had left to go travelling six months ago. She hadn't really cleaned the house since then. It was the house of someone who could just about make it to work, washed and in a clean outfit, but no more than that. The hallway window was steamed up and she wiped a hole in the condensation.

On the other side of the road, Davina Edgerton Davis swung out of the gates of the Old Rectory in a brand new Range Rover, number plate DAV1 V8. She wore large bug-eye sunglasses in spite of the gloom, probably off to a tennis lesson or to have some part of her body waxed or threaded. Davina had the word 'family' spelt out in large, gold letters above her Aga. She would no doubt have written a long list for the Filipino help to be getting on with. Bo wondered if she'd had time to look at Facebook yet. The ruddy faced, wholesome couple from the top of the lane were power walking past in hi-vis jackets. Dressed as usual for some sort of vigorous outdoor pursuit, sandblasted faces set in a smug half smile. She smiled and waved but they didn't see her and marched on.

It was a dismal day thank goodness. You wouldn't have a clue if it was dusk or dawn. How much worse to have been battling shame and melancholy with the sound of birdsong and lawnmowers outside. The rain had stopped briefly. A low hanging cloud clung to the top of the hillside in the distance.

She narrowed her eyes as she looked through the clear circle, even with her blurred vision she could just make out a bright yellow speck at the top of the hill. She squinted but still couldn't identify the unnaturally vivid, almost fluorescent shape. It must be two thirds of the way up the hillside on the path that led up to Devil's Chimney. She squinted again, it didn't seem to move. It couldn't be an animal, quite big though, what on earth was it? She walked down the stairs. The kitchen looked like it had been ransacked. The cat litter was brimming over under the kitchen window. She ignored it and pulled on a pair of purple wellington boots. Standing at the end of the garden, she could still see the luminous yellow shape, more of a streak now and drawing her closer as she walked to the bottom of the orchard, opened the garden gate and strode up the path.

It was spitting with rain but it felt good to be outside, walking purposefully up the hill. The rain had turned the dusty track to mud and she was out of breath from the unaccustomed exercise. The ground started to rise steeply and she picked her way up the rocky path, a sharp incline as it snaked around the hill.

The yellow flash was gone for a moment as she rounded the peak, then there it was again as she turned another corner. The path was narrower than she remembered, littered with scree and boulders either side. Her wellington boots weren't helping her progress as she slipped on wet rocks.

It must have taken ten minutes of uphill walking before she rounded the top of the hill. She stopped a moment to catch her breath. You could see the whole of Lower Hinton spread out below, but Bo could make out very little without her contacts in. She was panting and could barely speak as she turned the last bend and could finally make out the mysterious, incandescent body.

It was a young girl, perched on top of a rock jutting out over the edge of the hillside, no more than 17 years old. She clutched her knees under her chin and Bo could tell she had been crying. Her bright yellow lace dress was torn and muddy and her feet were bare. She clutched an iPhone in her left hand and a pair of very high black shoes were abandoned at the foot of the rock. She didn't even look round when Bo approached, but it was obvious she knew she was there.

'Oh hello.' It wasn't much of an opener, but Bo hadn't prepared for the fluorescent blob being a real person.

She didn't answer or look round.

'Hello there!' Now she felt really stupid. 'What are you doing up there?'

'Nothing,' standard teenage response, but a response at least.

'Have you been out all night?'

'What does it look like?' At last the girl lifted her head and turned to Bo. She looked slightly startled.

'Don't you think you should come down from there. It's actually a bit dangerous.'

No answer.

'Do you want to tell me what happened?'

'No.'

Bo stood for a moment, arms folded looking out across the downs. It was starting to drizzle again and she didn't exactly know what to do next.

'OK, well I'll just leave you to it shall I? It's about to piss down and as you may have noticed, I'm not exactly dressed for the outdoors either.' She turned away as if to leave.

'Why are you dressed like that anyway?' The girl was sitting up, slightly more animated now.

'Oh this?' Bo turned round. 'It's a long story. I suppose you'd call it a mid-life crisis. I've just found out my husband is shagging our old babysitter, I'm about to lose my job, I've put on two stone, I stayed up all night drinking wine, wrote 26 abusive Facebook posts. Oh and I haven't really managed to get up today at all really, except to go to the loo, which is when I spotted you up here.'

'Shit!'

'Yes, shit!'

'Do you want to come up here?'

Bo smiled and looked up at her. 'Why not.' There was a slightly undignified tussle as they both struggled to pull her up the slippery rock and she willingly took the hand the girl offered her. They sat side by side and stared in silence across the grey landscape for a little while.

Bo broke the silence. 'So, you tell me why you're up here first.'

'Oh OK. Well there's this lad, Dave from my estate who made out like he really fancied me, but it turns out he was only doing it for a laugh, him and this group of girls that hate me. Do you know what cyberbullies are?' Bo nodded. 'Well they send me messages and stuff and now they've set up an instagram account in my name so that they can post all this shit about me.'

'Oh right. And why are you up here then?'

'Well I was out in Izzy's in Brinton with some other girls and we saw them at the bar. They followed me into the toilet and said I was ugly and a lesbian.'

'And are you?'

'What? Ugly?'

'No, a lesbian.'

'No I'm fucking not.'

'Well there's no need to be like that. It's perfectly acceptable to be a lesbian these days, actually very cool. I mean look at Mary Portas and Claire Balding.'

'Who?' She looked at Bo like she was mad.

'Sue Perkins? Used to be on Bake Off? She's a lesbian.'

'Look I'm not a lesbian!'

'OK sorry, calm down. Well you're not ugly I can tell you that.'

'Fuck off, are you a lesbian or something?'

'No I'm feckin not. I'm married with a 19 year old son.'

They sat in silence again, both staring straight ahead. 'Let's have a look.' Bo reached across and gestured for her to pass her phone. She scrolled through the messages.

'Blimey I see what you mean. They've been busy haven't they? So how many girls are there in this little mob?'

'Three.'

'Is that all?' The girl didn't respond. 'And why did you come up here?'

'I don't know, to get away, maybe I was planning to jump off or something.'

'I see. Well no I don't actually. I mean jump off? Really?' Bo frowned. 'Some boy wanted to go out with you, you turn him down and now he's calling you ugly and a lesbian and sending you abusive messages.'

'Yes.'

'And you thought you'd end it all by jumping off a rock.'

'Yes.'

'Let's have a look at their posts then? Show me what they've actually been saying.'

The girl scrolled down the screen and handed it back to Bo. She squinted and held it away from her face to get a better focus. She had expected to see abusive words, but instead it was a jumble of meaningless letters. 'What on earth's this? Jesus, you'd have to have worked at Bletchley Park to crack any of this?'

'Pardon?'

'Forget it. What does IKR mean anyway?'

'I know right.'

'What about IYKWIM?'

'If you know what I mean.'

'JSYK?'

'Just so you know.'

'But what on earth's the point of bothering to say 'If you know what I mean?' What's this one? I know OMG, what's ZOMG?'

'That's sarcastic for OMG'

'NMU?'

'Not much you?'

'Let me guess, presumably in response to the equally fascinating, WYUP2?'

'Yeah that's right.' The girl looked reasonably impressed.

'Jesus wept, of course it is.' Bo started to laugh. 'This is moronic. None of them can even spell. Look at this one! You can't be upset by someone who can't spell 'frigid.' He's saying you're 'fridged!' I mean technically he's accusing you of being in a fridge. Message him back and say you're waiting for him in the vegetable drawer!'

'Shut up will you.' The girl snatched her phone back.

Bo laughed. 'Well I'm off then. I'm freezing my nuts off out here. I'd stay and chat if I thought there was anything I could say to help. If you're seriously going to give a toss what some loser thinks of you, there's not much I can say. You're extremely pretty which I imagine is what started all of this in the first place. Your life will most likely be plagued by little wankers.' Bo prepared to slither off the rock. 'You'd better get used to it.'

She turned to look at her before starting the downward slide. 'I mean for what it's worth, here's my analysis of the situation. SLW – that's Spotty Lowlife Wanker wanted to go out with you, felt like a proper prat when you turned him down and his pondlife posse are all jealous because you're PTT - prettier than them. I know I shouldn't say it but they're absolute mingers, all three of them. I mean she's boss-eyed for a start and I can only see the other one from the neck up, but double chins and nose piercings have never been a great combination. I dare say they'll be stacking shelves in Brinton for the rest of their lives.'

'My mum stacks shelves in Asda.'

'Sorry. I didn't mean to sound like some awful snob, I just …'

'You're vicious!' There was a grudging respect. 'Don't go yet. You're helping, sort of. In a funny way.'

'Oh right then. Where do you live?'

'Romney Leys. What about you anyway? What are you going to do about your husband shagging the babysitter? Are you going to leave him?'

'I don't know. I've got my son to think about, but he's pretty much left home. Trouble is I don't really feel anything. Not sure I even really care. I could make something up about cutting little pieces out of his suits or something, but I'd be lying.'

'Right.'

'I don't think I've felt anything for a very long time, you see. You're up here, crying, feeling pain because you're properly alive. I, on the other hand feel nothing most of the time, except anxiety, right here.' She pointed to just under her rib cage.

'Oh I see.' She obviously didn't.

'I think about killing him sometimes.'

'You what!!'

'I wouldn't obviously. It's just become something that I think about, to pass the time.'

'You're proper crazy!'

'That's rich coming from you.' They both stared ahead for a moment, before Bo carried on. 'Why don't you just switch it off, all of it, social media crap. It's like you're picking a scab. You don't have to look at it. Walk away! I mean the way I see it.' She stopped herself. 'Sorry I'm ranting.'

'No. Carry on.'

'Well the way I see it, your life hasn't even really got going yet has it. It doesn't have to be defined by some spotty loser and his three moron mates. I mean, he's laughable really. He can barely form a sentence.'

'It was Twitter. There's a limit on how many characters.'

'I know that thanks, but you can tell he's an imbecile from the first 10. I mean do you honestly really give a shit? Isn't there a tiny bit of personal responsibility? You can't control this kind of stuff, but you can control how you react to it. It's your life. Just close your account, STWO.'

'What does that mean?'

'Switch the wanker off!'

She was silent for a while taking this in. Bo realized she'd been too fierce. 'I'm just saying you don't need to live your life with all this baggage.'

The girl turned and looked her up and down. "Well you can talk."

'What's that supposed to mean?' Bo was startled by her tone.

'I'm not being funny right, but you've obviously let things go a bit haven't you, like what's that you're wearing anyway - a leopard skin onesie that's too small for you, your leg hair is actually minging! You're really good looking for your age, but you don't do yourself any favours. And I thought you said you had a job? I mean it's Monday right? Why aren't you at work?'

'Looks bad doesn't it?'

'Yeah actually it does... it really clings round your arse. Gives you a proper wedgie.'

'No I meant, my situation. Anyway, I wasn't planning on going out dressed like this. And I can't believe I'm getting fashion tips from someone in a black bra and glow in the dark dress.'

'Thanks a lot.' She looked hurt.

'Sorry. I mean, it actually looks good on you. It's just a difficult colour to pull off.'

'So's leopard skin on a woman your age.'

'Right. You're a complete cow and I'm bloody off! You'll be my age soon enough. I don't know why I'm freezing my arse off talking to you.'

'Wait a minute! Why aren't you at work anyway?'

'I threw a sickie.'

'Really!' She sounded impressed. 'Cool.'

'No, not really.'

'How would you kill him then, your husband?'

'It would have to look like an accident.'

'Obvs.'

'At the moment, I'm thinking of tampering with the brakes. If I knew where to find them, that is.'

'Oh right. Good idea. My cousin's a mechanic, he could show you. I'm Mel by the way, short for Melinda.'

'Bernadette, Bo for short. Nice to meet you.'

'So why aren't you at work then?'

'I don't know. I'm depressed. I'm bored. I'm fat, I'm forty, I can't get out of bed, I don't like my life anymore and I don't know what to do about it.'

'Oh right.' She paused for a moment. 'Have you thought about getting a tattoo?'

'Shut up!' Bo couldn't help but smile.

'What about your son, doesn't he come and see you?'

'He's travelling for a year, in Cambodia at the moment. This is him in India. Liam, my gorgeous boy.'

Bo zoomed in on her favourite picture of Liam on a beach in Kerala, grinning into the camera, with those bright green eyes and tousled black hair, broad brown shoulders.

'He's fit!' Melinda scrolled through the pictures. 'Are you going to show me your Facebook posts then?'

'Oh yes OK.' Bo laughed. 'Is this, you show me yours and I'll show you mine?' She took the phone back and clicked on the Facebook app. 'I can't work these bloody things. You do it!'

She waited while Mel flicked through each of the comments.

She snorted. 'Savage! Bit harsh on the little girl who passed her violin.'

'Yes, I know. I don't really remember writing it.' Bo snatched her phone back and tried to change the subject. 'So what else do you do, when you're not throwing yourself off cliff tops dressed in neon lace?'

'I'm doing an NVQ in hair and beauty, I want to open my own salon. And I play the guitar and sing a bit.'

'Well that sounds impressive. I'm just trying to imagine you in five years' time. What's your favourite car?'

'Pardon me?'

'What car would you buy if you could, I mean any kind of car in the whole world, money no object?'

'I don't know, maybe a Nissan Micra?'

'A Nissan Micra!? Oh for God's sake. I knew I couldn't help you.'

'Oh alright then, a red mini.'

'OK good, well this is how it's going to be then. Give it 5 years, and you'll be driving into a petrol station in Brinton in your red mini cooper, surround sound pumping, probably on your way to a film shoot or something where you'll be doing the hair obviously.'

'Obvs'. She sniggered.

'Yes obvs. And wanker is there. Dan or Darren or whatever you call him, will be in the petrol station shop and do you know what he'll say to you, 5 years after all this nearly made you jump off a cliff?'

'No, what?'

He'll say. 'Would you like to pop in your PIN?'

'You what?'

'He'll say 'Would you like to pop in your PIN' because he'll be behind the till.'

'Oh I see.'

'And you'll say 'Oh my God, Darren! It's really good to see you. You're still living in Brinton then? How long have you worked here? Six years! No, I don't have a Nectar card. Me? Oh I work on film sets, TV ads that kind of thing. What? Cash back? Oh no thanks. Yeah, really well thanks. Well, take care!'

'Take care!'

'Yes. Take care! Two of the most dismissive words you can say to anyone, especially ex boyfriends. And so you will erase the memory of Darren. And he will cease to exist.'

'Dave.'

'You will erase the memory of Dave, you will delete him forever. He will be archived in a folder marked 'non entity' 'can't quite remember who he was'. To the never ending petrol forecourt of oblivion.'

'Blimey! You can really talk. Are you Irish?'

'I used to be. When I was Bernadette Maloney.'

'Bernadette Maloney, I like that name! Baloney Maloney! Do you want a cigarette Baloney?'

'Why not.'

The fine mist of rain had turned into a drizzle, but neither woman made any move to go, perched on their shared rock, looking out over the wide expanse of greyness.

Bo stubbed out her cigarette and flicked it down over the cliff. The damp had started to penetrate her onesie. 'We should get going, it's going to tip down.'

Mel nodded. 'Well if you want my advice, you should get a tattoo and have sex with a much younger man. That would sort you out.'

'Well thank you Melinda, for your deep and insightful analysis, I'll bear that in mind.'

'I'm just saying. But I'd wax your legs first!' Melinda started to laugh unnecessarily loudly.

Bo remained expressionless. 'Well if you want my advice, you should work really hard at your NVQ and you should delete your Facebook and Twitter accounts while you're at it and Insta-thingey and Snapback.'

'Snapchat.'

'Whatever. Give up social media for at least 6 months.'

Mel gasped. 'You're joking, right.'

'No I'm not. We should go now, it's getting dark and it's going to chuck it down.'

Mel didn't move. You could see she was mulling over the idea.

A few rocks from above began to roll down the hill side. Bo looked up. 'OK, whatever. Let's go!'

Behind them, a cracking wrenching noise made them look up and both women gasped as they watched a huge mass of earth come crashing down.

It was as if the whole hillside was on the move, the rock gave way beneath them, they slid, arms and legs flailing, desperately trying to hold on to anything, earth, branches, rocks, anything to slow them down.

3

They had kept her in overnight. No amount of protests would convince them to discharge her before the morning. It's difficult to sleep when a nurse shines a light in your pupils every hour and they didn't turn the lights off in the ward. And then she had waited for 4 hours for the right type of doctor to come and check her over and finally agree to let her go.

She was desperate to know what happened to Mel but they wouldn't tell her. Now she wished she hadn't said they weren't related. It's not as if they were going to check. She had tried at three different reception desks. One of them looked like she was going to tell her and had started typing her name into the computer, but then Bo didn't know her surname and the nurse had eyed her suspiciously until she skulked away back to her ward.

She had switched on the news on the TV in the hospital common room. Luckily she was wearing a hospital gown, so the other patients didn't make the connection when the TV cameras zoomed in on her leopard print wedgie, jammed in the harness as she swung under the helicopter.

But the TV presenter with the very red lipstick had definitely said 'both women have been airlifted to safety, both women were receiving treatment!' She must be alive. Bo gasped with relief and turned to the other patients in the room. 'She's alive!' She was smiling as she left the room and they stared after her.

The purple wellies and onesie were returned to her in a plastic bag, so that she could change before she was discharged. And now it was almost exactly 24 hours since she had started her progress up the hill and she was back, pulling up outside her cottage in a Brinton minicab. The driver had been promised payment on arrival.

She had never been so grateful to see her home. It hadn't really occurred to her that she would be locked out, but it didn't matter because the kitchen window had been jammed open since last summer when she'd tried to paint it. She just needed to slide in and get some money for the taxi driver. She would have a shower, make a cup of tea and then all of this could be put behind her. She might even tidy up and put a wash on. At least the shock of the last 24 hours had broken through her inertia. She was feeling a lot better for some reason.

She slipped off the purple wellies and slid one foot through the kitchen window. The gap was narrower than it looked and she found herself lodged, with her right thigh squeezed between the wooden window frame and the sill, unable to persuade her right buttock to follow.

'Bernadette, what on earth are you doing?' Shit, it was Davina from across the road.

'I was worried. There were no lights on last night. Are you OK?'

'Oh yes, I'm good thanks.'

'Bernadette, are you stuck?'

'No, no I'm not. I'm just easing my way in. I've done it a hundred times. Nearly there.' She didn't like to tell her that her other bare foot, which she thought had made contact with the kitchen floor, was in fact lodged firmly in a litter tray brimming over with a week's worth of cat shit.

'Bernadette, what's that on your wrist?' She had that annoying habit of using your full name slightly too often.

'Oh this?' She bumped her head in her effort to snatch her arm away. 'It's a nightclub band. I went to a party, fancy dress.'

'But it says Brinton General Hospital on it Bernadette? And it's 11am.'

'Yes, it went on a bit.' Bo's face was red with the effort of trying to squeeze her bottom through the gap. Logic told her that if she could just get the one buttock through, the other should surely follow. Unless she had asymmetrical buttocks, which was possible. 'Have you seen the news at all Davina?'

'No Bernadette, you know I don't watch television.'

The taxi driver had edged up the lane to see what was holding her up.

'Come on, let's get you out of there Bernadette, you're not getting through that gap in a month of Sundays. Look I'm really flexible, why don't you let me have a go.'

'No!'

Bo clung to the window frame, but in spite of the fact that she was skin and bone, Davina had a surprisingly vice like grip. She reluctantly wriggled out of the gap. She would rather have amputated a limb than let Davina see the state of her kitchen, but she could think of no good reason to stop her.

'Oh God, what's that on your foot?'

'I must have stepped in something.'

'Step aside Bernadette!'

Davina slipped her child-like bottom through the gap in seconds. 'See what five years of Ashtanga yoga does for you Bernadette, you should try it!'

Bo stood silently waiting for the inevitable.

'Dear God, Bernadette! I'm so sorry, I think you've been burgled! Oh God it's absolutely disgusting. They've completely ransacked the place. Probably just young kids, but it's in a hell of a state.'

'No really?' Bo tried to sound shocked.

Davina's voice trailed off as she picked her way through the kitchen.

As Bo walked round to the kitchen door she tried to assume the expression of someone who has just been burgled.

Davina had her hand over her mouth as she opened the door. 'I'll send Angelica round to tidy up a bit.'

'I'd rather you didn't Davina.'

'It's no trouble at all, she's almost finished steaming the curtains, I'll get her to pop round in half an hour.'

'Please don't!' She had a desperate, inspired thought. 'I mean, I should probably let the police see this first.'

'Oh yes, no you're absolutely right. Let's call the police first and let them take finger prints.'

'Thanks Davina, I just need to be alone for a bit, I'll call them in a minute.'

'Understood Bernadette. Anyway, give me a buzz when you're ready for Angelica. I'm so sorry, if there's anything else I can do...' Davina stumbled away looking shell shocked.

Once she was sure that Davina was safely across the road, she sat down at the kitchen table and let out a deep, guttural sigh. Davina was right, it was a crime scene. What was previously a pretty, low beamed country kitchen was unrecognizable. Shattered glass and plates littered the floor. Snickers and Toblerone had obviously jumped into the sink and dislodged the mountain of dirty dishes and it was hardly their fault if they had given up on the litter tray altogether. Discarded takeaways, diet coke cans, and empty bottles covered the worktops, every drawer and cupboard was left open. She vaguely remembered having trouble finding the bottle opener last night. The notice board had come off the wall again and every postcard, shopping list and payment reminder was scattered across the floor. The cats had tipped the bin over, spilling its contents into the room and adding to the general smell of rotten things.

Bo sat there taking it all in. It was amazing the devastation that two cats and a pissed middle-aged woman could cause. She was startled for a second by the sound of a car horn. The taxi driver! She had forgotten that he was still waiting in the lane. She left the crime scene, clutching a £20 note and made her way over to the taxi.

But it hadn't been the taxi driver sounding his horn, it was Neil Spicer, sitting at the wheel of his BMW E series, unable to get past the taxi and into his drive. His face was red with anger as he stuck his head out of the window, pulling faces and gesticulating like a mad man.

She found herself slowing down to give the man a tip. 'Thanks for waiting, you've been very kind. Yes, see you again. Oh, do you have a card, that would be useful. Thank you.'

She thought Neil's eyes might pop out of their sockets as she wandered slowly over to his car. 'Hi Neil, how was the conference? I wasn't sure when you'd be back.'

'I can see that! Where the hell have you been, or do I need to ask. And dressed like that, for God's sake!'

'I've been to a party Neil.'

'No you bloody haven't. You're a liar.' He nearly ran her over as he swept into the drive. As he leapt from the car, the tirade continued. His normally florid complexion was a couple of shades darker than usual. 'The reason I know you are lying Bo, is that you were all over the bloody news last night.'

'Was I?' She knew how unconvincing she sounded.

'I'm in the middle of our international sales conference and my wife is hanging off a cliff in a fucking leopard skin onesie on the fucking national news. I walked in to the hotel bar to find out I was the fucking laughing stock. The CEO even mentioned it in his fucking wrap up speech.'

'Local news, Neil. It was only on the six o'clock local news.'

'Bullshit, it was on the regional news every hour. I don't know what you were doing up there, or why you were dressed like that, but you made a complete bloody spectacle of yourself and me. Do you know what Bo? You're pathetic. I looked at that TV screen last night and I thought, here we bloody go again, here she is making TV headlines twenty years later. I actually think it's time you got some proper help.'

'It's twenty one years. And you're never going to let me forget it are you?'

'Forget it? You were on probation for 3 years! It was a miracle we managed to keep you out of prison. You put everyone through hell and now you're at it again!' He shook his head. 'Well it looks like a leopard never changes its spots!' He was rather pleased with this last comment and threw his head back with a long, insincere laugh.

Bo wished she could shut him up. 'Do you know that I sometimes think about killing you Neil.'

'You do what?' It stopped the laughter at least. 'You've really lost it this time, Bo. You're not right in the head. We both know what you're capable of. You haven't changed in all these years. God knows I've tried to help you. And now you could lose me my job. You know what though? Your life might be spiraling out of control again, but you're not taking me down with you this time.'

He stopped for a moment, his fury momentarily spent. He looked at the ground.

'I'm leaving you Bo.'

'I know you are Neil.' She paused. 'Do you want to know how I know?'

He didn't reply.

'Someone wrote me a little note and shoved it under the kitchen door. Shall I go and get it?'

'What rubbish are you talking about now.'

'You and Mandy. How long have you been seeing her then?'

'Long enough to know that I'm in love with her. She's twice the woman you'll ever be.'

She was silenced for a moment by this body blow. 'Why wait til now, you've obviously been seeing her for a while.'

'We've both been worried about your state of mind to be honest.'

'My state of mind! You and Mandy Edwards. Shagging the babysitter! They can lock you up for that kind of thing Neil.'

'Look who's talking! She's 24 now Bo, so I don't think so. And she's a very smart and successful business woman. We're moving in together.'

'You're old enough to be her father. You sad, old fucker!'

'I don't have to listen to this. I'm going. I'll pack a bag and come back for some more things in a few days.' He looked around. 'This place is disgusting.'

She stood in the hallway looking up at the stairs, to the sound of him crashing around in the bedroom, not really knowing what to do with herself. What were you supposed to feel in this kind of situation, she wasn't sure. Was this really it, after everything they'd been through together? Her whole adult life. He stormed down the stairs and didn't meet her eye. She studied his familiar boyish features, his short muscular frame. He hadn't changed much in all these years. He seemed to hesitate as if thinking of something to say, but instead, lifted his jacket off the banister and walked out, slamming the front door behind him. She listened for the sound of his car in the drive. 'Goodbye Neil.' She mouthed the words silently and stared into space. She didn't feel like crying, not yet anyway. She was suddenly very tired and hungry.

'Hello, is that the Taj Mahal, yes it's Bernadette Spicer here. I'll have the Chicken Biryani, Aloo Ghobi, Peshwari Naan, Tarka Dahl and a couple of Poppadoms with chilli & mango chutney. 30 minutes? Thanks.'

There was a knock on the front door. *For the love of God, could she not just be left alone.* Whoever it was, was too short to be seen through the glass. It was too late to hide. She just stayed completely still, sitting at the kitchen table, hoping they'd go away.

The letter box opened and a small face appeared.

'You in there Mrs Spicer? Mrs Edgerton Davis sent me. She say you need deep clean?'

Bo addressed the little face in the letterbox. 'Angelica, I think that's probably an understatement.'

She went to open the door. Angelica looked her up and down. Bo noticed her checking out the hospital wristband. 'You alright Mrs Spicer, you got strange faraway look in your eye.'

'Yes I'm fine.' What was she supposed to say, that her husband had just left her? 'I've just ordered a takeaway curry, it'll be here in a minute, would you like some?' She was struck by how oddly we behave when our life is unravelling around us.

'No thanks Mrs Spicer.' Angelica ran her eyes over the straining material around the zip of her onesie. 'You ought to eat more healthy, like Mrs E-D. She don't eat nothing but bran flakes and fruit smoothies.'

Bo replied expressionless. 'Well, she must be very regular.'

'Pardon?'

'Nothing Angelica. What's it like in the Philippines? I've never been. I've heard parts of it are very beautiful.'

'I wouldn't know Mrs Spicer, I'm from Thailand.'

'Oh.' She thought for a moment. 'But I'm sure Mrs Edgerton Davis told me you were Filipino.'

'Pardon me, but she don't know arse from elbow. Mr Rupert saved me from bad marriage to fat old English man, he know my family.'

'I see. But doesn't Mrs E-D try to give you instructions in Spanish sometimes?'

'Yeah she do, I just ignore her.' Angelica had brought over a bucket with cleaning products and a mop. She put on a pair of marigolds, opened up a bin liner and leant down to pick up the cat litter.

'No, please, let me do that!'

'Mrs E-D say DEEP CLEAN WHOLE HOUSE!' Angelica was pretty much shouting at her.

'OK, I mean that would be really kind, but why don't you start upstairs and I'll do down here.'

'If you say so'. Angelica shrugged and disappeared off up the stairs.

Bo opened up the cutlery draw and found some scissors to cut off the wristband. Could she not just be left alone in her grief? *My husband has just left me and I'm being forced to deep clean my house by my passive aggressive neighbour.* She couldn't even phone the Samaritans, what with the sound of frenzied hoovering upstairs. She'd have had to shout over the noise. So this was what really happens when your husband leaves you, no serenity, not like the films. Real life tragedies played out with the sound of household appliances in the background.

Angelica popped her head over the banisters. 'Phewee Mrs Spicer, you got some dirty habits, you ever cleaned up here before?'

Bo gagged as she tipped the cat litter into a bin liner. There was soon a pile of black bags at the side gate. Angelica sang Take That songs loudly as she scrubbed and mopped the floors.

By the time the curry arrived, the kitchen was almost transformed. Bo had hoped for the solace of gorging in private, but it was not to be and it was a self conscious affair, with Angelica bustling in and out.

When they finally finished, Angelica left, still scolding her and shaking her head, as she walked down the drive, mop and bucket in hand. The smell of Dettol and pine toilet` cleaner wafted through the house. It smelt a bit like a hospital or some kind of institution. Bo ran herself a bath.

She picked up the onesie from the bedroom floor. It should really go in the bin. Would it not be cathartic to discard it, like shedding a skin. Perhaps she should burn it. She hesitated for a second and threw it into the laundry basket instead.

Tomorrow she would start again. She would brush her hair, put on her work clothes, paint on a happy expression and drive into the office. One inch at a time, she would try to reclaim her life. She caught site of her naked body in the bathroom mirror and thought of Mel's less than flattering words. Poor little Mel, barely an adult, already exposed to the crushing cruelty of life. Tomorrow she would find out what happened to her. Tomorrow she would do a lot of things. First she would shave her legs…

4

Familiar feelings of despondency always hit her as she pulled into the car park of HPS Ltd.

Hotel and Pub Solutions supplied interior fittings to the leisure and catering industry. It was not something Bo had known a lot about 3 years ago. Replica Boat Race oars, neon signage and all manner of Olde Worlde fixtures and fittings to dress the themed pubs and bars of the world.

The average member of staff stuck around for 6 months. Half the office was taking the piss and the other half was waiting for retirement.

It may not have been the dream job, but it was less than half an hour's drive from Lower Hinton and they had agreed to let her work part time. Finding part time work near home wasn't easy, especially as they had relocated several times for Neil's various roles, but he had insisted she keep working even though he was quite well paid. He was always apparently on the verge of redundancy on account of some global downturn or other, nothing to do with him of course. It occurred to her that he might actually just be shit at sales, he was after all quite annoying.

She hadn't in the end phoned work to say she was coming in. Torn between announcing her return and the advantage of complete surprise, in the end she had decided not to give Barry her MD, the opportunity to sack her over the phone.

Exactly the same two thoughts occurred to her every morning as she swiped her plastic entry card. Firstly, who on earth would want to break into this place? Surely it would be more appropriate to secure the building from the inside. And secondly, 'this is so far away from the glamorous career in London I had once envisaged.'

Bo was Marketing Manager, in name only, because every idea she had ever put forward was met by Barry's stone wall of resistance 'We tried that, it didn't work, too 'off the wall', I don't think so Bernie, wrong market, too risky, too expensive, doesn't align with our corporate vision, too 'labour intensive'.' And so her job consisted mainly of placing three, full colour, one page ads every month in the same hotel & catering magazines, to Barry's exact specification and manning the stand at a couple of hotel industry shows each year.

As she switched on her computer, she was aware that the whole office was pretending not to stare. Simon the new Operations Manager looked down at his screen and reddened when she walked past. The two new girls whispered and giggled. They were social media experts apparently. As far as she could see that consisted of tweeting every half hour that someone had ordered Krispy Kremes and persuading every pervert in the country with internet access to follow you on Facebook. So far that hadn't seemed to prompt a flood of orders, but it was early days. Barry was convinced that social media was the way forward, or rather that he didn't have a clue how to use it and had better get someone under 25 to show him how.

Who would be first to break the awkward silence.

'We saw you on the news Bo', stifled giggle from the younger of the social media girls.

'Yes, you would have.' Bo didn't give her the satisfaction of looking up.

Barry half opened the blinds in his office and peered through. Damn, she was hoping he wouldn't be in.

The door to his office opened. 'Ah Bernie, a word please?' He always called her Bernie for some reason. No one else called her Bernie.

Simon popped his head above the partition. 'There's someone on the phone for you Bo, it's a Katy Partridge, she says she wants to set up an interview.'

'Sounds like a recruitment agency. Can you tell her I'm in a meeting.' She shut the door of Barry's office behind her and he gestured for her to sit. He had one foot up on the desk and was rotating backwards and forwards in his revolving chair

She decided to try something light hearted. 'Hi Barry, how's it going?'

'Yeah really well actually Bernie, really well. Just had an order for 1500 Shakespeare waste paper bins for a hotel group in Shanghai and 400 of the mock bronze Churchill busts. He drummed his fingers on the desk top. 'And a hotel in Dubai phoned yesterday, interested in taking the whole heritage cricket range.'

'That's great Barry.'

'Yes it is.' He cleared his throat and took his feet off the desk. 'Look Bernie, I was watching the news on Monday night.'

'Yes I'm sorry.' She hadn't really planned what to say. 'They made me stay overnight in hospital. Such a fuss. I'm fine now. It's just great to be back at work.'

He raised his hand to stop her. 'The thing is Bernie, as you know, we don't really do the part time thing. We made an exception for you, but it hasn't really worked out if I'm honest? I mean I was checking the timesheets and you haven't actually completed a 3 day week for us since before Christmas.'

His phone rang, a brief reprieve. 'Yeah, it's the Amal hotels order I mentioned in my email, just an FYI really, no we opened up a dialogue with them last year, yeah great news, pushing into new territories. Yah, full knowledge share on Wednesday, great stuff.' – She looked at him, speaking too loudly into the phone, with his transparent ruler pressed against his face, splaying his nostrils so that you could see right up his nose. She felt an unexpected pang of pity. Here he was, sitting in his revolving chair, in his prefab office, nasty furniture and venetian blinds, thinking he was some kind of high flyer. Big shot Barry. And when has anyone called Barry ever made it big in business. Barry Branson, Barry Dyson, Sir Barry Sugar. She made an effort to return to the present. She must be seriously pre-menopausal if she was seeing Barry Perkins as a tragic figure.

'Sorry Bernie just giving Head Office the low down. Right, so where were we. Yes, I think we've reached a cross roads here Bernie and I think it's better for both parties if we agree to go our separate ways from here on in. I've talked to HR and I didn't want it to come to this, but really we are looking for you to leave HPS by the end of the week.'

When she didn't respond, he pressed on. 'The thing is Bernie, we are entering an exciting phase at HPS, marketing is going to be front and centre. It's mission critical that I have the full team on board, 110%, 24/7.'

Bo nodded. She couldn't help thinking about the full team outside the door, Simon looking at UniLad clips on Youtube, Brenda the bookkeeper, outside having her fifth fag of the day, while the social media girls compared shots of handbags on Instagram. Getting 50% out of them might have been a more realistic ambition.

'We are willing to pay you an additional 4 weeks and your references will be positive provided you act professionally and carry out a full and detailed handover.'

She stared out of the window, tuning out of the HR small print. She was sacked! There it was then. The sudden absence of a husband and a job. It occurred to her that Neil hadn't really said anything about money when he left yesterday. She tried to remember how much was in her current account. Enough for a couple of weeks perhaps.

There was obviously no point doing any work. She went back to her desk and stared blankly at her screen for a while and thought about Melinda. She googled 'Lower Hinton women on cliff'.

BBC News - *Two women were airlifted to safety on Monday evening after heavy rainfall caused part of a local landmark to give way. The women, Bernadette Spicer 48 and Melinda Cartwright 17…*

48! Forty BLOODY EIGHT! She was only 43 for God's sake. No one had even asked her age. Bloody bastards! An image finished downloading, a close up of her bottom, leopard print straining to contain her buttocks which were caught in a substantial wedgie by the straps of the helicopter harness.

For the love of God! She looked around the office, but no one had heard her. The story was everywhere. She ran down the list of news items - The Hinton Express, Wiltshire Times, South West Chronicle…

Party outfit pair in cliff rescue drama… Mailonline…Oh my God MAILONLINE, it was everywhere. And everyone had the buttock shot. Some local photographer must have made a fortune. *48 year old woman in cliff top rescue!* Every news piece reconfirming that she had an arse the size of Brinton and was in fact 5 years older than she thought.

But nowhere did they say what had happened to Mel. She supposed they didn't care anyway. Once they were plucked off the rock and the drama had subsided, it was off to the next story. But if Mel was in a critical condition, surely they would have reported it.

One new message in her inbox, from Barry. He wasn't hanging around. Probably about her P45.

To: Bernadette.s@hps.co.uk
From: barry.p@hps.co.uk
Subject: Friday night

Hey hot stuff

Looking forward to some spanking good fun on Friday night. Wear that nurse's outfit you wore last time. If you get to the hotel before me, treat yourself to something nice in the shop, charge it to the room. Do I need to bring cash again or can I pay the agency online.

Big bad Baz

Bo sat back in her chair in order to savour the moment. She smiled quietly to herself and started to type.

To: barry.p@hps.co.uk
From: Bernadette.s@hps.co.uk
Subject: Hanky spanky

Hi Barry/Baz

Thanks for your email. It took me a little by surprise if I'm honest, particularly in these challenging times for women in the workplace. I'm sorry but having checked my diary, I am in fact busy on Friday night, so I'm going to have to miss the spanking. Also, I should probably check my contract in detail when I share this email with group HR, as I'm not sure spanking is part of my job description. Thanks awfully for the offer of cash and something nice from the shop though. I'm guessing this means you want me to carry on working for HPS?

Bernadette

PS. Please don't ever call me 'hot stuff' again.

To: Bernadette.s@hps.co.uk
From: barry.p@hps.co.uk
Subject: Email error

Bernadette,

As I'm sure you are aware, you received that email in error, please delete it immediately. There is really no need to involve HR. We won't mention it again. What I was trying to say earlier, Bernie, is that you are a vital and valued member of the HPS 'family'. Let's use this as a platform moving forward. Feel free to take the rest of the day off. Business as usual tomorrow morning. 110%.

Barry

Bo slid her hand bag off the chair and sauntered out of the office smiling. She turned to the social media team. 'Actually girls I'm taking the rest of the day off to go shopping. You can tweet that if you like.'

Once she was in her car, the bravado quickly evaporated. Her hands were shaking and she couldn't make them stop. At least she had prevented one part of her life from unravelling. She just needed to get away from here. Maybe there was a kitkat in the glove compartment, no, must have eaten it already. She took a few deep breaths and started the engine. It was raining quite hard and all she wanted to do was get home and shut the door behind her. There was very little traffic as she pulled out of the business park, left on the roundabout and onto the A320. A white van was driving right up behind her. Such a strange turn of events. She would phone Lois and tell her all about it. God, why did people have to drive right up your arse!

She turned onto the road to Lower Hinton. The white van was still following her. At least she still had a job, for now anyway and the house was clean. Maybe see if she could get hold of Liam. She needed to tell him about Neil. God she hoped he hadn't got in there first. For the love of God this guy was close to her, a few feet at the most. Didn't these people realise what would happen if she had to brake suddenly. Stupid arse! She mouthed it into the mirror, not that he could see her. Obviously it was a 'he', no need to verify the gender of this particular moron. What an absolute prick! Her chest constricted. Neil, Barry, now this arsehole! She found herself slowing down to a near halt. White van man reacted by flashing his lights. Fecker! She was shouting now and made a 'tosser' hand signal in the mirror. Even in her rage she knew something had come over her, feelings of irrational fury which now made her pull over at an angle across the road and stop her car, so that he could not overtake her as he so obviously wished to do.

She waited, staring at the steering wheel like a woman possessed, her breath ragged. She heard the van door open. God knows what murderous paraphernalia he had in that van. A body bag, some duct tape and rope, a spade to dispose of her. She'd heard that if you're locked in a boot, you should kick out the rear lights and wave your hands through the holes. Maybe she should text his number plate to Lois. Too late oh my God, now he was walking over towards her car. Why had she done this, on a lonely country road. She must have a pre-menopausal death wish. She looked around for some kind of weapon. Two empty crisp packets and a cardboard nail file. *Just start the bloody engine and drive off for God's sake, find the lock button, start the engine.* Her hands were shaking badly now. He was standing at the door, his large frame stooping down and gesturing for her to wind the window down. She looked him in the eye. Goddammit, if she was going to die, she may as well go down fighting. She opened the window.

'Hi.' He was smiling, actually smiling at her, not in a killer way. 'You seem to have blocked the road and your driving just now was very erratic. Do you need some help?'

Help indeed! He had nearly run her off the road. He had very nice teeth she noticed.

'Erratic? So my driving was erratic was it? Well tell me something. Did you think I was a ferry back there?'

'I'm sorry?' He looked genuinely bemused.

'I was wondering if you mistook me for a drive-on ferry, given that you've spent the last 5 miles trying to get on board.'

'Oh I see. It was just that you were going so slowly. Are you alright?'

'I am absolutely fine, thank you.' He was all of 28, with big green eyes and a mop of blonde hair, asking her if she was alright. Patronising shite. 'At it happens at the moment when you were trying to kill us both, I was going at the national speed limit. 50 miles per hour, the legal limit. Obviously not fast enough for you as you were practically up my arse for 10 minutes.'

'It's 60 miles per hour and you were doing 40. At one point you were going so slowly I was worried you might stall.'

'Have you any idea what would have happened if I'd had to brake?'

'You already were braking, your brake lights were permanently on.'

'You flashed your lights at me. You are a dangerous driver and a road bully.' Now she knew she sounded like a member of the WI berating a 5 year old.

'Oh right and what was that sign you were making in the mirror, were you waving at me?'

'Tosser! I was trying to communicate that you are a tosser.'

'Well listen love, much as I'd like to chat about our different approaches to driving, I've got a sheep in the back that needs a vet, so if you wouldn't mind getting your car out of the way, I might be able to save its life.'

Listen love! Of all the condescending twats. But the mention of the sheep had slightly taken the wind out of her sails. Bloody pleased with himself young farmer. Cocky shit.

She started the engine in such a rage that she put it into third by accident and the car shuddered to a halt. Now he was actually laughing and shaking his head as he walked back to his van. She crawled off and stopped in a layby further up the road to gather herself. He swept past tooting his horn and waved in the mirror as he accelerated off.

Bastard men! Bloody bastard! After a few minutes, she switched on the engine. What would Lois say? Think positive, she had gone into work, saved her job, had not been murdered and it was still only 11.25.

She pulled out of the layby still muttering to herself, *Listen Love! Your driving was very erratic! Don't you Listen Love me!* She was driving when that shite of a man was still in nappies. *Sheep in the back of the van my arse, what was he doing with a sheep in the back of his van?* She had heard that drive-on ferry joke in a film, but it hadn't quite worked as well as she'd hoped if she was honest. It was a stupid thing to do but she was still alive at least.

It's come to a fine state of affairs when you are grateful to a man that he hasn't murdered you.

She was hurtling down the A320 now, mouthing imaginary responses. It was too late to see the policeman standing at the side where the road bent round, his speed gun pointing right at her. *Oh you have got to be joking!* She slammed on her brakes and another policeman waved her into a layby and signaled for her to wind down her window. She opened her door and an empty Monster Munch packet fell onto the ground.

He picked it up and handed it back to her. 'Good morning. Do you know what the speed limit is along this stretch of road?'

'50?'

'It's 60 madam.'

'Oh good.' She managed a smile. 'That's alright then, what was I doing?'

'73. Can I see your driving licence please.'

He went off for a moment and came back with a clipboard.

'If you could sign this form to confirm that we stopped you today. Since you haven't had any previous convictions you will be offered the chance to attend a speed awareness course and avoid any penalty points on your licence.'

Bloody, bloody bollocks. She crawled the rest of the short journey home at 30 miles an hour, still muttering and thinking how bully boy young farmer would be laughing.

5

She pulled up outside the cottage, looking forward to the calming prospect of a cup of tea and a phone call with Lois. Lois was going to love this. Where would she start?

There was a red mini parked right outside her front door and no sign of the owner. What now? Could she not just be left in peace? As she got out of her car a woman emerged from the side of the house. What was she doing snooping around her back garden? She didn't look much like a burglar, coiffed honey blonde hair do and very bright red lips.

'Hello there!' She was all smiles. 'Bernadette Spicer? I wasn't sure if anyone was in.'

'Yes?' Bo was hesitant.

'I'm Katy Partridge, from South West Tonight.'

Bo looked blank

'The TV news?'

'Oh, right.' Bo had a vision of the leopard print buttock footage. 'I saw your report. Are you the one who said I was 48?'

Katy smiled brightly. 'Absolutely! Can I come in for a chat?'

Bo looked her up and down. Her hairstyle was too old for her. Yes, it was a hair 'do'. She was only in her 20s but there was something of the Hillary Clinton about her.

'For the record, I'm only 43 and no you can't. I have nothing to say.'

'I just thought you might like to give your side of the story. You know, what really happened up there.'

'My side of what story? You've already done the story haven't you?' Bo rummaged in her handbag for the keys but the woman seemed intent on standing between her and the front door.

'Well I thought there might be a bit more to it. I've spoken to Melinda and she...'

'You've seen Melinda?' Bo looked up.

'Yes.'

'She's OK?'

'Yes, she's going to be just fine. If you let me come in I can tell you the whole story.'

Thank God Mel was OK. Finally she could find out what happened to her. Bo looked her up and down. She was just carrying a handbag, no camera or microphone. 'You'd better come in.'

Katy took off her coat and put her phone on the kitchen table. 'What a lovely cottage!' There was something very insincere about this woman.

'So do you live here alone?'

'Yes, as of yesterday I do.'

'As of yesterday?' Katy reached for her phone. 'Do you mind if I record this.'

'Yes I do actually.'

'It's only so that I don't get things wrong, you know, like your age for example.' She gave a little 'silly me' laugh.

'Oh OK.' Bo was starting to feel very uneasy. Having let this woman in, it might not be quite so easy to get her out.

'So do you want to tell me what happened yesterday?'

'No, tell me about Mel first.'

'Oh yes. Well she does have concussion, but it's quite mild and they put six stitches in the back of her head, but apparently it's not a deep wound. I think she was more upset that they had to shave a bit of her hair off to get to the cut.'

Bo thought about her beautiful, wild red hair. 'Where did you see her?'

'At her home in Romney Leys. I've just come from there.'

'Why did you go to her home? You've already done the story. I mean, what are you going to say now? Newsflash! Two women airlifted to safety, now at home living their ordinary lives.'

'Well quite. It wouldn't work on TV news. I just wanted to hear her side of the story.' Bo relaxed a bit and put the kettle on. Katy carried on casually. 'I wanted to get her reaction to what the RAF guy had told me.'

Bo looked round. 'What?'

'I caught up with the Search and Rescue team on Monday night, after you were taken to hospital.'

'You have been busy.' Bo was searching for a mug without a chipped rim.

'He told me that you risked your own life to save her, that you refused to let her go when he told you to release her?' Bo had a flashback to Mel's ghostly white face beneath her. She had been so sure she was dead. She suddenly felt sick and had to sit down.

Katy waited, face set in a sincere expression of concern. Bo had to hand it to her, this girl was a pro. She must have been about the same age as the social media girls at work, but what a difference.

Once Bo seemed to recover, Katy carried on. 'So did you think you were going to die?'

'Yes, I think I did.'

'But your first thought was to save the girl?'

'No, I mean, it was instinctive. Her fall was broken by some branches and I was able to prop her up for a while. I couldn't have held her full weight, could I?'

'But you were willing to die to save her?'

'What! Look, anyone would have done the same. It was the way we fell. I was able to prop her against the cliff. I don't think the search and rescue guy realized I wasn't taking her full weight.'

'But you risked your own life to save hers.' She looked Bo in the eye and spoke with an intensity that would have made Bo laugh if she hadn't been feeling quite so uncomfortable.

'Look, if you say so. How do you have yours?' This was such a strange conversation. Bo was quite glad to return to the business of making tea. 'Sugar?'

'No thanks. Coming back to what you said earlier. You live alone 'as of yesterday.' I don't wish to sound insensitive, but Mel did tell me a little bit about your personal circumstances.'

'Oh did she?' Bo was horrified. She hoped she'd skipped the bit about murdering Neil.

'Yes, well things have been a little tricky recently.'

'When you discovered your husband was having an affair?'

'Well yes, obviously that's never a good thing to...'

'And you're about to be sacked is that right?'

'No, absolutely not, no.'

'But the note through the door? The note that told you, perhaps what you already knew?'

'I'm sorry?'

'Was that when you hit rock bottom?'

'What? Well I've been very low, that's true, but I mean, who wouldn't be and you know…' Bo stopped herself. It was pointless. 'Look you're too young to understand any of this. It's my stage in life. I'm 43.'

'Yes, I'm sorry I got that wrong. Sloppy journalism!' She smiled and Bo slightly warmed to her.

'You see for a woman in my current situation Katy, adding 5 years to your actual age is really adding insult to injury.'

Katy nodded and seemed to understand. 'So was that when you hit rock bottom then?' Jeez, she was like a dog with a bone.

'No love, that was probably when your cameraman zoomed in on my oversized arse dangling from a helicopter and decided to flash it all over the bloody six o'clock news.'

This finally seemed to silence her. Bo continued. 'To be honest, I don't mind telling you any of this, I mean you are a TV reporter right? It's not like you've filmed me or anything for the Piers Morgan show.' They both laughed.

Katy smiled warmly. 'Oh yes mostly TV now, although I sometimes write stories for the weekend papers, you know women's interest features, that kind of thing.'

'Oh right.'

The conversation was cut short by the sound of the front door shutting. It was Neil, he had let himself in. Katy leapt to her feet, holding her hand out.

'Hi, I'm Katy Partridge.'

Neil looked confused and shook her hand 'Neil Spicer.' He looked at Bo 'I've just come to pick up some things.'

'Yes. Good. Go on then.' Bo followed him down the corridor

'Who the hell is that? I couldn't park in the drive.'

'Katy Partridge, you wouldn't know her.'

'Some new friend of yours is she?'

'Something like that.' Bo went back to the kitchen, seized by the thought that Katy might be rooting through her kitchen drawers.'

'So that was Neil? Your husband?'

'Yes, that's Neil.' There was an awkward silence. Bo cleared their mugs to suggest that it might be time for her to leave. Most people at this point might have got the hint, not Katy Partridge.

'Yoo hoo, the door was open so I let myself in!' It was Davina.

'Just checking that Angelica did a decent job, she can sometimes be a bit sloppy around the skirting...oh I thought you'd be alone.'

Katy shot to her feet, all Hollywood smiles again, her hand held out. Davina shook it as she scanned her clothes. You could tell she was impressed. 'Davina Edgerton Davis, I live in the Old Rectory on the other side of the lane.'

'Hello Davina.' Bo smiled weakly. 'Would you like a cup of tea?'

'Black coffee please. I don't mind instant.'

Just as bloody well, Bo found herself thinking as she rummaged through the cupboard for another unchipped cup. She gave up and washed the two in the sink.

Katy was gushing over Davina's sunglasses. She turned to Bo. 'I don't suppose I can trouble you for another cup of tea can I?'

'Of course.' Bo struggled not to roll her eyes as she sponged the red lipstick off the rim of the mug.

Katy was off again. 'We were just chatting about everything that poor Bernadette has been through.'

'Oh I know.' Davina sat down. She could tell this was going to be good. 'Which particular part?'

Katy leant forward. 'Well you know, everything that happened on Monday night. Did you not watch the evening news?'

'No I don't watch television. You mean the burglary of course.'

'The Burglary!' Katy took out a note pad from her handbag.

'The poor thing got back to find the place had been completely ransacked, I can't even tell you how disgusting it was. There was cat excrement everywhere.'

'Shit.' Bo dropped the mug, sloshing boiling tea down her hand.

They both ignored her. Katy was captivated. 'So she was burgled while she was in hospital?'

Neil popped his head round the kitchen door. 'Right I'll be off then. I'll leave you to your mothers' meeting.'

'Yes, fine. See you Neil.' Bo followed him out of the kitchen, grateful for an excuse to leave the room.

She watched him as he walked off down the drive, sports bag crammed with clothes and toiletries. He looked back fleetingly, 'I'll be in touch.' She was conscious once again of incongruous feelings. Should she have chased after him weeping? Instead she found herself wondering if he had remembered to pack his shaving gel.

Bo walked numbly back to the kitchen, in time to catch the tail end of the conversation.

'Can you believe it, she told me she'd been at a party all night!'

'I know, so modest. It's amazing really.' Both women were looking at her in a strange way, their heads tilted in shared compassion. It made her feel like a patient in a secure unit. She was relieved when they both got up to leave.

Davina left first. Katy grasped Bo's hand warmly in the driveway. 'Thanks for the tea and chatting to me. I think I've got all I need, but Davina gave me your phone number if there's anything else I need to know.'

Bo felt faint when she walked back into the kitchen. *I think I've got all I need, she'd said.* Oh shit. Phone Lois. That's what she needed to do. Phone Lois, the voice of wisdom. She would know what to do.

She dialed the code for Dublin. A familiar Irish voice 'Hi it's Lois Shaunessy, I'm not able to take your call right now. Leave your name and number and I'll get right back to you.'

Bo's voice shook as she left the message. 'Lois it's me. Listen I've really cocked up. Can you give me a call as soon as you get this. And if you want to know what's happened, try googling *'party pair airlifted off a cliff.'*

Four minutes later and the phone rang. Lois' number flashed up.

'Bernadette Maloney, I am logged onto the worldwide web and I am staring at a great big leopard skin arse that's bigger than my iPad screen. For the love of God, what have you been up to?'

'Thank you Lois.' It was strangely reassuring to speak to someone even more appalled than herself.

'Are you alright? What the feck were you doing up a cliff in the first place?'

'Yes, yes, I'm fine.' She struggled not to cry at the sound of Lois' worried voice. It was harder to deal with someone who actually cared.

'He's gone and left me Lois. He really has.'

'Well thank the Lord. Every cloud has a silver lining.'

'Oh stop will you.' She couldn't help but laugh. Bo described the moment she had found the note, right up to the departure of Katy Partridge. Prompted by Lois to expand on every detail and recap where necessary.

'And someone had pushed the note under the back door.'

'Good God! I never thought it would be this way round.'

'So he's left me Lois, after all this time. For Mandy, do you remember Mandy Edwards the babysitter?'

'How would I remember your babysitter?'

'And I saw this strange yellow object up above, so I followed it like a lunatic, right to the top of the cliff. You know Devil's chimney we went up there once.'

'Sounds like the three wise men Bo, did you take her some feckin frankincense?'

'Shut up Lois! So the Hanky Spanky email saved my job, would you believe it, so he couldn't sack me after all….'

'Jesus Bo, carry on.'

'And then the young farmer wound me up so much, I sped off and didn't see the police car…..so I was in a bit of a state when I got home, and she was waiting for me, Little Miss Anchor woman.'

'The one off the TV with the bright red lips.'

'Yes her. Loitering in my garden.'

'And she just kept on saying. 'Is that when you hit rock bottom?"

'They love that shite. She was trying to put words in your mouth. Go on.'

'So then she said 'I think I've got all I need!"

'Oh for feck's sake Bo! You sang like a canary, she's going to do a feckin story on you isn't she!'

'Do you think so?'

'Yes, I do! And we both know you really don't want to be in the papers again. I mean what if she does a bit of digging and finds out who you are?'

'I know Lois. What am I going to do? If the truth comes out I really don't think I could cope. You know I've never told Liam what happened. I don't think I could bear it. I can't bear him to know what I did.'

'OK let's not panic here. Did you tell her your maiden name?'

'No, she only knows me as Bernadette Spicer. But she could always look up my marriage certificate.'

'Yes, but why would she, Bo? There's no reason for her to do that. If she runs a story on you, it'll just be some soppy shite about your husband leaving you and saving the girl and all that. That's what that Rock Bottom shite was all about.'

'Do you think?'

'Yes I do, there aren't any pictures on the internet, well only the very blurred CCTV picture but you were wearing a hoodie and it was twenty years ago, so she'd never recognise you from that. Thank God it was before Facebook was invented! Look, I'll fly over at the weekend.'

'No don't Lois. It'll be fine, honestly. You've got your life. I'll wait to see if she writes a story. I just need some time, a bit of peace and quiet. It'll be fine I'm sure.'

6

The downpour was incessant and for once she had woken before her alarm. Dinner had been takeaway pizza and cookie dough ice cream, but she had at least resisted the wine box in the fridge. Rainwater formed small pools on the sill and she got up to close the window and make a cup of tea. It was nearly the end of the week. If she could just get through today in the office, she would have a long weekend to recover, speak to Liam, think about living the rest of her life on her own, without Neil. Today, she just needed to carry on, go through the motions and finally get home alone, to gather her thoughts about all that had happened, without the intrusion of others.

She brushed her teeth and opened the bathroom blinds. There were two cars and a silver van blocking the narrow lane. Without her contacts in, she could just make out a small group cowering under umbrellas outside the entrance to the Old Rectory. No doubt Davina was overseeing some vastly expensive home improvement. Bo smiled to herself as she gargled and spat. You couldn't help but like the woman. Davina lived in a Cath Kidston fantasy land, festooned with pastel bunting, a world in which choosing the right colour to re-tile your infinity pool was a source of genuine anxiety.

Downstairs she sipped her tea and switched on her iPad. Her anxiety was just about under control. She was dressed, clear headed on account of the lack of wine and even a little early for work. She stopped herself from looking at Facebook. There was an unread email in her inbox, most likely from Groupon or Pets At Home VIP club or some other such shite. She clicked on it, hoping that it was Lois with a late night message.

To: Bo.spicer@hotmail.com
From: Melindabeth99@gmail.com
Subject: ANGEL IN A ONESIE!!

OMG!!!!!!! You're so famous. Can't believe our story is all over the papers today! My mum saw it on the front page of the Mirror. She's dead proud. I asked the reporter for your email. She's a case isn't she! Asks loads of questions. I'm fine now! I haven't been on twitter or Instagram like you said!!!☺☺ ☺☺
Mel xx

Bo knocked her tea as her shaking hands typed in the words 'Wiltshire leopard print clifftop rescue'. No need to panic. She must have meant the local stories from Monday night. She could feel her chest constrict as she scrolled down the newspaper articles: BBC News, Mailonline, Mirror. co.uk, the Times, Metro, the Telegraph, The Sun, Sky News, Youtube.

Angel in a onesie - 'I won't let you go' says leopardess heroine, read more...

Metro.co.uk - These pictures capture the moment that a 48 year old woman saved the life of her stricken friend, helping rescuers to pluck her to safety...

Tearful teenager thanks plucky housewife...I owe you my life - mirror.co.uk

Oh fuck. Bo mouthed the words as she scrolled down.

Breaking news...Thieves trash heroine leopard woman's home as she fights for life in hospital!

My marriage is over, your life is just beginning. Hero housewife saves suicidal teenager - read more... sun.co.uk

She covered her face with her hands, unable to read any more. There wasn't a paper, magazine or radio station that hadn't covered the story. She was some kind of national heroine. Bo thought she was going to be sick.

She stood up. The people in the lane! They were there because of her. She rushed to the hall window. She could see them properly now with her contacts in, at least three times more of them than before. Vans with aerials on, TV cameras, reporters with microphones, reporters with cameras and long lenses. There was a shout as one of them spotted her at the window and they surged forward, cameras snapping. There were dozens of them. She fell to the floor and crawled back to the front door. Crouching down and hugging her knees she rocked back and forth, trying to stay logical. Should she call the police? But what could they do, you can't stop people hanging around outside your home can you? She sat up on all fours and tentatively looked through the keyhole. Pressing her face against the opening, she couldn't see much because the driveway was obscured by the silhouette of Katy Partridge facing the camera, her back to the door, familiar syrupy voice as she addressed the camera in front of her. Bo strained but could only hear snatches of her report.

'I'm standing at the front door of Bernadette Spicer, wife, mother, a very British heroine. As Bernadette's marriage lay in tatters.....a marriage ended by a scrap of paper pushed under her door....She literally put her life on the line to save a stranger...We've since learned, Declan, that thieves broke in and burgled her house while she lay helpless in hospital....'

Bo was sweating now, as she crawled on her elbows across the kitchen floor. She reached up for the phone and dialed the Dublin code. 'Hi it's Lois Shaunessy, I'm not able to take your call right now. Leave your name and number and I'll get right back to you.'

'Hello Lois, Lois. You've got to be there! They're all over my garden. Have you seen the papers? I don't know what to do.'

There were faces at the windows now, poking cameras in, photographing her kitchen, just like it had been 20 years ago, hunting her down, coming to take her away.

A lens appeared through the letterbox. She slithered on her tummy down the hallway to get away from it, clutching the telephone handset. From there she was able to pull the curtains shut from the floor and create a sanctuary in the centre of the house, away from the faces at the window.

The phone rang. 'Oh thank God, Lois.'

'Hi Bernadette, how are you this morning? What's your reaction to being called a hero by Harriet Harman?'

'Harriet? What! Who is this?' She put the phone down.

The phone rang again. Number withheld.

She tapped in Lois' number again, but the line was silent and no amount of hitting the keys could get a dial tone.

She opened the catflap. Katy Partridge had finished recording for now. She could see her talking to her cameraman. Probably planning the next instalment. From the hallway floor, Bo could see a man's leg appear through the gap in the kitchen window. There was swearing as he struggled to get his bottom through the gap. For God's sake, he was actually trying to break in. She crawled back into the kitchen on her hands and knees, he was inching in slowly. She could already see the belt of his trousers as he tried to wiggle his way in, doing a strange kind of limbo, camera in hand. He couldn't see her, as she looked around desperately for something to hit him with. He was nearly in. She panicked and tried to grasp his ankle. He couldn't see her from where he stood. He shouted and kicked himself free. In a desperate moment, she grabbed his calf with both hands and sunk her teeth hard into the exposed flesh. He screamed and shouted 'fucking animal' and the leg swiftly disappeared.

Bo crouched stunned for a moment at what she had just done, before crawling back to the safety of the hallway. A few moments later a selfie stick wired up with a small camera poked through the gap and hovered over the kitchen floor. She could hear a voice just outside the window. 'It's too dark, I can't get an image of her, I'll need to send in a flash but I think there's a dog in there, I don't want it to bite the lens.'

She realized now that her breath was coming in short, shallow gasps. She tried to control herself. *I am not a young girl any more, they can't do this to me.* Where the hell had she left her mobile? She couldn't get back to the kitchen to fetch her iPad, all contact with the outside world effectively shut off. The panic was overwhelming.

She flipped open the catflap and shouted just loud enough for only Katy to hear. 'Katy! Katy Partridge!' Nothing. Katy was too busy reapplying her lipstick for her next broadcast. 'Katy Partridge!' Katy looked behind her but seeing nothing, turned back to her cameraman. Seized by anger and desperation, Bo stood up, attached the security chain and opened the front door. She pushed her face through the gap and this time hollered. 'Katy Partridge! Katy! YOU GET IN HERE NOW!'

'Oh hi, Bernadette!' Katy was effusive. 'You're a national hero! Isn't this all so exciting?' Jesus! It was like she was talking to a four year old.

'Exciting!' Bo spat out the words. 'Get in here! No camera, no microphone, no phone. Got it?'

'OK fine.' Katy put her arms in the air theatrically. 'Look no wires, no phone!' Bo eyed her suspiciously but the rest of the reporters had seen her and started running towards the house. She hastily undid the chain and let her in, slamming the door behind them.

As she bolted the door, she stood with her back against it. 'What have you done?' Bo snarled.

Katy was all breezy and cheerful. 'Hilarious isn't it! Reminds me of *Life of Brian*. Have you seen it?'

'This isn't hilarious, you have no idea what you've done. What the feck was all that about my marriage? This is my life.'

Katy smiled with her head on one side. 'Look Bo, I know it's a bit of a circus, but you'll laugh about this next week. I just told them your story and the public did the rest. They're loving you! Even I didn't expect this kind of reaction. It's your fifteen minutes of fame! Enjoy!'

Bo looked at her flabbergasted.

In the absence of a response she carried on chirpily. 'I don't suppose I can grab a cup of coffee can I, it's freezing out there?'

'No you feckin can't!' Bo growled. 'You can go into my kitchen, pull down the blinds and bloody well make me a coffee, with a shot of brandy if you can find any'. Katy shrugged and disappeared off into the kitchen.

Bo shouted after her. 'And what was all that shit about me fighting for my life in hospital.'

'I know', Katy looked heavenwards with a little sigh. 'Not everybody has the same journalistic integrity as TV South West!'

Bo watched Katy struggle to shut the kitchen window. 'Don't bother, it's stuck, just pull the blind down.' Even when she was sure the kitchen was secure, she was reluctant to go back in.

The handset rang in her hand. Lois! She answered and immediately regretted it.

'Don't hang up. I promise I am not a journalist.' The voice was deep and husky. Bo was silent. 'My name is Betsy Levene and I can help you. I can sort all of this out. Just don't hang up and I'll explain.' The voice on the line waited.

'Who are you and how can you sort it out exactly?' Bo lowered her voice and moved away, so that Katy couldn't hear.

'Look, I'm guessing you're under siege, right? Journalists outside trying to speak to you? Cameras through the letter box, standard stuff darling. Are any of them on your property?'

'Yes, most of them. One of them just tried to climb into the kitchen through the window.'

'OK and did he get into the house.'

'No, I bit him.'

'Christ, OK, this is the thing darling. They are not allowed to enter your property. They can hang around outside, chase your car, talk to your neighbours, you name it, but anything else is trespass. We can sort that out in a moment. OK. Now have you spoken to any of them? I can completely control this, but only if you haven't given any more interviews.'

'Of course I haven't.' Bo spat. Who the hell was this woman anyway?

Katy shouted from the kitchen. 'Where do you keep your spoons?' Bo moved further away and whispered into the phone. 'Actually, I say that, but one of them is in my kitchen making coffee.'

'What! Oh Christ, OK, right, let's think. Put them on!'

'What?'

'I said put them on, pass the phone to the journalist.'

Bo passed the phone to a confused looking Katy and stood near the kitchen door so that she could hear. Betsy's booming voice was fairly easy to make out. 'OK, here's the deal. We get the two of them up the hill, same outfits, relive the whole episode, teenage crisis, mid-life crisis, I'm thinking like *super-size, super skinny*, the two of them talking about how they felt, how it changed their lives, the women's mags will love it.'

Katy's face hardened. 'I'm going to get all that anyway.'

Bo was strangely fascinated. They were talking about her and Melinda as if they were commodities, bartering for ownership. The woman on the phone didn't flinch. 'I don't think so. I'm representing her from now on. You get the clifftop re-enactment or nothing. It's a good offer.'

Katy wasn't beaten. 'She hasn't even signed with you yet.'

'Listen to me darling. I've dealt with your outfit before, Ian Stoddart right? Still head of news? We go back a long way. If I were you, I wouldn't fuck this up. You get the exclusive on the shots, the interview, the first reunion, the day a shy housewife turned into a national heroine, tears on the clifftop. Look, I'll even let you photograph the anonymous note OK? World exclusive. Leave her alone today and I'll sort the rest. Capiche? And tell Ian, Betsy says hi.'

Katy looked slightly shell shocked as she passed the phone back to Bo. 'She wants to speak to you.'

Betsy was still barking orders as the phone passed between them. 'Bo are you there? OK darling, are you listening? You speak to no one. I am sending a car and security for you right now. You're in Lower Hinton right? Where the hell's that? In Wiltshire? Give me your postcode. The car will be there in less than an hour. The security will knock on the door 9 times, in 3 short bursts of 3. We don't want to give away any free shots at this stage, so he will cover your head in a blanket and lead you to the car.'

'What!'

'Look I know, this is a circus sweetie, but what's done is done. I promise you this, they won't go away until they get their story. You have two choices. You can either take back control and make something out of all this, or hide in your bedroom for six months, while they hunt down your family, your auntie and your auntie's next door neighbour. Either way, this is your breakthrough moment sweetie, grab it now and ride the wave because pretty soon you'll be chip paper.'

'I beg your pardon?' Bo was having difficulty following.

'You know, chip paper, yesterday's newspaper, old news!'

Bo paused for a moment. 'But I have to go to work, I'm late already. I'm on my last warning.'

Betsy gave a little laugh. 'Work shmerk darling, this is show business. You listen to me and you won't have to go back to your tedious little job ever again.' As Bo hovered beneath the kitchen cabinets, her calves beginning to ache, her 'tedious little job' was looking rather appealing.

When Bo put the phone down, it occurred to her that she didn't even know who or what Betsy Levene with her baritone voice actually was or where 'security' was going to take her, but right now a secure unit in a mental wing would be preferable to this lunacy.

Katy Partridge had left looking slightly less chipper than before and Bo skulked back to her position in the hallway, cowering once again on the floor. *My name is Bernadette Spicer and I am sitting in the dark, on the floor in the hallway of my little cottage in the middle of nowhere, with the world's press outside and my life in the hands of a complete stranger called Betsy, who is 'sending a car for me'. This is a bad dream and I will wake up shortly.*

She dialed Dublin again. 'For God's sake Lois! Why won't you pick up the feckin phone!' The phone rang. Thank God!

'Hello?'

'Bo this is Betsy Levene again', the voice was booming. 'I thought I said, DON'T answer the phone! If this is going to work you will need to do EXACTLY WHAT I SAY.'

'OK yes, sorry.' Now this woman that she didn't know had got her apologizing!

'I forgot to say darling. The leopard print onesie?'

'Yes?'

'Bring it with you.'

'Right.'

Bo replaced the handset and caught her own startled expression in the hallway mirror. For a split second she was back there, almost twenty one years ago, huddled and sobbing in a hallway, blue lights flashing in the drive. There were no blue lights, this time she was besieged by cameras instead.

She peered through a gap in the blinds. Katy was standing in the centre of a huddle of reporters. Thank God, it looked like some of them were actually beginning to leave. Should she phone work? But what to say. Maybe listen to what this woman had to say first. Maybe she shouldn't go at all. No one to talk to, no one to tell her what to do.

Exactly 55 minutes after Betsy called, a long, black Audi A8 pulled up in her drive. A suited driver with an ear piece strode through the remaining journalists and knocked nine times on her door. He didn't have a blanket she was relieved to notice. As he ushered her to the car, he shielded her from the press and held the door open. A few reporters rushed forwards, microphones and cameras in hand, but she stared firmly at the ground and hurriedly got in.

As they cruised down the M4, she studied the back of his shaved head, the coiled ear piece attached to his ear, no doubt so that Betsy could bark orders without interruption. From utter mayhem they now sat in calm, air conditioned silence.

'Hello'. He didn't answer. She felt a bit foolish and wondered if he could hear her or was deliberately ignoring her.

There was a copy of Metro on the seat beside her. Not on the front page she was relieved to see. It didn't take long to find the story. She started to read but couldn't go on.

She decided to try to engage the driver. 'What's your name?'

'Lewis.' She wasn't sure if that was a first name or surname.

Silence.

'You're not very chatty are you?'

He looked in the rear view mirror. 'We're not supposed to talk to the talent.'

'Talent?'

'The VIPs.'

'Well that's OK then', she snorted 'I haven't got any talent.'

He smiled into the mirror but wouldn't be drawn into conversation. Bo pretended to look at her phone. Taking a biro out of her handbag, she started to fill in the Sudoku on the back of the Metro. Here she was, her life unravelling at alarming speed, rushing towards an unknown destination to put her fate in the hands of a stranger and what was she doing? Trying to work out if the second column, third row down should be a four, a seven or an eight. It couldn't be a one, a two or a five. You can't just guess at Sudoku. That could get you into terrible trouble. Neil had once told her that she was autistic, 'on the spectrum' he had said. It was true that she did sometimes count out loud to keep calm. Lois said that was rubbish, that it was 'disassociation', the tendency to enter a parallel universe when placed under stress. She chewed the end of the biro and tried instead to crack the fours.

They entered the outskirts of London and she began to recognize some of the streets. The car pulled up at a red light on the corner of Earls Court Road. She looked casually out of the window, glancing into a newsagent's shopfront. Good God, there she was, splashed across at least two of the front pages; unmistakable arse, dangling underneath the rescue helicopter.

She pressed redial on her phone. 'Hi it's Lois Shaunessy, I'm not able to take your call right now.'

'Hello Lois, please pick up the phone. I am currently speeding up the Cromwell Road in a chauffeur driven car with blacked out windows. Just gone past Harrods. Listen, if you can fly over, that would be great. Check the papers, look on Google, I don't know if it's got as far as Ireland yet but I'm all over the UK press. CALL ME!'

She put the phone back in her handbag as the Audi finally drew up outside a townhouse in Covent Garden. The chauffeur opened her door and she followed him up some steps, as he pressed a buzzer marked *Levene Associates*. The door clicked open and he led her up a wide sweeping, carpeted staircase. He reached for the gold handle of a large, oak door, but it swung open before his hand made contact.

'Bernadette darling! Welcome to my world!' The source of the baritone voice was a petite, impeccably groomed woman her arms held out in welcome. She had a perfectly coiffed dark brown bob, long red nails, a cardigan slung over her shoulders and her glasses on her head. It was hard to believe that such a deep, husky voice emanated from this little creature. She greeted Bo with a theatrical hug, kissing the air beside each cheek, like they were old friends.

Bo was tempted to see if she could lift her off the ground, a little sparrow of a woman. As she got closer the smell of expensive perfume mingled with cigarette smoke.

Betsy stepped back to appraise Bo. 'The pictures really didn't do you justice you know, you're beautiful darling! Well you and I are going to have some fun! Glass of Champagne?'

It was 11.45 in the morning. What the hell, anything to take the edge off the rising terror. Bo nodded.

The office was enormous, with double height sash windows overlooking the Piazza. There was a black and white picture of Lulu on the wall and Bo noticed a photograph on the large oak desk of Betsy standing between Richard and Judy.

Betsy opened the wine cooler next to her desk and pulled out a bottle of Pol Roger. She popped the cork expertly, without damaging her red nails and handed Bo a glass.

'Here's to a very successful partnership.' Bo stood self-consciously on a zebra skin rug, clutching the glass, her handbag and a Marks & Spencer's plastic bag containing the leopard skin onesie. She gulped the Champagne.

'Actually, could I just use your toilet.'

'Of course darling. Down the corridor, second on the right.'

Bo sat on the toilet seat and looked around her. She noticed in the mirror there was cat hair on her jumper. A fig & bergamot candle flickered on the window sill. The walls were covered in taupe suede and the sink and taps were made entirely from copper. Little rolled up flannels were lined up like perfect white sausages in a wicker basket. Bo picked one out and held it to her face. It was damp and smelt of rose water. What kind of people lived like this? People who paid a lot of money to smell only pleasant things. Davina would love it. Bo stroked a suede wall and looked in the mirror. She looked unkempt and out of place and felt annoyed for being intimidated by a lavatory.

As she came back into the room, Betsy's incredibly posh voice was booming down the phone.

'Hi Carl darling, it's Betsy.'

She winked and signaled for her to sit down opposite. Bo sipped her champagne awkwardly, not knowing where to look.

'So Carl, it's a little more than we thought, yeah! Teeth whitening, cut and colour, spray tan, threading? Quite a lot of facial, lip and chin, skin actually very good. If we thread now how long will she be blotchy? Bearing in mind I need her in a photoshoot at 2pm in Southwark. OK, well do what you can darling. We'll drop her round shortly. Love you!'

Betsy put the phone down, leant back in her chair and smiled broadly. She reached into a drawer and pulled out an iPhone, which she pushed across the desk to Bo. 'This is your new phone, the number's on the back. Only I will ever call you on this OK, so keep it on you at all times.'

This was becoming farcical and gave Bo the impetus to try to stem the flow of this woman. 'Can I just interrupt. You see, I really do need to call work and let them know.'

'Work! You're not going back to work darling.' Betsy snorted. You've got a photo shoot with Inside Story at 2pm. An interview with Good Housekeeping at 4, three radio interviews and that's before we've even done our own press shots. You've brought the outfit, yes?'

Bo nodded.

'Fabulous!'

Betsy's phone rang.

'Serge! Thanks for calling back! I'm going to need some of your magic. Serge, I'm sitting here with Bernadette Spicer, 'Angel in a onesie'? Do you not read the papers darling?

Google her, yah! Going to need some work. Yes. No, a bit more than that I think darling. I would say so. No darling, more than Bonnie Langford. We'll need you every day. OK, every other day? Ok, so if we say no wheat, carbs, sugar, dairy, red meat or alcohol in the meantime, when can you start. No quite.' She winked at Bo again and raised her eyebrows. 'Darling, I know you've worked with Kylie, you're the best there is, that's why everyone wants you. Ok sweet, we'll talk tomorrow, a bientot!'

Betsy put the phone down and rolled her eyes! 'Honestly darling, sometimes the support team are more trouble than the talent! Listen, I've drawn up a quick agreement, basic stuff really.' She raised her glass. 'The upshot is, we're going to make you rich!'

'What?' This was all moving very fast, but she imagined that was deliberate. 'And what if I don't want to talk to the press or do any of this stuff, photoshoots or anything.'

Betsy sighed theatrically and sat back in her chair.

'Can I be uber frank with you darling?'

Bo nodded. Betsy took her glasses off her head and leant forward. 'Here's the thing. Your husband.'

'Neil', Bo added.

'Yes. Neil. He's left you for another woman right?'

'Yes.' Bo was taken aback.

'And you work part time.' She was looking down at some notes in front of her. She twiddled her glasses around in her hand. 'I'm guessing you earn peanuts? Not much more than 20K if you're lucky?'

Bo nodded. 'So, when Neil comes knocking on the door wanting a divorce and half the house, things won't be looking too clever will they? You're looking at a fire sale of the house, the proceeds of which might buy you a small flat. In fact, you might want to think about going back to work full time.'

Bo looked at her. She really was ruthless.

'Like it or not darling, your star is in the ascendant. Today, you have a value to the media, next week you won't.'

There was a pause before Bo met her expectant gaze. 'What is it exactly that you do?'

Betsy twirled her glasses again. 'I do deals darling. Newspapers, magazines, tie ups with household brands, personal appearances. I use my substantial list of contacts and 25 years in the business to negotiate you the best possible deal, for which I take 20% of whatever you earn. Let me give you an example. *Inside Story*, you know it?'

'Yes.' Bo had read it in the hairdressers.

'They are offering you £10,000 for a photoshoot and interview this afternoon. Two hours work max.'

'What!'

'Yes, I'm guessing it's a bit more than you're used to earning in 2 hours.'

Betsy sat back, letting Bo take this in for a moment. 'Darling I'm talking about financial security for the rest of your life. I've got a high street clothing brand seriously interested in designing an entire leopard print range for the older woman called *Bernadette*. I can make sure you keep your house. If this all comes off, we can probably buy you another one as well. Rent it out, provide you with an income, or blow it on a yacht, it's entirely up to you. You have a son don't you?'

Bo said nothing and Betsy leant forward impatiently. Her voice had more of an edge now. 'Listen, the car is outside and you can get right back in it and we'll drive you home to

Lower Hinton, if that's what you really want. If you want to walk away from the opportunity of a life time, the last thing I'm going to do is force this on you. But all of this has happened and they'll hunt you down and write their stories, with or without my help and you can either get something out of it or nothing. Your choice.'

Bo looked out of the window. 'Can I have some time to think about it?'

Betsy sat back in her enormous chair. 'Like I said, you are today's news. You can think about it for about twenty minutes if you like, but I've got other fish to fry.'

Bo put her glass down on the desk. 'Would I keep control? I mean I wouldn't have to do anything I didn't feel right about?'

'Of course not darling. Trust me, it's all about building your brand. 'Bernadette' the woman next door, everyone's favourite housewife heroine. Profile raising yes, but we're not going to do anything to damage your brand values are we? It's all about the brand.'

Bo was starting to feel irritated by the lesson in branding. 'I do understand basic marketing.'

'Good then you'll understand the need to seize the moment, because this will all be very short lived.' Betsy reached into her drawer and drew out two copies of a typed up contract. She pushed the copies and a pen towards Bo. 'You'll have a personal trainer, make up artist, new wardrobe, stylist, dietician, use of a driver for work related appointments and media training.'

Bo felt sick and strangely excited at the same time. Here she was once more, a fault line in her life. Should she run and hide or try to take control? What would Lois tell her to do?

'And what about my cousin?'

Betsy looked bemused and irritated at the same time. 'Your cousin?'

'My cousin Lois from Ireland, can she come with me?'

Betsy smiled, sensing victory. 'I'm sure she can, some of the time and we can sort her out with a haircut and a few new dresses.'

Bo nodded her head silently.

'And the cats.'

Betsy was struggling not to look exasperated.

'What cats.'

'I'll need to sort out someone to feed the cats. I mean, if I'm going to be away a lot.'

Betsy edged the documents towards her. 'We'll sort the cats.'

Bo took a deep breath, leant forward and picked up the pen, signing the two documents in front of her. Betsy was smiling broadly now.

'Fabulous! Let's have some fun darling! Just one last thing, is there anything you need to tell me, you know, major drug abuse, tax evasion, prison records, that sort of thing? Never been in the press before?' Bo shifted uneasily in her chair. She could feel her heart move up somewhere towards her throat, but held Betsy's steely gaze.

'No, nothing.'

'Good, then it looks, my darling, like we have ourselves a deal.'

Bo's phone rang in her handbag. It was Lois.

'For the Love of God Bo, what are you getting yourself into now?'

'Lois! Hold on a moment.' Bernadette looked apologetically at Betsy. 'Could I just take this call somewhere? It's my cousin.'

'Sure, there's a meeting room down on the left.' Betsy waved her away dismissively.

Bo shut the door behind her, but continued to speak in a stage whisper.

'I'm in London, I've got an agent.'

'You've feckin what!!! You utter moron! Just don't sign anything Bo, please tell me you haven't signed anything.'

'Look, it's going to be fine. I had the press camped out in my garden, I couldn't leave the house. They had their lenses through the letter box. It was petrifying. At least this means I get to control what I do and make a bit of money. I can put it in an account for Liam. I can't turn back the clock can I, so I may as well ride the wave, it'll all be over in a week.'

'Sounds like you've been got at. I'm telling you now Bo Maloney, if they find out who you are, what you did, they'll feckin tear you to shreds.'

'It's going to be fine Lois.'

'Oh I'm sure it is Bo. And have you told your agent about your non-custodial sentence or your previous press coverage in every national newspaper?'

'Of course I haven't. Listen Lois, I was in a corner here and I made a decision. I'm not stupid, I know it's a terrible risk. But Lois, I'm sick of it. My whole adult life I've lived in fear and guilt and it's not as if hiding away has brought me any peace.'

Lois was silent for a while.

'Lois?'

'Well if you think you know what you're doing.'

Bo laughed. 'Of course I bloody don't, but it's done now. Come over and keep me sane Lois, for a few days?'

'I've already booked my flight. I'm arriving tomorrow, Heathrow 3.30 in the afternoon.'

'I'll pick you up, I've got a driver now. It'll be an adventure Lois. I've made her agree to a make over and new clothes for you too.'

'Who's 'her'.'

'My agent, Betsy Levene, she's got an office in Covent Garden.'

'Of course she has.' She could hear Lois sigh over the airwaves. 'May God help you Bernadette Maloney!'

'Bernadette Spicer, Lois! From now on, I can't be Bernadette Maloney.'

'I know.'

7

Her chin still felt raw from the previous afternoon's assault. She had been plucked and threaded within an inch of her life. Hair and make up had been less of an ordeal but she had drawn the line at false eyelashes. It was a bit too much of a 'hair do' if she was honest and she would mess it up later, but anything was an improvement and it did make her dark hair look thick and glossy.

After all that effort, it was only a shame that she'd been made to get back into the leopard print onesie, although this time with a spray tan and purple shellac nails.

They had photographed her in all manner of positions. The 'green screen' shot, arms crossed jauntily, one leg behind the other, head tilted, languishing on a day bed, legs straddling a chair, the chin resting on the arms shot, that was probably the silliest. It had taken bloody hours to get the shots they wanted. 'Look this way Bernadette, lovely, that's it, just relax, try not to look so uncomfortable, laugh into the lens.' It was hard to look relaxed, in a pair of magic pants, legs akimbo, with 7 people smiling at you benignly, but the glass of Champagne had helped.

By the time she had finished four interviews it wasn't worth going home. She was exhausted by the questions.

'Would you do it all again Bernadette? What advice would you have for Melinda now? What's your favourite tipple Bernadette? What foundation do you use Bernadette? Who's your favourite Apprentice? Is there anyone new in your life Bernadette!' Apparently she was refreshingly honest. Betsy listened in to every word, occasionally frowning and quite often taking notes. And there was always the reference to 'Rock Bottom'. They were bloody obsessed with it. It was clearly some sort of journalistic coup if they could demonstrate that you had reached it. *Bernadette Spicer, face down in the gutter, piss drunk, soiled and dribbling, still in her leopard print onesie.* That's what these people wanted. The rise and fall. Or the fall and rise. It didn't much matter as long as you'd reached the obligatory Rock Bottom somewhere along the line.

Betsy had given her the key to the company apartment in Soho. The waft of scented candles hit you as you walked in. There were Cowshed products in every room, the latest issues of Vogue and Tatler, a white leather chair in the bedroom. The showerhead was one of those big square ones that made you feel like you were standing in torrential rain. By the time she had used all the products, every window was fogged up and her skin smelt like Turkish Delight.

In spite of the Egyptian Cotton bed linen, she had slept badly, woken in the early hours by the sounds of drunken shouting and bottles smashing from the bar opposite. At some point as she floated in and out of sleep the voices across the street were replaced by her mother and Father Delaney, kneeling beside her hospital bed. 'The wages of sin is death' they both chanted over her. She crawled further up the bed to try to escape them. She woke up sweating, clutching the sheet tightly in her fists, taking a few moments to remember where she was.

Through the shutters she could see dawn breaking. Lois would be here soon.

Betsy had organised two more interviews, before she could even think about picking up Lois from the airport. Lewis the driver arrived at 9.30. She wondered if she was supposed to turn up in the onesie but decided against it. These ones were a bit more highbrow with their questions. 'Do you work out? Do you think Neil leaving you will make you a stronger person? How were you able to hang onto the cliff for so long? Do you practice mindfulness Bernadette? No! Yoga? No. Pilates? No. So where do you find your inner strength Bernadette?' *Inner strength! For Christ's sake!* She guessed they would write what they wanted in any case.

As Lewis sped up the M4 towards Heathrow, she felt shiny and buffed. This must be what Davina felt like every day. What a lot of work; bikini line, chin waxing, spray tans, eyebrow threading, gel nails, facials. And this was before you even got onto basic maintenance like opticians and dentist. The amount of appointments she must have to attend, there would be no time to do anything else, let alone work. No wonder these women were on Facebook so often. You'd want people to see the results of your efforts.

They turned off at Terminal 2 and pulled up at arrivals. The first few times she had reached for the handle herself, but now she knew to wait until he came round to let her out.

'If I'm not here, I'll be just up by the Meet & Greets.'

'Thank you Lewis.' She felt regal.

The flight from Dublin was on time and passengers were already coming out, most of them with carry-on bags. She scanned the crowd, finally Lois emerged with a trolley laden with very large pieces of matching luggage. They screamed loudly, arms waving as they spotted each other, continuing to scream as they embraced.

'You've lost weight Bo.'

'It's the spray tan.'

'Let me have a look at you. You look grand Bo! What have they done to you?'

'What haven't they done. My God Lois, are you planning on staying for a year! Come on, there's a car waiting.'

Lois was taller than Bo, five years older, not a sign of a wrinkle, blonde highlights and fabulously long legs. Their fathers had both been 6ft 4 and Lois was the image of them both. Bo looked more like her mother with her dark hair and green eyes.

Lewis held the door open. 'Lewis, meet Lois, Lois, Lewis!' Lois was clearly impressed. 'Well this is very nice I must say, so what's the plan.'

'We can stay at Betsy's flat tonight. And we've got invitations to a party.'

'What party? You didn't mention a party.'

Bo paused dramatically. 'I have a pair of VIP tickets to a National Television Awards After Party hosted by Simon Cowell.'

'Feck off!'

'I kid you not Lois. We are going to Simon Cowell's after party!'

'But I haven't got a feckin thing to wear!' Bo could see Lewis' shoulders lifting as he struggled not to laugh.

'Not a problem. It's all sorted. Betsy has arranged for us to be dressed by a personal stylist and we've got a private viewing of a handbag collection on Bond Street. We can pick what we want!'

'Jesus! I think I'm beginning to love this agent of yours. What is she anyway, some kind of celebrity ambulance chaser?'

Bo was conscious of Lewis listening in. 'Not quite, anyway, you'll meet her later.' Bo lowered her voice. 'Whatever you do, don't mention Max Clifford, she doesn't like it.'

'I'll be sure not to mention him.' They both started to laugh.

'So first stop Mua Mua in Bond Street.'

Lois laughed. 'It's not Mooah Mooah you daft cow, it's Mwah, like an air kiss!'

'Who cares Lois, they're giving us free clothes and handbags.'

It was just before 5pm when they pulled up outside the Bond Street store. They were ushered into a private area, damask wallpaper, chandeliers and circular mirrors.

'Hi I'm Fiona, senior stylist at Mua Mua. Can I get you a glass of Champagne?'

They both made a concerted effort not to look at each other or laugh. A younger girl appeared with a tape measure.

Fiona clapped her hands. 'Right, shall we get started? Annabel will take some measurements and then we'll get you a selection of dresses and bags.'

Annabel returned wheeling rails of dresses for each of them to try. Lois' head appeared between velvet curtains. 'What have they got you in then?'

Bo pulled back her curtains. 'Apparently it's a floor length peplum with embroidered bodice. I'm not sure about the black though?'

Fiona smiled indulgently. 'Betsy says black.'

'Oh right.'

Lois nodded. 'You look stunning Bo! Seriously.'

Fiona spotted them both stroking a raspberry velvet oversized clutch. 'Oh no, Betsy was quite specific, it has to be this one.' She handed Bo a leopard print clutch. 'And the shoes need to be leopard print too, let me get you some to try on.'

Lois snorted. 'Well I can see where she's going with the leopard print thing. Just be grateful your dress is black!' Lois was wearing a red lace floor length dress, with a scalloped bodice and a slit right up the front.'

Bo smiled. 'God Lois, fabulous!'

As they got back in the car, carrying their dresses, shoes and laden with gifts, including two raspberry velvet clutch bags and this season's tan leather tote in three colours, they started to giggle uncontrollably. Lois stopped first. 'This is unbelievable Bo. It's like winning the lottery.'

'I know! And Betsy has a hairdresser and make up artist waiting for us at the flat.'

'You're joking!' Lois looked out of the window as they drove up Bond Street. 'Let's hope this doesn't all come crashing down.'

Bo raised her eyebrows and threw a glance over at Lewis, but he didn't seem to be listening.

Lois carried on. 'And what about your job?'

'Betsy phoned them, I don't know what she said but they're holding it open for six months.'

'She's good this Betsy woman. And Liam? Have you heard from him?'

'No, he should be in Cambodia by now, he won't know anything about it.'

Lois nodded. 'Good. Poor love.'

At 8pm, Lewis held the door open and they slid into the waiting car. 'You look wonderful ladies. Betsy says I'm to pick you up at 11 o'clock sharp. You've got a meeting with The One Show producers tomorrow.' It was the most Bo had ever heard him say.

They swept along the banks of the Thames towards the O2, where Lewis pulled up in front of a crowd of paparazzi, lined up in banks along a red carpet. Bo leant forward. 'I'm sure we're not supposed to stop here Lewis. Isn't there another entrance round the back?'

He smiled. 'This is the only entrance.' And when he saw their bemused expressions. 'You go in here ladies, straight up the red carpet. The slower the better I believe.' He walked round and opened the door.

Lois and Bo looked at each other, mouths open. They just had time to mouth 'Shit' in unison, before getting out of the car.

'Have fun ladies. I'll be here at 11. Betsy wants you bright eyed tomorrow morning.' He stood back to let them pass. 'And try not to look quite so shocked.'

There were banks of photographers jostling for position, journalists standing on the sidelines with microphones, presenters talking to cameras, everyone shouting out names and instructions.

A young man with a clipboard and an ear piece emerged from the melee. 'This way ladies, if you'd like to follow me.'

'It's the angel in a onesie!' A voice in the crowd shouted. There was a ripple through the paparazzi, like a Mexican wave of recognition and suddenly all the lenses turned in her direction.

All these people were talking to her like they knew her.

'Bo, Bernie, Bernadette, look this way, who's your friend Bo?'

'Lois, my cousin.'

'Looking gorgeous ladies! Look this way, Bernadette, Bernadette, show us your leopard print bag! Lois, look over here!' They turned this way and that, blinking into the flashing cameras.'

Lois turned to the cameras, thrust one hip forwards and gave her best dazzling smile. She shouted over the noise. 'Well Bernadette Maloney, this is the craic!'

'Spicer, how many times do I need to tell you!' Bo muttered without moving her lips. 'I don't think I can keep this up much longer Lois, my smile's slipping off my face.'

'Can we have Bernadette on her own now!' The man in the black suit with the clipboard ushered Lois away.

Bo whispered under her breath. 'Lois stay right there. Don't you go off dancing with Simon Cowell and leaving me on my own.'

Lois hovered to one side as Bo stood awkwardly, turning towards whoever called her name. The entire cast of Corrie arrived and in one movement the photographers were gone. There were no more shouts for them and they tottered arm in arm up the rest of the red carpet towards the entrance.

'Oh my God Bo, it's Monty Don, I bloody love him!'

'Showing you're age Lois.'

'I'm going over to talk to him.'

'You're not.'

'I am.' Bo's grip tightened on Lois as they entered the huge hall, but luckily Lois was distracted as they were engulfed by a crowd of reality TV stars. They were handed a glass of Champagne as a platinum blonde with a dip dyed purple fringe approached them smiling. Bo vaguely recognized her as the daughter of an 80s pop star. She'd just come out of the Big Brother house.

She was smiling and talking to them like old friends. 'Oh yeah hi. What did you think of Ricky Gervais?'

It took Bo a while to realize what she meant. 'Oh we weren't invited to the actual awards ceremony.'

'Oh right.' She was a bit twitchy and kept glancing over their heads as she spoke. 'Who are you anyway?'

'Sorry, I'm Bernadette Spicer and this is my cousin Lois Shaunnessy.'

'No, I mean who are you?'

Bo was a bit nonplussed. 'You know.' Lois chipped in. 'Angel in a onesie!'

'Oh. I thought you were somebody.'

Bo could feel Lois' hackles go up. 'As opposed to?'

'Well, a nobody I guess!' Platinum reality star had already spotted someone genuinely famous and sashayed off.

'Bloody hell Lois, these people!'

'Cheeky cow!' Lois scanned the room. 'Come on Bo, we don't need some talentless reality TV star to tell us that we're 'somebody'. Two minutes on TV and she thinks she's Joanna Lumley?'

'Bo, it's Andrea Faustini. He's walking right towards us.'

'Who? How the hell do you know all these people Lois?'

'Don't give me that. You watch the X Factor, the cute Italian one with the novelty pug jumper.'

Andrea Faustini was indeed walking towards them and greeted Bo warmly, grasping her hands and kissing her on both cheeks. 'Bernadette, am I right? The 'Angel in a onesie'? I heard you'd be here. I'm so glad I found you.' He could see she was lost for words. 'You don't know who I am?'

'Of course I know who you are.' Bo was confident. 'You're Andrea. You won the X Factor.'

He pulled a face. 'Actually I came third.'

Lois looked despairing. 'Andrea was in the final, you daft cow, don't you remember? It was the fit van driver who won that series.'

'Oh yes, sorry.' There was a slightly awkward silence. 'And what are you doing now Andrea? Are you still working with Simon?' She assumed this was the sort of thing celebrities said to each other.

'I've just brought out my first album. Simon's been amazing.'

'Oh fantastic, well that's great isn't it. Any opera?' Bo felt herself flush as she said it.

'Sorry?'

'Any opera classics on the album?'

'No, no it's all original work, mainly gospel inspired.'

'Great.' She waited for an excruciating moment, but there was only silence. 'Well, we'll be sure to buy it, won't we Lois.' She was cringing even as she spoke.

He started to back away. 'Fantastic to meet you ladies! Amazing really!'

'Yes, amazing!' They both repeated after him.

They looked at each other as he walked off. 'Well that was awkward. I can't believe you said that! 'We'll be sure to buy it.''

'Shut up Lois! What was I supposed to say? What a lovely man! Just as I'd imagined. Can you believe he knew who I was!'

Lois wasn't listening. Her mouth was open and she was shouting above the music. 'It's Caitlyn Jenner!'

'Who?'

'Who! You know, Caitlyn who used to be Bruce Jenner, Kim Kardashian's stepfather!' Lois rolled her eyes. 'Listen to me Bo, we've hardly got any time until your man comes to pick us up. I'm not leaving without a selfie with Caitlyn Jenner! Come on, we need to dance.'

She was off. Bo struggled to keep up without tripping over her dress. Lois passed a waitress with a large tray of drinks and downed two Mojitos. 'Here we go!' Bo mouthed as she helped herself to a glass of Champagne. Lois was magnificent, with her blonde hair flying, red dress slashed up to her thighs, but even Lois was no match for the Kardashian security team.

Bo lost her for a moment and danced around on her own, trying not to dribble down her dress as she swigged from her glass of champagne. Mercifully the music was so loud that no one could hear if you sang along. She smiled to herself, how life can change in a week. Lois emerged from the crowd, whooping and hollering at the front end of a celebrity conga. 'Come on Bo, join the back!' Bo laughed and put her glass down. It was hard to keep up in four inch heels and a dress you might pop out of at any moment. She gave up after a bit and staggered around again in the middle. She had to concentrate quite hard not to click or clap when she danced, which Lois had said was absolutely off limits these days. There was Lois again in the middle of the dance floor, waving her arms in the air. She had somehow managed to dance her way into a tight circle of celebrities and was mouthing the words to 'Uptown funk gonna give it to ya'. Bo danced unsteadily towards her. The whole group had their arms up, punching the air. Lois and Olly Murs were holding hands, back to back and shimmying down to the floor together.

Lois was waving at her again and making whooping noises. 'Over here Bo! There's Paul Hollywood! Let's go and see if he's got a soggy bottom! Too hot, hot damn! Call the police and the fireman!'

Bo was quite near the Kardashian area now, which was raised up and cordoned off by a red rope. She took another glass of Champagne from a passing waiter and walked up to the entrance. Immediately a burly security guard stepped in front of her.

'Hi!' She smiled up at him. 'I'm Bernadette Spicer. You enjoying yourself?'

The security guard continued to look straight ahead, arms crossed. Bo struggled not to slur as she spoke. 'You might actually know me better as the Angel is a onesie?' She winked, which she was not in the habit of doing.

Still nothing.

'Can you see my cousin Lois, over there, dancing with Olly Murs? Well she's a huge fan of the Kardashian Jenners, Caitlyn in particular. Do you think he, she, could spare a few seconds to take a selfie with us?'

The security guard shook his head. 'Ms Jenner is not doing publicity tonight.'

It was unfortunate timing, but Lois' head popped up quite near to them shouting. 'Bo! Come over here! Paul Hollywood literally let me touch his bottom!'

Bo smiled up at him. 'She's not that pissed.' She pulled a face. 'She's a housewife from County Kilkenny, three teenage boys, doesn't get out much.'

The security guard shook his head but didn't reply.

'You know what, it's quite rude not to look someone in the eye when they speak to you? And you should uncross your arms. Your body language is very hostile.'

He continued to stare straight ahead. 'I'm asking you politely to move away from the area.'

'Do you think this is how celebrities should treat their biggest fans? Bollocks to you.'

Lois was by her side. 'Go Bo! I love it when she gets like this!'

The guard reached into his pocket. 'I'm calling security.' But before he could speak into his walkie talkie, a statuesque figure in a dark blue silk wrap dress and crystal chandelier ear rings, tapped the security guard on the shoulder. He immediately moved to one side. 'I think we can spare these ladies a moment, don't you, if they've come all the way from Ireland. Do you have a phone ladies?'

Bo and Lois' mouths hit the floor. Bo recovered quickly enough to find her iPhone in her giant clutch bag.

Lois rested her face against Caitlyn Jenner's arm. 'God you're even more beautiful in real life!'

'Lois!' Bo raised her eyes. 'I'm sorry, she's from Kilkenny.'

They huddled either side and Caitlyn handed Bo's phone to the security guard to take the shot. Bo tried not to smirk. When she had gone, the guard handed it back to her. 'You got your shot ladies now beat it.'

The party was only getting started when Bo's mobile phone alarm went off. They reluctantly found Lewis waiting for them at the entrance.

In the back of the Audi, Lois sighed. 'I will never have a word said against Caitlyn Jenner. Did you know she won the Olympic decathlon?'

Bo rolled her eyes. 'You had mentioned it.'

'The feckin Olympic games Bo, a gold medal for Christ's sake! The woman is sainted.'

'She is indeed Lois.'

'Some people say it's not right and d'you know what I say to them Bernadette?'

'What Lois?'

'I say get over your feckin self and get a life! Because everyone deserves the chance to be true to themselves right Bo?'

'Right Lois. D'you know what I think?'

'What?'

'I think it's a blessing you didn't catch up with Monty Don.'

They snorted with laughter. 'Christ Bo, I think I've wet myself.'

Back at the flat, their dresses lay in a crumpled heap on the floor. Lois was already asleep but Bo sat up in bed and scrolled through the pictures on her phone, trying to take it all in. A message popped up from Facebook. Talia Grossman was in the First Class Lounge at BA again. Bo's hand hovered over the shot of her and Caitlyn Jenner. She wondered why she cared about these bloody awful show offs anyway. She hesitated for a second and then pressed 'Post'. *Bernadette Spicer was at the National Television Awards After Party with Caitlyn Jenner.* Stick that up your infinity pool Talia Grossman!

Next to her, Lois slept soundly, snoring lightly in spite of the night time noise. She imagined she should feel elated, riding on a celebrity high, but instead she started to feel the anxiety return and this time it was far worse than anything she had experienced before.

Bernadette Maloney you will be found out...and when you are, may the Lord have mercy on your sinful soul.

8

'Last night everyone's favourite housewife hero, Bernadette Spicer mixed with stars of stage and screen at Simon Cowell's glittering post Awards bash.' Betsy was reading out loud from the screen in front of her.

It was hard to read her expression as she skimmed the headlines. 'Good work Bo. Yes, very good. You're in most of the key ones. Mailonline, aceshowbiz, Reveal, Getty images, Popcrush. Yes, this is all good news for us.'

Bo squinted as she studied the pictures over Betsy's shoulder.

'Good grief.' Betsy took off her glasses. 'One has to ask if there was anyone you didn't take a selfie with. Olly Murs has posted the picture with you and Lois on twitter and you and Caitlin Jenner are trending on #youbeyou.'

'This looks like a good one.' Betsy paused on one of the pieces and read it out loud. 'Digital Spy caught up with 'Angel in a Onesie' Bernadette Spicer. We asked her what it felt like to be partying with the stars.'

Betsy put on her reading glasses and read slightly theatrically. 'To which you replied, 'The drinks are free and I'm very pissed, but not as drunk as my cousin.'

She sighed. 'There's a picture here of you and Lois on either end of a conga with the entire cast of Geordie Shore.

At least they've put quite a nice picture of you on the Geordie Shore website. And what's Lois doing in the background with that ice sculpture?'

'Oh yes.' Bo had forgotten about that one.

Betsy closed her laptop and took off her glasses. 'Well I don't suppose we'll get the Mua Mua gig again, but it's all good. The whole 'over excited girl next door', down to earth thing plays right into our hands. It seems the whole world wants to meet you or get your advice on something or other! We've had 2,500 messages overnight on Facebook and Twitter, most of which are asking for your thoughts on everything from cushion covers to whether or not to ditch their husband. I'll get one of the juniors to answer them.'

'I can answer them.'

Betsy looked up, slightly surprised.

'If people have asked my opinion then shouldn't it be me that answers them?'

Betsy shrugged her tiny shoulders. 'If you like, I mean it's not really how it works. It's very time consuming.' She sighed. 'I'll get Toby to show you how to access the account.' She flicked through some papers on her desk. 'So, we've got a meeting with the One Show at 12. We're seeing Dorothy Perkins at 3 and Zest magazine want to know about your pelvic floor?'

'My pelvic floor? It's Lois' pelvic floor you want to worry about.'

'Ah yes, Lois. County Kilkenny's favourite 'it' girl. How is she this morning? A little under the weather I imagine?'

'Sleeping it off.'

'Good, because you're really going to have to focus today. I've printed off some key messages we can work on.'

She handed Bo a sheet of paper. 'Think of it as building a brand. *The housewife heroine.*' She leant forward and looked at Bo intently. 'You're gutsy, uncompromising, likeable, self-deprecating, very British, think 'Loose Women'. You just did *'what anyone else would have done.*' Betsy did that speech mark thing in the air. 'Only we all know that's crap don't we. Most of us wouldn't cross the road to save a stranger.' Bo was fairly sure that Betsy wouldn't.

'Can't I just be myself?' She felt stupid even before the words had left her mouth.

Betsy looked up from her desk. 'Yourself with bells on sweetie! Of course we need you to stay 'real'. No harm in some lovely little glimpses of your life back home. You know, struggles with your weight, favourite TV soap, husband leaving you for a younger woman, your cats, that kind of thing. All great stuff! Helps establish how very ordinary you are Bo. On second thoughts, don't talk about the cats, too tragic!'

'I won't mention the night sweats and binge drinking then?' Betsy, oblivious to irony, looked at her blankly.

'If the One Show meeting goes well, they're thinking of putting you on tonight's show. And if we can get them to commit to that before the Dorothy Perkins meeting this afternoon, I don't need to tell you that would be a huge added pull. Your value would go stratospheric darling! And we need to sort out a photoshoot at some point, with that bloody little upstart from TV South West.'

'Katy Partridge?'

'That's the one. We need you and Melinda for a clifftop photoshoot sometime this week if possible.'

'I'm not sure I can do this Betsy.'

'Do what?' Betsy sounded faintly irritated.

'Any of it.'

'You'll be fine, just do as I say.' Betsy didn't even look up.

Bo fiddled with the tassels on her new handbag. 'I didn't sleep at all last night. I could hardly breathe at one point.'

'It's called a panic attack darling. Perfectly normal.'

Betsy studied Bo picking at the tassels for a moment. 'Look, let's put you in touch with Vishal.'

'Vishal?'

'He's a mindfulness coach. He's worked with a lot of my clients.' Betsy reached into her desk drawer. 'Take these, you need to listen to both CDs tonight and I'll get him to call you tomorrow. He's based in San Fran, it'll probably be tomorrow afternoon.'

Betsy was still coaching her as they walked into the offices of The One Show. 'Be yourself, but think about the brand. Gutsy, modest, straight talking and real. We need you to be on this show tonight Bernadette. If we can take your story to 3.5 million people, we'll have retail brands biting our arm off.'

If Betsy's pep talk was supposed to keep her calm, it wasn't working. Bo's mind was reeling when the two producers greeted them in reception. There was a lot of awkward air kissing before the one with the clipboard showed them into a meeting room.

'So, we're just going to ask you all about what happened up there. Really amazing what you did, huge fans here at the One Show. Alex and Matt would love to have you on the show. Can you just talk us through how you came to be up there in the first place?'

'I was looking out of the window and I saw this yellow shape.' Bo focused on Betsy's bony knees as she recounted the story. It sounded more distant and unreal each time she told it. 'I guessed she must have been about 17 and I could see she was very upset.'

The producer's eyes narrowed. 'Did you think she was going to jump?'

'No not really, I was more worried about the weather.'

'Right. And you held onto her until the search and rescue team arrived.'

'Anyone would have done the same.' Bo couldn't look at Betsy, but she could see her nodding vigorously.

'OK great.' The producer was making notes. 'Well we'd absolutely love to have you on the show Bernadette. You're amazing, really inspirational. Tell it just like that! We'll put you on the sofa at about 7.15. If you can be back here in make up for 5.30pm, Matt and Alex will come and have a chat with you before we go on air.'

She could sense Betsy's triumph as they got up to leave. She swung out of the revolving doors in her Chanel suit and enormous sunglasses.

Lewis was waiting for them outside. Bo's stomach was churning, it could no longer be called anxiety. 'Live TV Betsy! What if I'm too petrified to speak?'

'It'll be fine. We'll run you through the key messages so many times you'll be saying them in your sleep. Anyway, petrified is good. Helps keep it real. We don't want you to come across as too slick or rehearsed. Right let's focus, we've got one hour before Dorothy Perkins.'

'I think I'm going to be sick.'

'Deep breaths Bo!' Betsy looked at her and sighed. You could tell she was trying to keep a lid on her irritation. 'Look darling, if it helps to focus your mind, Dorothy Perkins are talking about a plus size leopard print 'Bernadette' lingerie range for the over 40s. Their first punt was £50K up front with another £20K for five PAs in the next six months; store visits, photoshoots, sky's the limit. I'm sure I can get you double that and if it sells well, who knows after that.'

'Did you say fifty thousand pounds?' Bo's eyes widened.

'Minimum!'

'And would it absolutely have to be a plus size range? I'm only a size 12.'

Betsy looked vexed again. 'Look darling, for that kind of money it can be a morbidly obese, hunch back, bloody elephant size range for all we care. It's not about you, it's about *Bernadette the brand*. That reminds me, we need to talk about your weight darling. I've got you booked in with Serge for your first session at his studio, first thing tomorrow morning.'

Bo stared straight ahead. 'I need to go home tonight.'

'What for? We've sorted the cats. Your neighbour's cleaner is coming in twice a day.'

'I'm booked in for a speed awareness course tomorrow.'

Betsy snorted. 'Cancel it!'

She looked out of the car window, anywhere but at Betsy. 'I can't, I've already confirmed.'

Betsy sighed deeply again and picked up her phone. 'Right!' She looked down at the schedule in front of her and started punching the keys with her thumb. 'I'll have to see if I can reorganise Serge. And while you're at home, I suppose we might as well sort out that bloody cliff top exclusive.'

Bo couldn't help but break out into a broad smile. It was strange to be excited by the idea of home.

Betsy could sense her relief. 'Only a few days though, then it's straight back to work. And you'll have to do at least 3 radio interviews over the phone while you're home.' She flicked through her notes. 'The Metro Q&A we can do by email.'

The Dorothy Perkins meeting was a breeze by comparison. There were no searching questions and this time it was Betsy's turn to perform. She was predictably impressive. She felt a bit like Betsy's stooge as she sat by her side in the swanky office. By this time, she was seriously hungry and her main concern was trying to suppress the noises her stomach was making in the quieter moments. She sipped her water and listened reverently to Betsy's monologue.

'Bernadette Spicer, safe, ordinary, loved. Think Delia Smith, Lorraine Kelly, Colleen Nolan; all hugely influential women. I don't need to tell you what an association with any of them would do for a high street brand. They speak and millions of British women listen. What we have here is a fledgling star. When I last checked, just before we came here, twelve thousand people had been in contact to ask for her advice.' Bo looked suitably surprised by this latest revelation.

Betsy let them take that in. She looked around the room. 'This is a potential phenomenon and we want to work with a few, select, high street brands to capitalize on her influence.'

The marketing team looked at each other and nodded.

'And how committed would you personally be to the brand Bernadette?'

Betsy butted in. 'She would be all over it. Completely integral to the brand. The PR exposure we're getting would double your marketing investment. She's on the One Show tonight, we've done 6 magazine spreads and 14 interviews in two days. I've got media biting my arm off to speak to her, find out what she watches on TV, where she shops, her beauty routine, what she eats.'

'Absolutely.' Bo nodded. Would this woman ever let her speak.

The more senior looking marketing bloke piped up. 'And you'd be prepared to invest time to promote the brand. You understand how much work that could entail.'

Bo took another sip of water. 'Oh yes.' At this point, if someone had promised her a burger and chips, she would have signed up for a Playboy centrefold.

As they walked out of the office, Betsy once again buoyant, Bo's phone rang. She walked swiftly ahead up the street, out of Betsy's earshot.

'Lois, I'm going to be on the bloody One Show! Tonight! Live!'

There were a few seconds silence at the other end.

'Bo, do you not think this has gone far enough? I mean the higher you climb, the harder you'll fall.'

'Thanks for the pep talk.'

'I'm just saying, if you get found out!'

'I know, but it's too late Lois.' Bo looked over at the car where Betsy sat impatiently pointing at her watch.

Lois was still talking. 'You could just quit now, you know. You must have made a few grand already. No one need ever know.'

'I can't Lois. They're waiting for me. Anyway, how's your head? Have you been out of the flat?'

'Not yet, but Betsy's organized a personal stylist and makeover at Selfridges later on, can you believe it!'

Bo felt sick. 'I've got to go now Lois. I'll see you back at the flat later. Don't forget to tune in!' She added rather weakly.

'I'm just coming.' Bo snapped at Betsy as she walked back to the car.

And there was Lois telling her to quit the limelight, while she thoroughly enjoyed the trappings of fame. As she stared out of the window, Bo had the strong impression that Betsy was beginning to control her every move.

She turned to Betsy. 'You were very impressive back there. Very persuasive. Do you always get what you want.'

'Yes, mostly.' Betsy smiled.

'And what about Mr Betsy? Is there another half at home?' She felt bold even asking.

Betsy smiled a little condescendingly but was surprisingly candid. 'No, not a Mr, no.' She paused. 'There's a Mrs. I share my life with Perdita.'

'Oh right.' Bo flushed. That would teach her to pry. More than ever, she felt like a gauche, unworldly housewife from Lower Hinton, sitting next to this woman, this clever, urbane woman. She should have guessed. Betsy had something of the Mary Portas about her, very direct, knowing exactly what she wants. She imagined Perdita was tall and willowy, with a job in the media and very cool clothes.

Bo's tummy rumbled again. Betsy didn't seem to stick to regular meal times. They eventually stopped at an organic café in Carnaby Street and Betsy ordered her a bowl of lettuce and edamame beans. It didn't even take the edge off. Betsy ordered the chicken Caesar salad, without the dressing and a black coffee.

By the time they arrived back at the studio, Bo was word perfect, the responses drilled into her. 'Yes Betsy, no Betsy, it's what anyone would have done Betsy.' 'Me? I'm just a no-nonsense house wife.' 'I can't believe the reaction of the British public, it's been amazing.' She was on automatic pilot as they applied a thick layer of orange make up to her face. It was only when she sat on the famous lime green sofa, the neon lights behind her that her hands began to shake. She hoped the camera wouldn't zoom in, but resisted the temptation to look at the monitor.

Matt Baker turned to her and smiled reassuringly.

So, one week ago, you were Bernadette Spicer, an ordinary Wiltshire housewife and today you are the nation's sweetheart, hero, agony aunt, friend of the stars. Has all this taken you by surprise?'

'God yes!' She relaxed a little.

They both laughed at her candid response.

'What an incredible story. Just to recap, although I doubt there's anyone who hasn't heard about it this week. You spotted a young girl sitting at the top of a local landmark, you climbed up in torrential rain and tried to talk her down and when the rock gave way and you both fell down the side of the cliff, you managed to somehow hold onto her until the rescue team could winch her to safety.'

Bo pulled a face. 'Yes, but that does make it sound better than it was. To be honest, I feel like a bit of a fraud.' She imagined Betsy's face. This was not what they had rehearsed.

Matt smiled. 'You saved a life.'

'I suppose so.' She paused, wondering if she should say any more. 'It was instinctive, you know, it wasn't brave or anything.'

Alex joined in. 'Well I think a few people would disagree with you. Mel was quoted in the papers today saying you made her laugh at her problems, like they were very small. I hope you don't mind me saying this, but you had literally just found out that your husband was leaving you. Do you think that gave you more empathy?'

'Maybe. Everyone's struggling with some kind of heartache aren't they?' No key messages.

It was Matt's turn again. 'And while you were recovering in hospital, I believe your house was burgled! What do you say to the people that broke into your house?'

Bo flushed bright red. 'I don't know, thanks for tidying up?'

Alex was serious again, 'Joking apart, what advice would you have for a young girl in Mel's situation, Bo?'

'Well I told her to switch it all off, all that social media stuff. It's not real life. Try living without it for a bit.'

Alex leant towards her, 'But is that the right thing to do? Shutting down your connections with the outside world.'

'Oh yes, Facebook and Instagram. I think it can actually make you feel even more lonely and inadequate.'

Matt narrowed his eyes. 'That sounds like it's spoken from the heart. And do you take your own advice when it comes to living your life.'

'God no! I'm a disaster!' Dangerously off brief again.

Alex smiled. 'Are you surprised by the number of people turning to you for advice. I think it's now in the tens of thousands.'

'I think it's lovely!' *Lovely! Where did that come from.* 'I just hope they'll be patient because I'm going to try to reply to as many as I can.'

'You're going to be busy!'

Well, they've set up different forums on my website so that people can talk to each other and I can offer advice, for what it's worth.'

'Fantastic!' Finally, she'd got one of Betsy's precious key messages in. She could feel her heart thumping through her shirt.

'Wow! Amazing story. Well good luck with it all Bernadette.' Matt turned to face the camera and she was off air. 'Let's find out what the weather's got in store for us this weekend.'

One of the production team ushered her off the sofa and unclipped her microphone. Betsy was waiting for her in the green room. She actually looked quite pleased. 'Excellent Bo! Completely off bloody script, but perfect all the same!'

'Thank you, Betsy.'

9

Lewis had driven her straight from the studio. It was just before 9.30 when she finally got home. She stood with her back to the door, looking around her own hallway as if she'd been away for a year. She called to the cats. 'Hey Snickers, Toby, where are you?' They skipped down the stairs and curled around her legs. What would Betsy say about her cats? Tragic! Who cared what Betsy thought anyway.

She picked up Snickers and went into the kitchen. The house was spotless, every surface shining and the smell of pine freshness wafting from every room. Angelica's mop was propped up by the fridge, next to a post-it note sellotaped to the kitchen door.

I DEEP CLEAN. Mrs E-D say you call her as soon as you back. Cats fed. DON'T MESS UP HOUSE.

She kicked off her shoes. A glass of wine, some TV and a takeaway pizza. She searched the cupboards for a bottle of wine and dialed the pizza delivery number. Lois was staying in London with a friend, so tonight would be perfect, uninterrupted peace. There were 18 unread Facebook notifications on her iPad but she resisted the strong urge to look. Instead she put her feet up on the sofa and switched on the TV. Monty Don was sponging down his greenhouse and potting on some lavender cuttings. The sight of his soil covered hands plunged into a bucket of well gritted earth was strangely comforting. He really was very attractive for his age. She smiled to herself. Thank God Lois hadn't caught up with him. She looked at her bare feet. The waxed calves and perfect shellac nails were the only clues that the last few days had actually happened, that and the £25,000 that Betsy had deposited in her bank account. £25,000! And that was just the advance, the rest could go in an account for Liam. She would have a few glasses of wine and think about how to spend it. Maybe she should go away somewhere very hot and take a lover, foreign obviously, like Shirley Valentine. Monty was talking about jobs for the weekend. 'And if you haven't yet pruned your fruit trees...' 'No Monty I haven't pruned my fruit trees. You can come and prune them if you like.' She wondered how many thousand middle aged women were shouting something inappropriate at the screen at exactly the same time.

The phone rang. It was international, probably one of those nuisance cold callers, but she answered it anyway, just in case it was Liam.

'Hello.'

'Hi, Bernadette!' The voice was American. 'My name is Vishal.'

'Sorry, who?'

'Vishal. Betsy gave me your number.' There was an awkward pause. 'I'm a mindfulness coach.'

'Oh yes, right.' She thought about Monty and the glass of wine waiting for her in the other room.

'Betsy told me you've been having some issues with anxiety.' She was feeling quite anxious now, but only because she wanted to get him off the phone before the pizza arrived.

'Have you listened to my introductory Podcast? It's a unique approach, I've patented it, '*Vish-ful thinking*.' It's a mix of cognitive behavioural therapy, mindfulness and yogic breathing.'

'Oh I see, yes, Vish-ful. Very good.'

'Have you listened to the Podcast?'

'To be honest, no. I'm sorry Vishal, I'm going to have to call you back another time.' She was struggling to think of a good enough excuse.

'I'm sensing a lot of anxiety in your voice right now Bernadette. Are you really busy? Too busy to start the journey toward an anxiety free future?'

'God no.'

'OK then, let's examine how you feel right now. Are you anxious Bernadette?'

'Yes I am.'

'OK. How would you rate your anxiety on a scale 1 through 10?'

'I'd say a 7. To be honest though, now isn't a good time.'

'Hey but now is always a great time! Are you subconsciously blocking Bernadette?'

'Blocking?'

'Yes. I need you to open up, before we can start this journey together. We only need 15 minutes for our first session.'

'Oh OK.' May as well get it over with.

'I need you to empty your mind, concentrate on your breathing. In and out, in and out. Have you emptied your mind Bernadette?'

She wondered if she should say yes or should it appear to take a bit longer. 'It's empty.'

'OK great, now I want you to pick up on what you can hear all around you? As you breath in and out, in and out, listen to your breathing and concentrate on the small everyday sounds around you.'

She could hear the theme tune for *Gardeners' World*. Bugger, she'd missed the whole bloody episode!

'It's 10 o'clock at night, I can't hear anything really.'

'Empty your mind Bernadette and listen deeply.'

'OK then, I can hear the noise of a radiator.'

'Good, go on.'

'It's sort of gurgling, sounds like it needs bleeding but Neil used to do that, so I'll have to get someone in. And my neighbour's dog's barking, probably a fox going through the bins again.'

'Keep going.'

'And my National Trust 'Birds of Britain' clock ticking. It's quite faint and the second hand pauses too long on the Mistle Thrush, I should replace the battery, but I keep forgetting to buy four AAAs, need to write it down. And I can hear the theme tune for Coast on the TV in the next room with that Scottish presenter – the one that need's a haircut, he's too old for a pony tail – I sound like my mother!'

There was a brief silence at the end of the line. Was it too much to hope that he'd put the phone down. 'No Bernadette, do you see what you're doing? You're creating a mental 'to do list', ramping up your anxiety levels. Here's how this works. I want you to listen deeply, hear the sounds but give yourself permission to drop them and move on to the next. I want your mind empty, do you understand?' She was picking up a slight undercurrent of tetchiness. 'And Bernadette, switch off the TV!'

'Right OK.' If she was to do a bit of amateur psychology herself, she appeared to have allowed yet another random, bossy person into her life, telling her what to do. It was 10 o'clock at night for God's sake. She turned down the TV volume – how much more relaxing to have watched Monty Don applying a bark mulch.

'Let's try that again. Breathe in, and breathe out, concentrate on the rhythm of your breath, in and out.'

She could hear the sound of the pizza delivery van in the drive. Best not to mention that. 'No, I see what you mean Vishal, that's very insightful.' *Insightful? She'd never used that word in her entire life.* 'It's just that my neighbour is about to come round for dinner, you see.'

Just as she said it the door bell rang. 'There she is now! She's been through a terrible time poor love.' She walked to the front door. 'And I'm busy tomorrow, so maybe later this week?'

There was a slight sigh at the other end of the phone. Could mindfulness coaches be short tempered? 'OK Bernadette, but you need to make time for this. I'm sensing resistance. You're withholding.'

'Absolutely Vishal. Here she is now!' She opened the front door, not wanting the pizza delivery man to go away.

She greeted him loudly. 'How lovely to see you!'

He looked a bit taken aback. 'Extra pepperoni and cheese, no olives. Side order of coleslaw?'

She nodded and gestured for him to keep his voice down, speaking loudly into the phone. 'You poor love. So good to see you! Come in!'

'Sign here please.' Pizza man looked at the ground and shuffled nervously, it wasn't the first time he'd been asked in by a lonely middle aged woman. He waved the screen in front of her and mumbled. 'You don't need a pen, just use your finger nail.'

'Come in, come in. I'll pour you a glass of wine.'

He backed off hastily down the drive, shouting as he got in the van. 'We're running a promotion on the stuffed crust pizzas. There's a £2 voucher in the box off your next order.'

She gave him a thumbs up sign. 'I'll speak to you next week Vishal!'

'Yes, I can hear that you're busy.' Sarcasm now. 'Listen to the Podcast Bernadette, do the exercises at the end, I'll call you on Monday.'

'Will do, great.'

She sat down on the sofa and opened the cardboard pizza box, a full, dewy glass of white wine on the coffee table and the cheesy meltingness of the pizza now dripping slightly down her chin. Anxiety levels were down to a 5, maybe even a 4. The cats jumped up beside her.

'Mindfulness my arse!' She shouted out loud. Of course she was anxious. In the last 24 hours, she'd sold herself to a major High Street brand, danced with celebrities, posed in front to the nation's press and appeared on live television. Anxiety wasn't the word. Cold, hard fear would be a little more accurate. Surely there wasn't anything left to be anxious about, but she knew that wasn't the case. Vishal was right, the mental 'to do list' would be back soon enough, plaguing her with feelings of unease and hopelessness. For now the wine would keep it at bay.

She switched over to the History Channel, nothing on that she hadn't already seen five times. How ironic that 12,000 people had asked for her relationship advice. What a fraud! Neil would be sharing a bottle of wine with Mandy in the open plan kitchen of her executive home. Mandy probably knew all about the vineyard and the correct temperature to serve it. She wondered why she didn't feel more pain, but she knew the answer. He had left her a long time ago and she had learned to live alone, without even noticing.

Toby had emailed her some sample questions. She opened up the page.

Dear Bernadette,
I think I'm gay, how can I be sure?
Dear Nathan,
If you want my opinion, there's no such thing as 100% gay or straight. That would be far too simple. Aren't we all just on a spectrum? 'Shades of gay!' A friend of mine described it to me the other day. He said he can be very attracted to women, but only really love a man. I thought that was a lovely way of putting it…

Betsy would be furious if she knew she was answering these half pissed.

Dear Bernadette
I am 48 and have been feeling down for several years now. My sex life is non-existent, I have no energy, I'm short tempered and have feelings of low self worth…

Dear Justine

You poor love. Have you ever thought it might be the menopause? I only say this as I swear to God I've been menopausal since my mid 30s. I know it's not for everyone, but ever since my cousin started the HRT she's been hard to …

Dear Bernadette

I've been having feelings lately that make me think I hate my husband. I only ask because a magazine article I read said that you were planning to kill your husband too. Could you give me some advice…

Bloody hell! She decided to ask Betsy about some of the more complex ones.

There were now 21 Facebook notifications. She could no longer resist.

Lois Shaunnessy shared **Geordie Shore conga**
652 likes

Lois Shaunnessy shared **Caitlyn Jenner, Bernadette Spicer & me!**
324 likes

Talia Grossman commented: Gorgeous girlies!!!
Davina Edgerton Davis commented: Stunning!
Liam Spicer commented: Mum?! What the hell are you doing and who's that?
Poor Liam. She should call him.
Lois Shaunnessy updated her profile picture
206 likes

Lois Shaunnessy likes Selfridges personal shopper

Lois Shaunnessy is drinking margaritas at Cantina Bar, Soho

There was a message from Liam.

Mum what on earth were you and Auntie Lois doing at the National TV Awards and who was that tall woman with you? I've left Cambodia and I'm in Koh Pan Yang beach internet café, this is the first time I've had wifi for a week. What's going on?'

She began to type.

Hello! Glad you're back in contact. How was Angkor Wat? Nothing to worry about here. I've been having a few adventures of my own!

The phone rang again. *For the love of God.* She didn't pick it up.

'Bernadette, I know you're there.' It was Vishal again. 'It's important that you understand that I accept you, whether you are stuck and aimless or purposeful and committed to action.' Message left at 10.31pm…

'Well that's bloody good of you Vishal.' She shouted at the phone, because by now she'd had most of the bottle.

10

The Battle of the Somme

She was already 10 minutes late when she drove into the car park. Anxiety levels had been a constant 7 the entire journey as she struggled with the SatNav. The man at the security gate had given her an A4 pink sign to put on her dashboard 'SPEED AWARENESS PARKING', just in case there was any doubt at all why she was here.

She swung into a space, next to the entrance, not entirely parallel to the white parking lines, but the car park was only half full so she hoped it didn't matter as she hastily grabbed her hand bag.

Before she had a chance to get out, a woman pulled up right next to her in a duck egg blue mini. She could have chosen anywhere else in the car park, but instead she parked pedantically close to the white line, as if to point out Bo's parking deficiencies. The woman shook her head disapprovingly and made a bit of a scene as she got out of the car, holding her cream coat away from Bo's mud splattered bonnet. She thought she saw her mouth the word 'filthy'.

Well at least she wasn't last to arrive. They both looked a little furtive and avoided eye contact as they walked towards the entrance. Bo noticed mini woman had a flower in a vase on the dashboard, right next to the big pink parking badge of shame. She realized she was scowling and tried hard to assume a more positive expression.

They were greeted at the door by a suited man with a clipboard. He had very shiny black shoes and a perfect crease in his trousers. They were pointed to a room at the end of a long corridor. Only two seats left. She instinctively picked the one on the back row, leaving duck egg mini woman the front row position and slid into a plastic chair with clip-on tray attachment. There was a pen and paper in front of her.

As they waited for the course to start, she had the chance to look around the room at her fellow offenders. Two rows of plastic chairs and probably 16 people, shuffling around in their seats, some looking awkward, others looking like they wanted to chat. There was a bald, heavily tattooed man with two deep folds of flesh on the back of his neck. He was sitting next to a man in red cords and a barbour jacket, who looked very ill at ease. Duck egg blue mini woman, pulled out an iPad from her handbag, with a duck egg blue iPad cover.

An older lady sat next to mini woman, probably in her early 80s. Bo had a vision of her speeding all the way here, Beastie Boys blaring out of the stereo, with a handbrake turn into the car park. Anxiety had dissipated and there was now a real danger of hysteria. A tall, slightly brassy blonde with thigh high black suede boots was at the far end and next to her a younger man with dark blond hair, quite tanned, in jeans and a white shirt, nice watch. She couldn't see his face until he turned towards the door.

OH MY GOD IT'S HIM! Anxiety level 9. It was HIM. The young farmer, her would-be murderer, 'sheep in the back of my van', sarcastic young upstart, the reason she was here in the first place.

Please don't look round, please don't look round.

The course leader came in and shut the door and all heads turned to the front.

'Good morning one and all. My name is Bob Pargeter. My background? Six years in the military followed by fifteen with the police force.' He had very short bristly badger hair, cut into a stiff, geometric shape. She imagined him standing over her shouting abuse, while she did 150 press ups.

'I'll start with a few housekeeping rules. No hot drinks to be consumed in this room for health and safety reasons.' Her mind wandered. She was now in a sub category of human being who could no longer be trusted to control a cup of tea without causing grievous injury.

'So no doubt each of you has a very good, perfectly rational reason why you were speeding on the day you were caught.' They all nodded in agreement. Bob raised his eyebrows and nodded along with them. She sensed that this was a well-rehearsed routine.

'On the desk in front of you, you will find a form. On that form, you will write down in a phrase or short sentence, why you were speeding.'

Bald tattoo man started writing immediately. A few people chewed their pencils, another gazed out of the window. Young farmer looked around the room. She stared down, fixated by the piece of paper in front of her.

'The fact is...' Bob carried on, pacing the room as they gathered their excuses. 'You probably think you were unlucky to be caught. But you weren't unlucky. About 10-15% of speed cameras are functioning at any one time and believe me, traffic police have far better things to do than set up speed traps for people like you. Think about it! The truth is, all of you in this room are repeat offenders.'

The old lady rolled her eyes! Bo was sure of it. In spite of the anxiety, she had a warm feeling of respect.

The rest of the room looked cowed while Bob continued. 'So each of you now will read out to the rest of the group, why you were speeding.' *Oh my God!*

'Who's going to go first.' Silence in the room.

Bob pointed at bald tattoo man. 'You.'

Bald tattoo man turned out to have a very thick Eastern European accent. 'I'm from Poland. I don't know UK speed limit.' There were a few sniggers, but Bob chose not to rise.

'You?' He pointed at brassy blonde.

'I was late for the school pick up.'

She didn't think they'd have to read them out. There was no time to change her answer. It was her turn. She tried to keep her voice low as she read. 'I was being tail-gated by an aggressive young farmer.'

'Lucky you!' Brassy blonde woman had the whole room laughing. Bo couldn't look up as she sensed his eyes on her.

The laughter subsided and Bob pointed at the old lady. Bo glanced sideways. She had white, perfectly styled hair and very red lipstick. Old lady held eye contact with Bob as she spoke. 'I was running late for my yoga class.' She caught Bo's eye and winked.

A few hands were going up now as the room relaxed a little. She noticed young farmer hadn't been yet. So did Bob. Young farmer paused slightly before answering, his lips twitching. Bo held her breath. 'I'd just had an exchange with a complete nutter. I was accelerating to get away.'

Brassy blonde and old lady exchanged glances. Bo's eyes widened. The room looked suitably impressed.

'Interesting! OK,' Bob was animated. 'Not an excuse, but you bring up an interesting point. How many of you have let your emotions get the better of you on the road? We know what we're talking about, the gesture in the mirror?' They all giggled. 'But the rule is simple, DON'T. You are not safe just because you are inside a vehicle. As this gentleman puts it, there are a lot of nutters out there and they've all got a driving licence. For all you know, it could be the Kray twins in that car.'

Young farmer was looking over at her now, he caught her eye and raised his eyebrows. Her full body blush of shame turned into defiance. Bo felt her hand go up. 'So what should you do then, if some complete idiot is driving literally a foot behind you?'

'Nothing at all. Don't let it alter your driving in the slightest. Observe the speed limit and if you continue to be concerned, pull over and let them past.'

She could see young farmer nodding.

'OK let's move on. We'll come back to your excuses a bit later, when we've looked at some of the consequences of speeding.'

She looked out of the window at the uninspiring, 70s office block. It was a miserable day, grey and raining heavily. Betsy had plans to re-enact the clifftop scene tomorrow with Melinda and the TV South reporter. She wondered if they'd call it off because of the weather. Probably not.

Bob was pacing again, in full flow. 'The reason we know this is successful is that only 16% of people that attend this course go on to reoffend.'

'Bollocks!' Everyone looked up. It was posh bloke in the red cords.

Bob was on to him. 'I beg your pardon Sir?'

'What you mean is only 16% get caught again.'

'Not true, this course has been proven to cut reoffending significantly.' Bob's cheeks had coloured slightly. He obviously decided it was time for the video interlude and hastily pressed play. They were supposed to be noting down driving hazards. Most people were studying the film footage earnestly and scribbling. She glanced over at young farmer, he wasn't writing either. He looked at her and smiled.

Bob made them shout out the hazards. It was like one of those 'objects on a tray challenges' at children's birthday parties. Some people were genuinely enjoying themselves. 'Poorly lit road!' 'Cyclist.' 'Blind corner!' 'No road markings.' She looked at them all, with their eager faces. 'Stockholm syndrome' wasn't that what they called it, when you started to bond with your captor, something like that anyway.

Bob moved on. Another video. This time it was accompanied by the screeching of wheels, tyre marks across the road, a Vauxhall Corsa with a teenager sprawled across the bonnet, people on life support machines. Bob ran through life expectancy rates and probable injuries based on how badly you were speeding. It was confession time and Bob wanted each person to publicly acknowledge the extent of their crime. Here we go, this was the interesting bit.

Brassy blonde was up first, '36 in a 30 zone.'

Posh bloke was next, '50 in a 40.'

Bob pointed at her: '73 in a 60 limit.'

Old lady: 'Apparently I was doing 58, when the limit was 50.'

Bo put up her hand, almost without realising.

'Yes?' Bob turned to her.

'Well, nobody here seems to have been doing what I would call serious speeding. I mean where are all the people you caught doing 60 in a built up area? What happens to the real offenders, the ones doing 80 or 90 in a 50 speed limit, the joy riders?'

Bob looked at her blankly. 'They're not offered the course. They just get the points.'

'What, so because we're all decent, law abiding citizens who were barely over the speed limit, you can count on us to go online, book our course, pay the fee and turn up on time.'

'Quite dear!' Old lady piped up. 'I think they call us the 'squeezed middle''.

Bob opened his mouth as if to say something, but decided not to and moved on. 'In a moment, I'm going to give each of you a handheld device to register your answers to a simple screen based multiple choice. Use the device to answer A, B, C or D.'

The first question flashed up on the screen.

How many British people are killed in road traffic accidents every year?' Is it a) 18,000, b) 1,800 c) 420,000 or d) 420

Bob looked around the room. Mini driver was surprisingly animated. She had her hand in the air. Bob pointed at her.

'Is it 420,000?'

'What!' Bo felt herself snort, one of those involuntary laughter ones that shoots right out of your nose, without having to open your mouth. She didn't think anyone had heard, but the whole room was looking at her.

Duck egg blue mini woman turned round in her seat. She had a face like thunder.

Bo tried to keep her voice down, but she was right at the other end of the room. 'I'm sorry, it just sounded a bit daft that's all. I mean 420,000 British people killed in road traffic accidents every year?'

'No it's not.' Mini woman spat the words out. 'There are people killed on our roads every day.'

'I'm not disputing that, but 420,000! I mean that's the same amount of British troops that were killed in the entire Battle of the Somme?'

Mini woman's eyes had narrowed to angry pin pricks. 'Are you calling me stupid?'

'Not at all, I'm just saying that it was unlikely, if you think about it.'

'You're the rudest person I've ever met.' The room was silent apart from the shifting of people in their seats.

'Well lucky you, if I'm the rudest person you've ever met!'

'And quite unlike your TV persona if I may say.' Now everyone was transfixed. Out of the corner of her eye, she could see young farmer throwing his head back laughing.

'Ladies please! Let's keep this positive and collaborative.' Bob stood between them so they could no longer try to out stare each other. He moved on to the next question. 'OK, I think it's going to be best if I leave you to answer the questions as they flash up and we'll run through the correct answers at the end.'

Bo's phone vibrated, a text from Betsy.

Radio 5 want u back on, talking regular slots! Phone in agony aunt! Cliff scene with Melinda and TV reporter tomorrow. Meet at yours ETA 10am. B

Betsy in Lower Hinton! Bo thought of all the empty pizza boxes and chocolate wrappers. She would have to do a sweep of the house. It hadn't occurred to her that Betsy would be coming along. Betsy vs Katy Partridge – the live rematch. And Lois was arriving tonight. Anxiety level 9.

'So what do you think is the correct answer?' Bob was looking right at her.

'Sorry?'

'Two lane dual carriageway?'

'Fifty.'

'Seventy!' Bob was triumphant.

'Really!' She hadn't meant it to sound sarcastic.

Her phone vibrated. Betsy again. **I'm bringing Perdita she has a cut & blow dry 1ˢᵗ thing so have rescheduled TV South ETA now 12.**

So Perdita was coming, this was going to be interesting.

Bob was starting to wind up the course. She looked at the clock. They only had to do one last multiple choice on the handheld gizmo and that was it. 10 more questions and she would be out of here. Probably best to let Young Farmer leave first.

What is the speed limit in a built up area? What is the braking distance at 40 mph? They had gone over these again and again. She pressed the buttons and put down the device. Bob waited for everyone to finish. He went over to his laptop and looked up scowling. His cheeks had gone bright red again.

'Right, one of you obviously hasn't been listening. We're going to try that again. I've reset the programme, everyone pick up your device and take the quiz again please.'

There were groans and cries of 'what!' from the group.

She whipped through it again. 10 questions, by now almost impossible to get wrong.

Bob tapped his shiny shoes nervously, while he assessed the results. 'So....it seems we have a joker in the pack.' They sat in silence looking round the room. There were a couple of nervous sniggers, which only seemed to inflame Bob further. 'Let's see how funny you find it when I tell you that none of you are leaving until the results are 100% correct... from everyone.'

Once again, sighs, rolling of the eyes. Old lady mouthed 'outrageous!' Bob went back to his laptop and started the test again.

After a few minutes, everyone had completed the quiz and put their devices on their trays. Bob returned to the laptop and scowled at the screen. His cheeks were on fire. She prayed for deliverance. He cleared his throat. 'It's very clear to me, that someone is deliberately answering every question wrong.' Lois was going to love this.

Mini driver woman looked at Bo accusingly. Bo turned to her 'What? It's not me!' Some of the others started to turn round and look at her.

Bob reprogrammed the quiz. There was silence while people retook the test, no laughter any more. They looked round shiftily at each other between questions, trying to identify the enemy within. How quickly you could turn people against each other.

Once again, Bob scanned through the answers. By the look on his face, she guessed they weren't leaving in a hurry. He scowled as if thinking about how to handle a deliberate challenge to his authority. He paced the room and then quite suddenly his expression changed, he smiled broadly and tapped his pen on the table.

'Good good, 100% correct at last! Thank you, ladies and gentlemen. You may now go, drive home safely and I hope I don't see you again.'

There was a general rush to leave the room. Young farmer wasn't hurrying. Should she loiter for a while or make a dash for the door. She decided on the dash.

Duck egg blue mini woman sidled between their cars again. Her face looked like she was sucking a lemon and she was doing one of those exaggerated 'you've parked too close to me' walks with her arms and handbag held aloft, tutting as she eased the driver door open. Bo wound down her window and waited until mini woman looked at her. 'I'm sorry!' She mouthed through window. It was just a general apology really, but mini woman chose to ignore it and turn away, stoney faced. She continued to stare straight ahead, as she reversed out and drove away.

Bo raised her middle finger in a futile gesture that no one saw. No one that is, except young farmer who was walking casually towards her car, smiling broadly.

He bent down towards her open window. 'Now what did Bob say about obscene gestures at the wheel? Were you not paying attention in there?'

Bo tried very hard not to smile. He had his hands in his pockets and didn't seem bothered that she hadn't answered.

'She didn't seem to like you very much did she?'

'I can't say I blame her.'

'What did she mean calling you a 'TV persona'? I didn't know I'd been abused by a celebrity.'

Bo willed herself not to blush. 'I'm not a celebrity. I just did some stuff recently that attracted a bit of attention that's all.'

'What's your name?'

'Bernadette, Bo Spicer.'

'Ben Hardy'. He offered her his hand and she shook it rather awkwardly through the window. 'Impressive knowledge of World War One battlefields by the way.'

'Thank you.' She was about to wind up the window but couldn't help herself. 'It was you wasn't it?'

'Me?' He looked confused.

'You were the one deliberately answering the questions wrong, weren't you?'

He smiled. 'As if I would do something so childish!'

'And I know you didn't answer them correctly the last time either! We could've been in there for hours.'

He shrugged. There was a silence. They both looked at each other and she struggled not to laugh.

He turned to go. 'Well if I don't see you on the road, give me a call. He took a piece of paper from his pocket and handed it to her. 'We should have a drink some time. Drive safely.'

He walked away and she put the piece of paper in the cup holder without looking at it. It was scrunched up, but she could see it was the Driver Awareness form they had filled in with their reason for speeding. She would wait until he was safely out of the car park before looking at it. She saw him drive off in a battered old Land Rover Defender. Off to his farm no doubt, to attend to his silage or whatever they did.

Her mobile buzzed again. A text from Vishal.

Bernadette, sometimes we need 2b stuck for a while b4 we find the willingness 2 move on.'

'Oh shut up.' She switched off her mobile and threw it on the back seat.

Once young farmer was gone, she reached for a packet of maltesers in the glove compartment.

As she pulled out of the car park, she noticed Bob standing rather stiffly under the front entrance having a cigarette. Poor man, she hadn't taken him for a smoker.

Handing back the pink parking sign to the security guard, she picked up the piece of paper and read the handwritten scrawl.

Speeding to get away from complete nutter. Terrible driver, VERY pretty though. Ben 07899 261384

11

If you reveal your secrets to the wind, you should not blame the wind for revealing them to the trees. Khalil Gibran

It was the same dream, her mother, Father Delaney, shouting over her as she lay, restrained in the hospital bed. But this time Sister Marianne was there, a kindly face, arms outstretched, the only person who could offer her salvation. She woke up with a start. It took her a few minutes to recover.

She got out of bed and went downstairs to put the kettle on. She had tried to contact Sister Marianne once, a couple of year's ago. There was a nun's retirement home next to her old school on Gladstone Road. They wouldn't let her see anyone. Apparently, it upset her too much. Bo had waited in reception for nearly an hour before one of the nuns had come to talk to her. 'She has severe dementia I'm afraid, can't remember anything, just talks a lot of nonsense.' The nun shot Bo a meaningful look. 'If she sees anyone from the past, it sends her into a terrible state of confusion for days and we have to cope with the consequences, so no we can't let you see her. I'm sorry.'

Bo sat at the kitchen table and sipped her tea. Lois was still asleep upstairs. She looked through her emails.

To: Bo.spicer@hotmail.com
From: Melindabeth99@gmail.com
Subject: THIS IS MENTAL!!

OMG BALONEY!!!!!!! R they making u wear ur onesie? That Betsy keeps calling me, says she wants to represent me… whatevs
C u later. Mel xxx☺☺ ☺☺

By the time Lois woke up, Bo was dressed in the leopard print. She stared into the bathroom mirror, blotting newly purchased BB cream around her nose. She stood back and addressed her reflection. 'I am a 43 year old woman who can still attract 28 year old young farmers.'

'One young farmer. That's singular.' Lois walked into the bathroom.

'Thank you, Lois.' Bo laughed.

'Are you going to phone him then?'

'Certainly not.'

'Oh go on with you, it would do you good to have a drink with him.'

'I have no desire to go out with a man young enough to be my son.'

'God, I have.'

They both laughed. 'Lois, I'm overweight and he's probably never even seen cellulite.'

'Of course he has, he's a farmer! Anyway, you're not overweight, a couple of pounds if that. I've told you before, you can't go picking some random number which you haven't weighed since you were 13 and call it your ideal weight.'

Bo smiled. 'You know I love you Lois!'

'I know. That's not the most flattering outfit though, it has to be said.'

They both looked at Bo's onesie. It was particularly tight around the thigh and belly area. Lois pulled a face. 'We could try and stretch it? What are you doing anyway, I thought they were bringing a make up artist.'

Bo gave up on the BB cream. 'I know but I don't want them to be shocked at the state of me without make up.' She picked up her mobile. 'We've only got half an hour.' Katy Partridge was coming to pick them up in a minibus with Melinda, the photographer and the make-up artist. She had wanted to return to the cliff top scene for the photo shoot, but the whole area had been fenced off since the accident. Katy had found a farm up on the Ridgeway instead. It was suitably high up and remote, with plenty of rocks and ledges for the photoshoot. It was a bright day, cold but sunny and Bo wasn't convinced that any of this would look very authentic. She cringed as she imagined the sorts of poses she and Melinda would be asked to assume. Betsy and Perdita were meeting them there. At least Betsy would vet the pictures before she let them go in the magazine.

Lois wiped away some BB cream from the end of her nose. 'Who's this for anyway?'

'I can't remember, one of the Sunday supplements I think she said.'

Lois shook her head. 'Blimey. Is there any publication you haven't been in?' Lois disappeared off into the spare bedroom and came back waving a newspaper. 'Look, I brought you the Metro from the train. It says here that you're 48 years old. Are you going to sue?'

Bo snatched the paper from her and frowned as she read it. Lois ran through her check list. 'Right I've got a thermos of tea, a packet of jaffa cakes, 2 towels, wet wipes and a packet of Haribo Starmix. The weather might change, where's your raincoat?'

As they walked down the stairs there was a knock on the door. Before Lois could open it, the letterbox flapped opened 'Yooooo hoooooo!' It's only me!' They both looked at each other. It was Davina. Lois opened the door.

Davina looked a bit taken aback. 'Oh! Have I called at a bad moment? What are you wearing that for?'

Bo explained. 'We're off to do a photoshoot Davina, for a magazine. They want me and Melinda dressed as we were when we were up Devil's Chimney, only we can't get up there anymore so I think we're off to a farm, up on the Ridgeway.'

Davina looked thrilled. 'How exciting! I don't suppose I can come along can I? I've never been to a photoshoot. I promise I won't get in the way.' Davina was wearing white jeans, ballet pumps and a pink fur trimmed parka.

Lois snorted with laughter. 'Well I don't see why not. You can keep the cows off us.' Lois had a pathological fear of cows.

Bo wasn't convinced. 'You're not really dressed for it Davina. We are going to a farm you know. Do you have any outdoor clothes.'

Davina looked a bit confused. 'These are my outdoor clothes. And Bernadette, if you don't mind me saying, you're not exactly dressed for it yourself.'

Lois laughed. 'Well quite. A bunch of women inappropriately dressed on a farm. What could possibly go wrong?'

A silver minibus drew up at the end of the drive. Melinda was sitting on the back row, wearing the neon yellow lace dress. She was having her make up done. She screeched with excitement when she saw Bo. 'Baloney! It's you!' Bo sat the other side of her and they hugged warmly. Bo held her face in her hands. 'Beautiful girl, let me look at you. How's your head? Did they do a neat job of sewing you up?' Melinda laughed. 'Oh yes, the hair's starting to grow back. How's my make up? This is so awesome, isn't it!'

Katy was sitting in the front, next to the driver, her bright red lips mouthing instructions as she studied the map on her phone. She wore a red Ilse Jacobsen raincoat which perfectly matched her lips. 'Morning! Betsy's running late. She's meeting us there, let's get going!' The photographer was younger than Bo expected, she sat behind Katy, playing around with her camera lens.

Once they were off the main road, the minibus wound its way higher and higher up the chalky escarpment and the road turned into a single stone track. They bumped along for 15 minutes until they finally reached the entrance to the farm. As they drove in, the buildings looked semi derelict. The driver opened the sliding door and as each of them emerged, they gasped and put their hand over their mouth. An enormous slurry pit the size of three swimming pools gave off a smell that could almost choke you.

'Wait there!' Katy took charge. They watched in respectful silence, as she picked her way through rusting farm equipment shouting 'Hello! Hello there! Is there anyone here?'

A man dressed in a brown boiler suit and wellington boots emerged from a stable. Katy, all smiles, held out her hand. 'Hi Katy Partridge, TV South West! We spoke on the phone yesterday?' The farmer wiped his palm on his boiler suit and shook her hand. He looked her up and down and grunted.

'OK super! Thank you so much!' Katy gushed. 'So where would you suggest we go to find the best rocks, cliffs, that kind of thing.' She wrinkled her nose.

'There's a steep drop, if you head off towards the White Horse.'

Katy looked blank.

'Through that field with the cows in, walk around, keeping the copse on your left, you'll see it when you turn the corner.'

'Great!' Katy set off at a pace, striding ahead, mobile in one hand, pen and notepad in the other, trailed by the young photographer.

By this time the farmer had been joined by a younger boy and they both leant on the fence watching expressionless, as first Katy and then the photographer struggled awkwardly to climb over the gate and into the field. 'You could just open it!' The younger boy shouted, both men sniggered.

Melinda helped Bo over but Lois hung back. 'Do we seriously have to go through that field Davina?'

'Come on, they're only cows Lois. They're more scared of you.'

Lois shook her head. 'People have been killed by cows, trampled to death, it genuinely happens.'

Davina took her hand. 'Come on Lois. I promise you will come to no harm. Just keep looking straight ahead.'

'I can't.'

'You've got to Lois. Bo needs us!' Lois might have found it comical if she hadn't been quite so petrified.

'Look, I'll go first. We'll keep to the side of the fence. They're miles away.'

Lois' legs shook as she climbed the gate. They hadn't even made it half way across the field when the cows began to follow them. Davina looked furtively behind her. 'Shoo, go away, shoo!' One of the cows did a little buck as it started to trot.

The farmer and his young sidekick were now openly laughing, not wanting the sport to end. 'Ladies! Don't you go upsetting the bull!'

Katy was the first to break rank. When she heard the word 'bull', she started jogging ahead of the others towards the gate at the far end. Sensing panic, the cows started to canter towards them. Lois risked a backward glance and screamed at the sight of the advancing herd. She started to sprint faster than she had moved for many years, choking and panting as she threw herself over the iron gate and landing ungainly on the other side. One by one, they cleared the gate, only looking back once they were safe, glancing sheepishly to where Davina stood alone, stranded in the middle of the field, arms outstretched, single handedly holding off the 30 strong herd. Their heads were down and snorting as they nudged tentatively towards her. She made strange, guttural noises as she waved her arms, her ballet pumps and white jeans now encrusted with mud.

'Are you OK Davina?' Lois shouted unhelpfully from the other side of the gate. 'Clap your hands!' 'Try shouting at them!' 'Don't turn your back!' The farmers made no move to help. Davina's ballet pumps made sucking noises in the thick mud as she attempted to back away. Her feet were released but the ballet pumps remained fixed in the gunge and they watched in horror as she lost her balance and one perfectly manicured bare foot after another broke through the crust of a warm, dark green cow pat.

'That's disgusting.' Mel muttered.

'Just leave your shoes and run Davina!' Lois shouted.

The cows looked up, momentarily distracted. At the other end of the field, a man in a smart grey suit held the gate open for a tiny figure in a monochrome checked jacket and skirt. She wore very clean lace up rubber boots in cream and strode right up to where the cows encircled Davina, waving a Louis Vuitton golfing umbrella in front of her.

'My God it's Betsy.' Bo muttered.

Lois nodded. 'It is indeed and I think she's wearing Chanel.'

'Get away! Gertcha!' Betsy clutched a small ball of white fluff under one arm, with a handkerchief held to her nose. The cows parted like the Red Sea as the diminutive figure marched between them.

Davina picked up her ballet pumps and limped bare foot towards the gate.

Betsy looked at the group, who were watching open mouthed. 'What on earth's the matter with you all. Open the gate will you?'

Katy pulled the bolt back and Betsy picked her way between two cow pats, looking disgusted. 'I'm sorry we're late, Perdita's appointment ran on. Katy did you have to pick a farm right next to a giant, liquid pit of animal faeces?'

Katy was breezy once more. 'It's a slurry pit Betsy, I think they all have them.'

Lois reached for the wet wipes in her bag as Davina staggered towards them clutching her shoes. 'I'm so sorry love!' Lois rubbed one of the pumps with the wipes but it just seemed to spread the stains around and Davina snatched it back. She shook her head and whispered to Lois. 'The buckle's come off. They're Ferragamo!' You could see she was struggling not to cry.

Melinda looked at the ball of white fluff Betsy was clutching under her right arm. 'And who's this little fella?'

'This is not a fella. This is Perdita, she's a Bishon Frise!'

'Perdita! Of course.' Bo blushed at the realisation.

Perdita was dressed in herringbone tweed with navy velvet trim. Fresh from the salon, she was whiter and fluffier than any dog Bo had ever seen. Melinda reached her hand towards Perdita. 'Isn't she gorgeous.' Perdita snarled and curled her upper lip back to reveal perfect white canines.

'She doesn't like the countryside.' Betsy turned to Katy and the young photographer. 'Right where are we shooting this.'

'This way Betsy.' Katy was upbeat and efficient, leading the way. 'We're turning left at the copse.'

Betsy, Katy and the photographer walked ahead. Bo and Mel linked arms and followed close behind. They rounded the corner and the narrow track led to a crescent of rocks and boulders, beyond which the path dropped steeply away to the patchwork fields below. Bo gasped at the view beneath them. The photographer started taking light readings. Katy looked very pleased with herself.

'Come on then!' Betsy looked at her watch. 'Let's get this over with!' I expect you can do the interview while the photographs are being set up.' Mel and Bo were ushered towards a rock and giggled as they draped themselves over it.'

'Well this is a bit different to the last time we met isn't it.' Bo laughed.

'You look WAY better.' Mel took in Bo's make up and newly cut hair. 'And you've lost weight.'

Bo laughed. 'I haven't actually. It's the spray tan.'

Betsy settled herself on a nearby rock. Lois sat right next to her. She tried to strike up a conversation. 'Why don't you put the dog down and let her have a little run around?'

Betsy didn't even look at her. 'Don't be ridiculous, she's wearing Harris tweed.'

Betsy leapt to her feet, still clutching Perdita. 'No, no, she can't sit like that, it's all stomach! Take the shot from below.'

Lois mumbled under her breath. 'She's a dog for God's sake! She's supposed to run around.'

Davina sat on a tree stump, stained pumps back on her feet, taking it all in.

Betsy shouted again. 'No! No! Double chin!' The young photographer looked petrified as Betsy jumped up from her rock, prodding a perfectly manicured red finger nail into the air as she spoke. 'I'm approving all of these shots before they go anywhere.'

Clearly exasperated, Betsy turned round to Lois. 'Look after Perdita for a moment will you, I'm going to have to take over.' She handed the white ball of fluff to Lois and strode off.

Bo and Mel both assumed artificial smiles and carried on chatting as the photographer snapped around them.

'So you know Dave, who was sending me those messages.'

'Yes.'

'Turns out he really likes me after all.'

'You don't say. Next you'll be telling me that you're going out with him.'

Mel laughed nervously and looked a bit sheepish.

'You better not be!' Bo frowned.

Katy took out her notepad and started the interview. 'So how do you feel about your new found fame.'

'Awesome!' Mel answered before Bo could interject.

Katy cleared her throat. Bo felt a bit sorry for her. The presence of Betsy was obviously making her nervous. 'So just to recap Bernadette, it was that morning that you received the note under the door, telling you about your husband's affair?'

Bo nodded.

Katy narrowed her eyes. 'And was that when you hit rock bottom?'

Bo could hear a disdainful snort from Lois' direction.

Katy carried on. 'Why do you think you both climbed up there in the first place? Did you mean to jump? End it all? Two women on the edge?'

Davina leant forward, not to miss anything.

Betsy was on her feet again. 'Listen darling enough of the rock bottom, suicide tosh! She's an ordinary, gutsy, housewife heroine. I can see exactly where you're going with this, but you listen to me. If your story even hints at mental issues, this will be the first and last national magazine article you ever write. Capiche?'

Katy nodded. Betsy pointed at her notepad. 'Housewife heroine, write it down.'

As Betsy dictated the rest of the interview, Lois walked away, the ball of fluff tucked under her arm. She tickled Perdita between the ears. 'Come on then Fluffkins, let's go and have some fun!'

The photographer wanted them both to stand on the highest boulder, holding hands, waving, jumping. It was a struggle to get up there, but at least Betsy had retreated to her rock. They were supposed to scream and shout out their names to make them look more animated, but this just made them all the more self-conscious and giggly. The holding hands thing didn't really work either and Betsy was on her feet again. Apparently it looked too much like they were about to jump. They tried a back-to-back pose and finally settled for a relaxed, smiley shot of them sitting on the boulder, arms interlinked.

As they struck the final pose, Bo and Mel were the first to see Lois. She was running towards them, screaming, frantically waving her arms. As she reached them, she struggled to catch her breath. Bright pink in the face, she waved the dog lead at them. 'I've lost the feckin dog. She slipped the lead.'

Betsy's face was thunder. 'What do you mean she slipped the lead. You didn't put her on the ground?'

Lois leant on a rock to catch her breath. 'She wanted a run. I was throwing her sticks.'

'A run? She doesn't run. She's never been alone in the countryside. She'll be petrified, you stupid woman.'

Bo slid off the rock. 'Calm down, it'll be fine. She'll be easy to spot. Lois, which way did she run?'

'Back the way we came. I couldn't follow her because of the cows.'

Bo shook her head. 'For God's sake Lois!'

Betsy looked like she might kill her. 'Stupid, stupid woman!'

Davina stepped between them. 'Come on, you're wasting time. She's probably heading for the car.'

'My poor darling.' Betsy gasped. Davina and Betsy strode ahead, with Katy, Mel, Lois, Bo and the photographer just behind.

As they jogged past the cows, it was like some kind of mad carnival scene. They hollered and clapped their hands to keep the herd at bay; Davina's pink fur hood flapping, enormous bug-eye sunglasses, Mel struggling along in tight neon lace, Bo in leopard skin and Katy in a full length scarlet raincoat. The cows looked up disdainfully and a few farm workers emerged from an outbuilding to find out what was causing all the noise. Betsy and Davina caught up with them first.

Bo was panting momentarily lost for words by the time she got there. There was a split second of recognition when she got up close to the group of men. It was Ben. He was the third farmer.

When she finally caught her breath, all she could think of to say was, 'It's you.'

'Yes, it's me.' He grinned. All three men stood with their arms crossed.

Davina whipped off her sunglasses. 'Her dog, it's gone missing, a small fluffy white dog, have you seen it?'

The youngest farmer, the one who had been laughing at them earlier nodded. 'Yeah I did, little white thing, it was sniffing round the slurry pit a couple of minutes ago.'

'My God!' Betsy was appalled.

All eyes turned towards the giant liquid cesspit. The thick dark green crust which had earlier been intact, was now broken by small dog sized craters, revealing the thick stenching liquid below. As they stared in horror, the largest crater in the middle gave off a few solitary bubbles, popping as they reached the surface.

'I think we've found your dog.' Ben started to run towards the edge.

Betsy's hand covered her mouth. 'She's going to die! My poor baby is going to die!'

The older farmer turned to the younger one. 'Run and fetch a rope from the barn.'

Ben waded in. The stinking dark slime was well over his waist.

'That's disgusting!' Bo held her hand over her mouth. He was already a quarter of the way across the pool.

The photographer took the lens cover off her camera and started to snap away.

Bo turned to her angrily, 'Jesus, stop it! He could die.'

Betsy shouted after him. 'We're coming Perdy, on our way my darling!'

'For God's sake!' Bo was pacing the edge of the pit. 'He's going to drown. We should have stopped him.'

As Ben went deeper and the tide of liquid shit rose further up his body, Bo ran forward. 'He's going to get stuck.' Lois grabbed her shoulders and tried to restrain her. Ben was now almost up to his neck.

With a sharp tug Bo broke free of Lois' grip and launched herself into the green liquid. She made slow progress through the stenching slime, as the warm liquid started to penetrate the velour of her onesie and drag her down. She wretched into one hand as she attempted to push forwards but couldn't move, her boots already fixed to the bottom.

One of the farmers ran out of the stable clutching a coil of rope. He launched it at Bo and she caught it with one hand. Ben's face was so close to the surface, his cheek was smeared, as he dipped down into the slurry, feeling around with both arms for the body of the small dog.

The women stared in horror. Katy held her notepad over her nose.

Lois shook her head. 'I don't feckin believe this.'

'This is your doing.' Betsy snapped at her.

Finally there was a triumphant cry, as he seized a handbag sized dripping lump and lifted it with one hand above the surface. It was impossible to see where he ended and the lump began. He clutched the dark green bundle under his arm and Bo threw him the rope. The two farmers picked up the end and started to ease them both in, little by little back towards the edge.

'Perdy!' Betsy exclaimed. 'Baby!'

Bo was first to emerge, her onesie soaked from the chest down. Ben was just behind, but when he reached the edge, he didn't stop where Betsy stood, arms outstretched, but ran with the bundle towards the stables.

'Perdy! Where are you? Mummy's coming!' Betsy was shrieking as she ran after him, running from door to door. 'Where are you Perdy?'

'She'll be alright Betsy. Calm down.' Bo looked at Betsy's spotless cream boots as liquid shit dripped down her arms and legs.

When he reappeared, it was through a different gate, the disheveled shape under his arm, now clearly discernible as Perdy. Her white fur, a lighter shade of brown and she was shaking violently.

He handed her to Betsy. 'She's going to be fine. Just keep her warm and make sure she's drinking plenty.'

Lois looked awestruck. 'My God, you look like the creature from the black lagoon.'

'Lois! He's just risked his life to save a dog.' Bo scowled.

Lois ignored her. 'I've got some wet wipes in my bag, if you want me to run and get them.'

He smiled. 'That's very kind, but I think we'll be needing more than wet wipes.'

He unzipped the soaking boilersuit and started to unbutton his shirt. Lois' eyes were on stalks. Bo was mortified.

The farmer shook his head like they were all mad. 'There's a hose in the yard. You two had better come with me.'

Lois stepped forward. 'Shall I hold the hose?'

'We'll be fine thanks.' Ben gestured for Bo to go in front and the farmer led them to the stable yard.

'I'll get you some towels.' The farmer disappeared as Ben dropped his soiled shirt on the ground to reveal a perfectly honed, tanned upper body. Bo made a conscious effort to remove her eyes from his chest. 'Are you working here?'

'Yes, I am.' He smiled. 'Shall I hose you down, or do you want to do me first?'

'I'll be fine thanks.' She tried to sound nonchalant and started to unzip the front of her onesie, realising in time that she only had her underwear underneath.' Self-consciously clutching the onesie to her chest, she splashed a little water from a bucket over her arms and chest, it was very cold and completely ineffective.

He watched her smiling and picked up the hose.

'You didn't call me.'

'No, well it's only been two days.' She carried on flicking water down her front. 'I wouldn't want to look too keen.'

'God forbid.' He put his finger over the spout. 'You know I think all you probably need is a good soaking!' He blasted freezing water right in her face and over her chest.

She gasped in shock as the icy water cascaded inside the onesie and down her stomach and legs.

She saw the bucket of water out of the corner of her eye, it was only a couple of feet away. Ducking under the spray of water, she grabbed it with both hands and launched the entire contents into his face.

He looked shocked and she was suddenly afraid of how he was going to react. She stood defiantly in front of him, her black hair dripping, trying not to laugh.

He wiped his hand across his mouth and looked her up and down. 'It's Bo Spicer isn't it?'

'That's right.'

'Well I wish I could say it's been a pleasure meeting you again.' She shrugged.

'Have you picked up any speeding tickets recently?'

'I haven't.'

'You're a terrible driver.'

She opened her mouth to reply, but he carried on. 'Thank you for coming to save me back there. Completely unnecessary, very impressive though.'

'Well it's the thought that counts. Next time you're neck deep in liquid shit, just call me.'

'I would if I had your number.' Silence. He switched off the hose. 'But you've got mine.'

'I wouldn't call you.' She could see he was slightly taken aback. 'I'm too old fashioned.'

He shrugged. 'Well you'd better go back to your friends. Don't let them go though, I need to talk to the one that owns the dog.'

'OK.' She walked back through the gate, conscious that she was smirking.

Lois was standing waiting. God Bo, you're soaking wet. Come on, I've got some towels in the mini bus.'

'He said we had to wait.'

'Did he!' Lois exchanged a glance with Davina.

'Wasn't he just like Mr Darcy?' Lois sighed. They all looked blank. 'You know that scene where Colin Firth comes out of the lake in Pride & Prejudice, all wet and gorgeous.'

Bo shook her head. 'I do. Except that he was covered in shit Lois.'

'Indeed.'

Bo half whispered. 'Lois, do you realise who it is. It's him. Young farmer!'

'I know.'

'No, I mean it's HIM. The young farmer I told you about, from the speed awareness course. It's THE young farmer.'

'You are joking! You didn't mention that he looked like that!'

'Do you think you could stop ogling him Lois, it's actually quite gross.'

He returned a couple of minutes later wearing a clean boiler suit and Bo was struck by the thought that he was probably naked underneath.

Ben turned to Betsy. 'Right, she belongs to you does she?' Betsy nodded. 'I performed a tracheal intubation to clear her airways, so she'll be a bit sore for a while. I would get her checked up by your local vet in the next couple of days. If you see any signs of infection, raised temperature, off her food, that kind of thing, you need to phone the vet immediately.'

Betsy cradled Perdita and flashed Ben her best showbiz smile, 'What can I do to repay you?'

Bo couldn't help thinking it was typical of Betsy to see everything as a transaction. She was surprised she didn't reach for her wallet.

He really was very good looking. Lois piped up. 'You seem to know an awful lot about this sort of thing, for a farmer.'

He looked slightly confused. 'Yes. Probably because I'm a vet.'

Davina stepped forward and flicked her hair. 'Thank you so much for what you did.'

'No problem.' He hovered for a moment but Bo didn't speak, still mulling over the vet disclosure.

'So, why the party outfits?'

We were doing a photoshoot. Mel gushed. 'It's for You magazine.'

'Oh right, well I'll be sure to read it. I suppose I'd better get back to work. Ladies.' With that he strode off back towards the stables.

It took them a few moments to close their mouths and finally speak.

Betsy quickly regained her composure. 'I need to get Perdita back to London, she's shivering. Katy, send me the draft copy and the pictures. Bo, I'll call you tomorrow.' She marched off down the driveway towards the waiting car.

Lois shouted after her. 'I'm sorry Betsy.' She didn't turn round.

They strolled to the minibus together, Mel and Katy a little ahead of the others.

Mel started laughing. 'That was sick! And Baloney went in after him!'

Katy giggled. 'Yes, what a story! If only we'd got a shot of him with the dog. I should be able to write it up for the local paper.'

'Oh right, yeah.'

'By the way Mel, why do you keep calling her Baloney?'

'Because that's her real name, before she got married, Bernadette Maloney. Sounds a lot better than Spicer don't you think!'

12

Eat drink and be merry, for tomorrow we die.

Lois had stayed longer than she had planned and there had been several heated phone calls back and forth from Kilkenny. Patrick and the boys could no longer manage without her. Bo walked Lois to the departure gate at Heathrow. They hugged each other warmly. 'Now you take care!' Lois patted her back. She felt desolate as she watched her walk away. It was easy to be brave with a friend like Lois at your side. Lois turned around before going through the gate. 'Be careful!' she mouthed and waved good bye. Bo missed her even before she turned out of view.

She walked back slowly to the waiting car. Lewis had picked them up this morning and now waited patiently beside the door. They were heading back to London, to the string of appointments Betsy had organised.

They pulled back onto the M4. Lewis looked in the mirror. 'Alone again?'

Bo smiled. 'Looks like it.'

That would normally be it, but Lewis continued. 'She's quite a woman, that friend of yours.'

'She is.'

'Reminds me of the wife.'

'Really! Well good luck to you in that case.' This was the most she'd ever got out of Lewis. She decided to press on. 'Is Perdita OK now?'

'Oh yes, good as new. Betsy took her to a specialist vet to be checked out.' Bo wanted to say 'as opposed to the one who saved her life,' but she kept quiet.

'You know, I thought Perdita was her other half!' She blurted out and immediately regretted it.

'I beg your pardon.'

'I mean like her civil partner. When she kept talking about Perdita and her hair appointments, I thought she was a person.'

'Oh Lord, no!' He caught her eye in the mirror and they both started to laugh.

'So how long have you worked for Betsy?'

'Gosh it must be nearly 10 years now. I used to work for the CEOs of a few London companies, but Betsy's business grew and she needed me full time.'

'I expect you have to be very discreet.'

'Oh yes. All part of the job.' His lips twitched and she saw him chuckle again in the mirror.

'Come on Lewis, I bet you've got a few stories you could tell me?'

'My lips are sealed.' She obviously wasn't going to get any indiscretions out of him.

Lewis pulled up outside the Jessica Stamford store on Sloane Street. As she pushed open the big glass door, she was greeted like an old friend by the sales girls. They had a rack of clothes waiting for her to try on. The good thing was, Betsy's idea of a housewife heroine involved some very expensive clothes.

When Bo had asked her if an everyday housewife would really wear Prada, Betsy had looked a little weary. 'Sweetie, we are not talking about real housewives, we're selling a dream. Thin, stylish, well groomed, it's about aspiration, an ordinary woman with the potential to transform herself, that's the story, do you see?' Bo obviously didn't see. 'Look my darling, no one wants a photoshoot of you in a cat hair covered baggy jumper, with your stomach spilling out over your jeans. We've got the shots of you looking chubby in your onesie and that's all fine, but it's time for the transformation, yes? Selling the dream darling, the potential for the very ordinary to transform. That's why the brands will want you. Yes?'

'Yes Betsy.'

She wondered if anyone ever said 'No Betsy.'

Her food was now delivered to her in little boxes, the daily calorie intake dictated by Betsy: quinoa, salmon flakes, wild rice, soy beans. At first she had been excited at the idea of delicious food and the chance to lose weight effortlessly, like celebrities must do, until she realized that they were just very small portions. She had lost a bit of weight, but Betsy was frustrated by the slow progress. The protein came in tiny little squares, the size of a postage stamp. The cats were getting more food than her. She had been forced to add in a few more courses, just to stop herself from fainting; a lion bar at 4 o'clock, cheese on toast at 6, half a bottle of wine and so forth.

She opted for a cream dress with matching three quarter length coat. The girls sent her off with a box of knitwear in layers of tissue and two pairs of trousers. There was no question of paying for anything. It seemed you only got the free things when you could finally afford to pay for them. She'd got the trousers in Lois' size.

Next it was hair and make up in a salon in Chelsea. She walked back to the car with perfect french manicured gel nails and bouncy hair. Everyone was so nice to her, it was actually embarrassing. The photoshoot was to launch an endorsement Betsy had negotiated. She just had to pose in front of an ironing board, pretending to iron. They had already written the interview in which she was to mention how much she loved their kettle and toaster set. In another shot, she smiled as she buttered toast. They were paying her £15,000! For buttering some toast. It was beyond belief.

And this lot were even more gushing. It was no wonder genuine celebrities went mad, in this bubble of deference, where everyone laughs at your crappy jokes. You'd lose your compass.

Of course, she knew it wouldn't last. Betsy had been very clear. She had short term appeal, based on one accidental, heroic act. There could be no longevity. 'It'll be over in a few months, possibly weeks. In the meantime, let's build you up a substantial nest egg, something to fall back on.' She wasn't dumb, she knew all that. She had already formulated a plan. There was a derelict outbuilding at the bottom of the garden in Lower Hinton, an old apple store. She almost had enough money to do it up and rent it out. She could make a small income. University fees and a deposit on a flat for Liam. She had to think about the future and work out how she was going to get by on her own. But first she would take Lois on holiday, somewhere very hot with a swim up cocktail bar. There had been no word from Neil since he'd come to pick up his things.

She pressed the buzzer at the offices of Levene Associates. Betsy buzzed her in and greeted her at the top of the stairs. 'You look fabulous darling. It's amazing what a well cut suit can disguise.' Her voice boomed down the stair well.

They sat on the sofa in Betsy's office. Bo, Betsy and Toby, the graduate trainee. It was a working lunch, no sandwiches Bo noted, just a quinoa and soy bean salad. Toby passed round a typed up agenda with her name at the top and today's date. 'Current retail opps', 'warm leads', 'media', 'book deal', 'website responses', the list went on.

'Now I've got a bit of interest in a 'Bernadette' branded diet, but you'd obviously need to shed a lot more weight before we could do a deal.'

'Wouldn't that conflict with my plus size clothing range?' Bo's lips twitched.

Betsy took off her glasses. 'You said you didn't want plus size, so I renegotiated. It's a range of leopard print leisurewear in standard sizing, you'll be pleased to hear.'

Seeing her surprise Betsy explained. 'We are doing all of this on your behalf Bo, but you must realize that you remain very much in charge.'

Bo nearly spat out her coffee.

'And besides', Betsy carried on, 'a plus size range wouldn't do us any favours when it comes to all those other branding opportunities out there. We need you looking gorgeous!'

Bo frowned. 'And what's this book deal?'

'Bernadette... the day that changed my life.'

'You think I can write a book?'

This prompted another weary look. 'Of course not! No one writes their own book these days! You'll just have to sit down with a ghost writer a few times. They write it, I approve the content and front cover.'

Bo stifled a yawn. It had been particularly difficult to get Vishal off the phone last night. She was beginning to suspect he was paid by the minute. They had been working on getting her centred. She was trying to sound cooperative, but didn't have a clue how to locate her centre. It was a bit like strengthening your core, or locating your pelvic floor. They were probably in there somewhere. These things remained a mystery to her.

She tried to pay attention to Toby's agenda. They were up to 'website responses'.

Toby handed them both a piece of paper. Betsy put on her glasses and sighed as she read the words. She started to read out loud rather theatrically.

'*Dear Bernadette, I think I'm gay, how can I be sure?*

'To which you answer...'

'Dear Nathan, if you want my opinion, there's no such thing as 100% gay or straight. That would be far too simple. Aren't we all just on a spectrum? 'Shades of gay!''

'Shades of gay!' Betsy took off her glasses. She paused as if working out how she could make herself understood. 'Look Bo, if we are building a brand, we can't have you shooting your mouth off on every subject from exploring your sexuality to the menopause. There's one here where you talk about wetting yourself on a trampoline.'

'That wasn't me, that was actually a friend of mine.'

'And there's another one where you tell a middle aged woman to go and get a tattoo.' Betsy was flicking through the responses. 'Here's one where you've asked someone round to your house for dinner. You can't just ask people round for dinner!'

'Can't I?' She realized she sounded like a sulky teenager.

Betsy closed her eyes in exasperation. 'You have to understand Bo, when you reply to a woman with weight issues that she should have a glass of wine and never weigh herself again, it makes it quite difficult for me to get you a six figure deal with a diet food brand. Capiche? I told you that Toby would answer these for you, didn't I Toby.' Toby looked sheepish and stared at his notes.

Bo sat up straight on the sofa and crossed her legs. 'So, that bit about me being 'very much in charge?" The cream power suit and bouncy hair seemed to have strengthened her resolve. Toby looked mortified. It wasn't very often that anyone answered back. He wasn't sure if he should include it in the minutes.

'Of course you are in charge Bo, but it's my job to advise you and get you the best possible deals. And that includes being up front, when I believe you are compromising our ability to get you lucrative endorsements.' There was something of the Margaret Thatcher about Betsy today.

An awkward silence followed and Bo stared out of the huge sash window at the offices opposite.

She turned back to Betsy. 'I do understand that I need to eat what I'm told, wear what you tell me, turn up to the interviews, deliver the key messages, 'gutsy housewife heroine' and all that. But there are a few areas where I'm afraid I won't compromise.'

Toby pretended to read his notes. Betsy looked genuinely surprised.

Bo uncrossed her legs and flopped back into the sofa. Power dressing was all very well but she couldn't keep it up. 'You see Betsy, I would never for example, endorse a diet brand. You might have noticed that I don't believe in withholding food. And I think women on the whole are far too hard on themselves and I genuinely don't believe that everyone is 100% straight or gay.'

'Alright!' Betsy held up her hand in mock surrender. 'How about you submit your responses to Toby and we can just tweak them a little bit.'

Bo shook her head. 'No tweaks.' Toby noted down 'no tweaks' and Betsy shot him a look.

Bo carried on. 'You said this will all be over in a few weeks anyway, so surely it doesn't really matter that much.'

'Well that would normally be the case, but there does seem to be an endless appetite for your brand of 'ordinaire.' We could be looking at another year of this.' Seeing Bo's horrified expression, she leant towards her. 'I'm not talking hundreds of thousands anymore Bo, we could be looking at millions.'

Bo's mouth dropped open and Betsy looked suitably pleased to have regained control. 'Vanessa Feltz wants you on next week. This could run and run.'

After Bo's momentary defiance, Betsy was straight back to the agenda, name dropping producers and TV programmes, peppering the conversation with 'I'm a celebrity', 'Strictly...' and 'Big Brother.' The list was endless and the impression was that Betsy would simply have to pick up the phone.

Bo walked down the enormous staircase in a daze. She didn't speak as they drove to the flat. *We could be looking at millions.* She thought about Liam. He wanted to be an engineer. She could already pay for most of his University fees. And Lois and Patrick had been struggling for years, she could put aside some money for the boys. And she would take Lois somewhere she'd never been. They would sit at sunset on the water's edge, like Shirley Valentine, listening to the waves. And how they would laugh about all of this as they shared a bottle of local wine.

Back at the flat, she changed into a fluffy white dressing gown. She had planned to go shopping or sight seeing, but after the meeting, the anxiety was back. The fridge had been stocked with the little cardboard meals which were fine if she combined two on one plate. There were no proper snacks just some Wasabe peas and quarter bottles of Pol Roger Champagne. She opened up the Wasabe peas and popped the cork on a Champagne bottle. There were harder ways to make money that's for sure. If she could just go with the flow, try to enjoy the experience. She took a handful of peas and nearly choked. Her eyes watered and she swigged from the Champagne bottle to get rid of the burning sensation on her tongue. Wasabe peas! For God's sake, what was the matter with these people!

The phone on the coffee table rang. It could only be Betsy.

'Great news darling!' She was buoyant. 'Katy Partridge has come good! We're in the paper tomorrow, exactly what we wanted, word for word. Let me read you a bit. The headline's perfect, *'Everyone's talking about…Bernadette Maloney'*

'And it goes on…

The hottest new celeb about town is a housewife heroine called Bernadette Maloney. The latest twist in the public appetite for reality tv celebs, an everyday accidental hero has been turned into the hottest property in town.'

'It goes on to say...*High street brands are queuing up for a piece of the action...* I made her put that bit in. Bo are you there? What do you think. Fabulous, no?'

'My God.' Bo's voice could only just be heard over the line.

'I know. I thought you'd be pleased!'

Bo sat back on the sofa. Don't panic, keep your head, there must be something she could do.

'Betsy, I need you to change it.' She tried to breath normally.

'What darling, it's word for word what we wanted.'

'Can we make any changes, they've used my maiden name, how did they get my maiden name?'

'I noticed that too, slightly annoying but nothing major. The brand is 'Bernadette' after all, really doesn't matter if they occasionally mention surnames.'

'Can you get them to change it?'

'No darling. It's too late to change anything.' Betsy laughed. 'It's gone to print. Even I can't recall a national newspaper weekend supplement! It'll be in a million households by tomorrow morning.'

So here it was then, her come uppance. Should she have confessed to Betsy? Too late now. She looked around at the apartment, faded linen sofa covers, Jo Malone room diffusers, copies of Vogue scattered on the glass coffee table. It may as well have been the Tower of London.

She reached for another bottle of Champagne and looked in the mirror. *Eat drink and be merry, for tomorrow we die.*

13

Ladies who lunch

Repeat after me, 'I am purposeful and committed to action.'

'I am purposeful and committed to action.' She wasn't but she hoped he couldn't tell from her voice. She had agreed to another phone session with Vishal to try to control the overwhelming anxiety which had gripped her since Betsy had read out the contents of the interview. It was Tuesday afternoon and the article had been out since last Saturday. There had been nothing but an eery silence, no reaction, none of the expected disclosures. Apparently Melinda had told Katy Partridge her maiden name. Lois seemed to think she was in the clear, if they were going to find out, it would have happened by now.

If you googled 'Bernadette Maloney', which she hadn't for years, you could hardly find her now. In the 21 years since she last hit the headlines, she had literally been buried. It seemed a thousand Bernadette Maloneys had been born, crowds of them all fighting for space on LinkedIn, Facebook, Instagram and Pinterest. You had to scroll through three full pages of Bernadette Maloneys before you finally found those blurred CCTV pictures, the faceless criminal in the burgundy hoody, clutching what looked like a blue bag and slipping unchallenged through the foyer.

'Have you listened to your PodCast this week Bernadette?' She had forgotten that he was on the other end of the phone.

'What? Yes Vishal.' *No.*

'I'm sensing an energy change Bernadette. I'm trying to point you toward your own resourcefulness in this situation. Does that make sense?'

'Absolutely.'

'The impetus for action needs to come from within you. An over reliance on the coach could replace your own internal commitment.'

'I know that Vishal.' *I don't have a clue what you're on about and this isn't helping at all.*

'So we're breathing deeply, in and out and you're going to tell me what can you hear around you Bernadette? Accept the sounds and let them go.'

'I can hear the dishwasher, I can hear next door revving his motorbike, I can hear the lavatory flushing because of the faulty stopcock, it's been 20 minutes since I went to the loo and it's still going.'

'No, Bernadette, stop with the stopcock. You see what you did. Let's try that again!'

'Sorry, OK. I can hear birdsong.' She couldn't actually hear birdsong.

'I can hear the front door bell.' *Blessed relief!* 'I'm sorry Vishal I've got someone at the door. I'm going to have to call you back.'

It was Davina. 'Bernadette! Oh good you're here. You have remembered you're coming for lunch haven't you! Very informal, just a catch up over salad with some gorgeous girlies! Talia and Sally Ann are coming. You know them. And Claudia Floyd Roberts from the tennis club.'

'OK lovely thanks.' Why had she said that? It just slipped out. Maybe Vishal could help her with her inability to say no.

Last year Davina's house had been in one of the more upmarket interiors magazines. There was a six page spread featuring her newly refurbished home. *'Returning from the Far East, Rupert and Davina Edgerton Davis wanted a relaxed family feel to their 1800s former rectory.'* Davina was pictured leaning on her kitchen island. *'They set Interior Designer Sally Ann Harper an interesting challenge, how to make sense of a home full of cherished pieces brought back from Asia and annual trips to Tuscany and Provence...'*

Bo put on the cream Nicole Farhi jumper then changed her mind, she was bound to splatter food down the front. At least she had all these new clothes now, but it didn't seem to make it any easier to pick the right ones. There was a pile of rejected outfits on the bed.

She looked in the bedroom mirror and assumed a pleasant expression. 'Say nothing and smile.' Lois's voice was in her head. 'It'll do you good to get out and meet some people.'

Her phone buzzed – a new text message. It wasn't a number she recognized.

I finally tracked down your no, drink this Friday night? don't reply for a few hours, don't want to look too keen Ben

She looked back at the bedroom mirror and noticed that she was smiling foolishly. She would have a drink with him, why the hell not. Lois was going to love this. They had now started referring to him as SV (Sexy Vet) as opposed to YF (Young Farmer).

As Bo walked up Davina's drive, clutching some hastily picked daffodils from her garden, she walked past a row of shiny Range Rovers, all with cream leather seats and personal number plates. The others must have arrived.

Davina answered the door. 'Oh darling how sweet of you!' Davina took the daffodils and put them on the hall table. Bo noticed that everyone else had brought a scented candle.

She followed Davina through the flagstoned hall to the enormous, double height kitchen. 'Bernadette, you know Sally Ann and Talia. There was a lot of air kissing which always made Bo uneasy. Lois had told her you weren't actually supposed to kiss on the skin and it was never clear how many kisses were appropriate anyway. Talia gripped her fiercely. 'Hello gorge! Haven't seen you for ages!' Talia had a glossy curtain of dark chestnut hair, so highly brushed it was giving off static. 'I've been out of the Country for ages. Can't wait to hear what I've missed!' Bo tried not to think about what she'd written on Facebook that night.

There were two huge glass vases with white flowers displayed on a grey console table, either side of giant gold letters spelling out the word 'family'. Angelica was pouring Champagne into flutes and handing them round. Three sets of perfectly honed buttocks perched on breakfast bar stools.

Davina led her round. 'And I play tennis with Claudia.' One set of buttocks swiveled round to greet her. Claudia was nut brown and sinewy with arms like biltong.

'Hi Claudia.' Bo thought she might actually be thinner than Betsy. 'Claudia is a yoga instructor.' Davina explained. She wore the tiniest pair of white jeans Bo had ever seen on an adult. Claudia kissed her three times and Bo was engulfed by expensive perfume.

Sally Ann had only recently finished the refurb of Davina's entire ground floor and the lunch guests were keen to examine every detail. As they bandied around the names of fabric designers and table lamp brands like familiar friends, Bo sat silently. They were players in a well-rehearsed orchestra and any attempt to join in was bound to sound clumsy.

Claudia got up to admire the action on Davina's wash drawers. She looked suitably impressed. 'I must say Davina. You and Sally Ann have done the most amazing job with this house. It felt quite pokey when you first bought it. You've really opened it up.'

'Thanks.' Davina didn't look entirely thrilled.

Sally Ann turned to Bo smiling. 'Have you been to Talia's house?' Seeing Bo's blank expression, she explained. 'It's spectacular! 600 acres with an Italian sunken garden and a Tudor moat.'

'A Tudor moat!' Bo found herself repeating, for want of a better response.

The conversation turned back to Davina's kitchen island, which had the words *Epicerie Du Centre* painted on the front.

'Sally Ann found it in Paris. It's a vintage shop counter.' Davina explained. 'She replaced the work surface with hammered zinc.'

'How clever! Amazing!'

'I know, we're thrilled with it. It's 15 foot long. Any standard island would have looked ridiculous in this kitchen.' They all nodded. 'Can you believe I was really worried it wasn't going to be long enough' Bo had a vision of her lying in bed in a cold sweat. She thought about her own mock marble, 70s formica counter tops, held together with toast crumbs. Davina carried on. 'When they first put it in I was in floods of tears. Poor Sally Ann! I was in pieces wasn't I?' Sally Ann rolled her eyes.

Seeing that Bo was struggling to join in, Davina turned to the rest of them. 'Now Bo has been having a very exciting time, haven't you Bo! She's been interviewed in every magazine in the country. And she's been up and down to London, to all sorts of celebrity bashes!'

Talia looked interested. 'How fabulous! Who have you met?'

Bo thought about it. 'Well Olly Murs was lovely! And Caitlyn Jenner. And the entire cast of Geordie Shore.' Talia looked completely blank. Bo tried again. 'I saw Monty Don the other day, didn't get to speak to him though.'

Talia nodded. 'Oh yes we absolutely adore Monty, he's been to supper a couple of times. He was really helpful when we wanted to reinstate the knot garden.'

Davina was a very attentive hostess. 'And Claudia has just come back from the Ethiopian Highlands where she has been working to protect Gelada Baboons, photographing them for charity.'

'I'm running a charity ball in aid of the Gelada Conservation Trust in June. Absolute bloody nightmare to organise.'

Davina nodded, 'You must come along Bo.'

Angelica started to lay out the food on the kitchen table. 'Girls, grab a plate and come and sit down. We've got potato and anchovy soufflé, grilled chorizo and plantain salad, Halloumi, beetroot and pomegranate salad. Claudia I know you're wheat and dairy intolerant, so Angelica's made this one without the halloumi just for you.'

There was much admiration of the salads. Bo was careful to watch how much the others put on their plates, so that she didn't over pile. Talia turned to Davina. 'This is absolute heaven. Skye Gyngell?'

'Thomasina Miers! Actually I can take no credit whatsoever, Angelica made absolutely everything. I even burnt the toasted pine nuts so she sent me out of the kitchen!' They all laughed.

'Isn't Angelica wonderful!' Sally Ann enthused.

'Wonderful', they chorused. Claudia nodded. 'I don't know what I'd do without a Filly! Bernadette, do you have a Filly?'

'I beg your pardon?'

'A Filipino help.' Claudia explained.

'No, I don't. But I think Angelica's from Thailand actually.'

Claudia shook her head. 'No, she's from the Philippines.' Bo decided to leave it at that. She was busy struggling to free a pomegranate seed from between her teeth.

Through the course of the lunch it became clear that Sally Ann had a fairly serious crush on Talia. Most of her anecdotes started with 'Talia and I.' But Davina also seemed to be vying for her attention. You could tell that Talia rather enjoyed the situation. There was a definite pecking order.

'I love the tufted fringe on your ottoman Davina!' Talia shouted as Davina cleared the salad plates.

'Yes, Sally Ann found it in Rajasthan.'

'Gorgeous! And are your flowers from Willow & Grey?' Davina nodded.

Talia frowned. 'I've been having a few problems with them lately. Ever since I gave them my weekly order. I just think they've got a little bit complacent.'

'You do have to watch them.' Davina replied. They all nodded in agreement. Bo noticed that her daffodils, which she had wrapped in damp kitchen roll and tin foil, had been swiftly whisked away.

Angelica brought the pudding to the table. 'Sky Gyngell's Sweet Chestnut cheesecake!' Davina declared.

Claudia waved the plate away. 'Not for me thanks.'

Sally Ann pulled a guilty face. 'Just a 'girlie' portion for me thanks hun!'

Davina sliced up the cheesecake and passed round plates. 'Bo, I imagine you want a proper portion.'

Bo smiled weakly. 'Yes, thank you Davina!'

Davina passed her a plate. 'Sally Ann, can you pass Bo the cream.' The conversation turned to an organic café in London they had all frequented.

Bo stood up. 'Actually Davina, can I just use your loo?'

Sally Ann's magic touch was evident in the lavatory as well. The wood paneling was painted in a very tasteful dark green. There were pictures of Rupert on the hunting field dotted around and a large framed black and white photograph of Rupert and Davina, flanked by Chloe, Felix and Imo. They were all wearing jeans and white shirts, in one of those casually orchestrated studio shots. Bo tried to imagine herself, Neil and Liam posing for a black and white photograph in matching linen shirts.

The loo smelled heavenly on account of two giant scented candles flickering away. They had 18 wicks each. Bo counted them as she sat on the loo. She had seen them in magazines. Some of them were more expensive than an all-inclusive holiday to Greece. She really must stop being so chippy, they were all being very nice to her. She wondered if she would ever have a weekly flower delivery. She looked in the mirror and checked her teeth. She stared at her reflection and pulled a face. 'Would you like to come and see my Tudor moat?' *Stop it. Be nice! They're just trying to be friendly.*

On the way back to the kitchen she spotted Angelica polishing the table in the dining room. She went over to speak to her. 'Thank you for the lovely food Angelica. It was delicious!'

Angelica shrugged. 'Mrs E-D gave me the recipe. It look like bird food to me.' She carried on polishing and singing quietly to herself.

As Bo walked back into the kitchen, she heard her name. 'So Bernadette and I were running through the field, chased by a herd of cows, when this utterly gorgeous vet came out of nowhere. Ben Hardy I think he's called. And he literally waded into 6 feet of slurry, followed closely by Bernadette, to save the dog!'

'Oh my God I know him!' Talia squealed. 'And you must too Davina, he looks after Rupert's hunters.'

'Does he?' Davina looked blank.

'Yes! He's gorgeous looking! I went to school with his wife Jo. She's an absolute stunner too, legs up to her armpits and lovely with it. They live up in Hardy's Barn, apparently she did an amazing job converting it when they first bought it. I should get her to show us round. They really are the dream couple, totally devoted. Makes you sick!'

They all laughed. Bo struggled not to look as deflated as she felt. So Sexy Vet was a married Sexy Vet and she wouldn't be running off into the sunset with a younger man after all. That was short lived. She stared out of the window, wondering if it was her age that made her feel so foolish.

The conversation turned to children. Talia sighed deeply. 'Nessie's doing Prue Leith for the summer, I think she's hoping Imo will too. God knows what we're going to do with Caspar. He's retaking his A levels, thick as two short planks. Marcus is going to have to pull some serious strings in the City.'

Bo hadn't spoken for ages and Davina tried to bring her into the conversation again. 'What about Liam, Bo? What's he up to these days?'

Bo tried to sound upbeat in spite of the revelation. 'He's travelling at the moment, in Cambodia. He's about to start an engineering degree.'

Claudia nodded. 'Oh fab. Building bridges and that sort of thing.'

'More of a biochemical engineer' Bo explained. 'He wants to specialise in renewable energy, building power plants.'

'Oh, super.' There was a silence.

'How's Imo's lawyer friend, Davina?' Sally Ann whispered theatrically.

'Imo's bagged herself a top, international lawyer!' Talia explained. They all looked suitably impressed.

Davina returned to the table with a glass tea pot. 'She's completely besotted. Very successful Argentinian barrister apparently.'

Talia sighed. 'Oooh do you think he plays polo?' They all giggled.

'Mint tea infusion anyone? The mint's from the garden.' Davina started to pour. Bo took a glass tea cup. If she was honest, it tasted like luke warm piss, but she drank it all the same.

Once she had drained her cup, she saw an opportunity to leave. 'That was absolutely gorgeous Davina, but I've got a call I have to take at 3.30.'

'Oh of course!' Davina looked impressed. There was a round of air kissing and Claudia promised to send her an invitation to the Gelada Baboon Conservation Ball. Davina walked her down the corridor. Now Bo, I'm having a big party in the garden next week, you must come and do bring Lois.

'Of course.' She managed to keep the smile on her face until she was safely through the front door. As she walked down the gravel driveway, she wondered if she had ever felt so lonely in her whole life.

Reaching for her phone, she reread the text. There was the familiar sensation of disappointment. Neil the cheating bastard and now Ben, but what exactly had she expected at 43, 'Colin Firth on a fucking unicorn' as Lois was fond of saying. She punched out a response before she could change her mind.

'Too busy this week, another time.'

She was almost at the gate and about to cross the lane back to the cottage, when she saw a blonde head ducking suddenly behind a low, orchard wall. She poked her head round the corner of the wall.

'Imogen? Are you OK?' Imogen was surrounded by a cloud of smoke. She hastily removed the cigarette from her mouth and threw it into a patch of nettles.

'Shit! Mrs Spicer!'

Bo smiled. 'You didn't have to stub it out on my account.'

'Oh thanks Mrs Spicer. You won't tell Mum then.'

'No. Imogen, you're 19 aren't you? I think it's legal.'

'I know, but Mum's ridiculously strict. I thought her little lunch 'do' would go on longer.'

'Oh I see. Well the others will be in there for a while I expect.' She realized she sounded a bit off hand. 'I hear you've got yourself an Argentinian lawyer friend. That sounds exciting!' She felt awkward as she said it. It was exactly the sort of intro she would have hated as a teenager.

'Oh Christ! Is that what Mum's been telling her friends.' Imogen shook her head and lit another cigarette. She offered one to Bo and looked slightly startled when she took it.

Imogen lit Bo's cigarette. 'So, Mum's in heaven because she thinks I'm seeing some minted lawyer and I'll go and live in Chelsea and make souffles and play tennis and live happily ever after and be just like her.'

Bo shrugged her shoulders. 'Doesn't sound too bad to me.'

'Anyway, he's Brazilian.' Imogen dragged on her cigarette. Bo said nothing, she sensed there was more to come.

'And he's not a Barrister.'

'Oh.'

'I told Mummy that he's a Barista and she misunderstood.'

'I see.' Bo tried very hard to keep a straight face, but it was no good. Their eyes met and they both started to laugh.

They stopped laughing briefly, long enough for Imogen to say, 'Bar-ista – he serves coffee.'

'Yes, I got that.'

'He works at the Costa Coffee in Brinton train station. Mummy would die if she found out. She's told all her friends I'm hooked up with some South American top lawyer.'

'Well that's awkward isn't it!' Bo nodded and dragged deeply on her cigarette.

Imogen was serious again. 'I mean imagine if she had to tell all her tennis friends that I'm going out with the bloke at Costa that serves them skinny lattes on their way to London. I mean it's ridiculous because he's really intelligent and he's going to be very successful, but Mummy's such an unbelievable snob and now she wants to meet him.'

'Come on, she's not that bad. Can't you just tell her the truth. Bring him home and introduce him.'

'And hope he won't notice my mother's disappointed face. He's the most gorgeous man ever. He doesn't deserve that.'

'You're being a bit unfair. She just wants the best for you. That's all it is. Just tell her.'

'I suppose you're right.'

'Do a really quick introduction, so it's not too awkward. You could get him to pick you up before you go off somewhere.'

'Do you think?'

'Yes.'

Imogen looked at her with new found respect. 'How's Liam these days?'

'He's good. He's in Cambodia. I really only find out what he's up to on Facebook.'

'Does he have a girlfriend?'

'I don't think so. Well he probably wouldn't tell me anyway, would he!'

'Probably not.' Imogen smiled.

Bo stubbed out her cigarette. 'I'd better go. Just do me a favour Imogen. Don't have any secrets, they become a terrible burden.'

Imogen wondered what she meant as she watched her cross the lane, walk back into her cottage and shut the door.

14

Bo held up a flowery dress and looked in the mirror.

Lois shook her head. 'No, too pretty. You want something sexier.'

Lois had just arrived and they were trying on clothes for Davina's party. Bo frowned as she rifled through the cupboard. 'Do you think it's going to be quite formal?'

'Oh God yes, they'll be dolled up to the nines.'

'You're right. She's had caterers and flower arrangers arriving in vans all day and last night she had a white grand piano winched onto the terrace by the pool.'

'A white grand piano!'

'Yes!' Bo applied bronzer, without really looking. 'And I wouldn't be surprised if Elton John was flying in to play it.'

Lois sighed. 'She's quite a woman isn't she.'

'She is indeed.'

'What's it in aid of anyway?'

Bo lowered her voice. 'She says it's her freedom party.' They both raised their eyebrows.

Lois wore a deep red Diane Von Furstenberg dress, a gift a couple of months back, from the Selfridges personal shopper. Bo finally settled on black jeans, her wedge heels and a floaty black top. Lois surveyed her. 'Much better, sophisticated and yet sexy. Nail polish?'

'I can't be arsed Lois.'

'Fair enough. Shall we have a little sharpener before we go?'

'Why not. We're going to need a drink if it's all the twiglet women from the tennis club.'

An hour later, they walked hesitantly up the sweeping drive of the Old Rectory, both suddenly a bit intimidated by the sight of the torchlit path, flower festooned archway and waiting staff dressed in white uniforms either side of the entrance.

They each took a glass of Champagne and knocked them back quickly as they entered the enormous white pavilion.

Their mouths dropped open simultaneously. 'It's Chelsea Flower Show!' Lois mouthed incredulously. Every pole was covered in jasmine and white roses, upside down flower arrangements hung down from the ceiling, white Mongolian throws covered chairs and sofas. Displays of white jasmine and candles filled the air with a heavy perfume and tiny candles floated on the swimming pool at the other end of the marquee. Angelica had scattered white petals all over the marquee floor. The guests were head to toe in white: floaty dresses, hotpants, white lace tops, sparkly clutch bags, white thigh high boots.

Lois and Bo stood at the entrance, conspicuous in black and red. 'Did she not tell you it was a white themed party?' Lois whispered under her breath.

'No she didn't!'

Lois surveyed the room. 'It looks like an 80s tampax ad!'

Bo took a step back towards the door. 'We'll go home and change?'

It was too late. Davina came rushing towards them, arms outstretched. She was perfectly toned in a floor length white maxi dress. 'Girls! You look fabulous!'

'You didn't tell us it was a white party Davina!' Bo spoke through gritted teeth. 'Yes I did.' Davina laughed. 'Anyway, no matter. Come and meet some gorgeous people! Nessie Staniforth-Cummings is here! I've told her all about you.'

Lois pulled a face at Bo as they followed Davina through the enormous white structure towards the swimming pool. 'Nessie!' Davina squealed as she kissed an Amazonian blonde in a white silk jump suit.

'Girls, come and meet Nessie! Bo, Lois this is Vanessa Staniforth-Cummings. Nessie this is Bernadette and Lois, who I told you all about.' Davina was gushing. Vanessa didn't look quite so enthusiastic.' Poker-faced, she air kissed them both at least a foot away from their heads. A recent round of Botox had deprived her of facial movement.

'Amazing tent.' Bo attempted to fill the awkward silence.

'Yurt.' Vanessa replied. Her swollen upper lip making it quite difficult to be understood.

'I beg your pardon.' Bo looked confused.

'It's a oroccan yurt.' The lip wasn't helping at all with the consonants.

'Right.' They both nodded.

Lois looked around impatiently. 'Well it's been lovely to meet you Vanessa. Heard so much about you from Davina.'

'Ya cool.' Bo was transfixed by her completely smooth face and incredibly deep voice. 'You drove up from London, ya?'

'No, I live just over there. And Lois is staying with me.' Bo added.

'Cool.' There was a silence.

You could tell Lois was itching to get away. 'Right well we'd better go and say hello to your neighbours Bo, there they are!'

'Oh yes.' Lois pulled Bo away.

'Jesus Bo, it's all stick insects with boob jobs!'

'Keep your voice down!'

They walked straight into Claudia Floyd Roberts and Talia Grossman. Claudia was wearing children's white jeans again. 'Hello Bernadette. You didn't get the email about the white dress code then.'

'No, we didn't.' Bo smiled. 'Aren't the flowers amazing!'

'Yah!' Talia pulled a face. 'Shame about the Chincherinchees though, she couldn't get them flown over in time. Had to settle for the Jasmine.'

'Shame.' Claudia and Talia both nodded in agreement as they accepted tiny morsels of sushi from a passing waitress.

Claudia frowned. 'Oh no, I do wish she'd told me. I've got a darling friend in Cape Town, I could have had them flown in.'

Lois snorted. 'I could've got her some orange begonias in plastic pots.'

They both just looked at her blankly. Bo gave her a look.

There was a shriek from the other end of the terrace. Sally Ann had spotted Talia and was approaching at speed, waving her arms like a typhoon. She was so excited, Bo thought she might actually knock Talia over.

'Hi Gorge!' Talia managed to extricate herself from Sally Ann's powerful embrace. 'You look stunning hun! Alice Temperley?'

'Maria Grachvogel.'

'Hi darling!' Claudia air kissed Sally Ann.

'Lovely party!' Bo mumbled as Sally Ann kissed her.

'Talia had a WONDERFUL party last year.' Sally Ann was breathless. 'We floated lotus flowers down her moat.'

Bo thought Lois might spit out her drink. 'Did you. I'd love to have lotus flowers floated down my moat!'

'Lois!'

Claudia looked at Lois with renewed interest. 'Have you got a moat?'

Sally Ann oblivious, sighed at the memory. 'It was magical!'

Lois shrugged her shoulders. 'It's lovely, but where I come from, you can have a perfectly good party with an 80s disco mix, a couple of bottles of Frascati and a packet of Doritos.'

Tania, Claudia and Sally Ann stared at her nonplussed.

'We've got to say hello to my neighbours Lois!' Bo led her away. 'Lois, you don't have to be so confrontational.'

'Well really! What do they think they're like?'

'They think they're normal Lois, just like we think we're normal.'

'Yes but we are! Will you look at that Bo.'

They both looked over at the shiny white grand piano.

A woman in a white Kaftan swayed and clutched onto it for support as she sang 'Summertime', loudly and slightly out of tune. '*The fish are jumping, And the cotton is HIGH…*' Her voice was getting louder and more pronounced with every line. The pianist was playing a completely different tune, but nobody seemed to notice, least of all her.

'Why do pissed middle aged women always sing 'Summertime' at parties Bo?'

'I guess it's one of those songs that makes you think you've got a really good voice and that you should have been a famous jazz singer. And after three pints of champagne, you don't care who knows it.'

'Quite.' Lois shook her head. 'But someone needs to tell her she's as flat as a witch's tit.'

They wandered over to the pool, their pathway scattered with flowers. Angelica stood at the end holding a silver tray, dressed up in white tuxedo and trousers. She looked furious. 'You want WHITE RUSSIAN!' She barked aggressively at passing guests.

'Thank you, Angelica.' They both laughed and took one.

Lois waved her drink at Bo. 'Look over there!' A very good looking man in tight white jodhpurs led two miniature white ponies on ribbons around the pool. There was a collective sigh from the crowd. 'Oh Falabellas! How adorable!' They both started to giggle.

'Girls! Are you enjoying yourselves!' Davina strode up and they both felt guilty for laughing.

Lois sipped her White Russian appreciatively. 'It's an amazing party Davina.'

Bo couldn't speak as she struggled to swallow a Chinese pork dumpling.

'Oh I do hope it's going well.' They both nodded vigorously. Davina looked relieved. 'Well I am good at this sort of thing. It's what I do! Putting my OCD to good use!'

Bo finally got the better of the dumpling.

'Where's Rupert?'

Davina's expression changed. 'We're having a bit of a break Bernadette.' Bo noticed she wasn't wearing her wedding ring. 'Don't look so surprised, it's for the best. It's not that dramatic, we hardly see each other as it is.'

'I'm so sorry Davina!'

'No, it's fine. Now you go and have a dance. And make sure you're out here at midnight for the releasing of the doves! Enjoy!' She marched off, instructing caterers as she went. They looked at each other.

A small crowd was gathering around the woman at the piano. 'You're Daddy's RICHHHHH, And you're Momma's good LOOKING.' Lois rolled her eyes. 'Of feck, she knows the second verse!' A few other women started to join in.

'Come on then, let's go and dance!' Lois strode ahead, but Bo spotted Imogen waving her over. Lois disappeared off towards the dance floor.

'Mrs Spicer! Bo! There's someone I really want you to meet.' Imogen was accompanied by a tall man in his twenties with shoulder length dark hair. 'This is Mateus! He's from Brazil.' Bo held out her hand and he grinned and shook it. 'Hello Mateus! Lovely to meet you. I'm Bo, I live across the road.' He almost bowed as he shook her hand. He was very good looking and Imogen radiated happiness.

'You introduced Mateus to your mother then?'

'Yes, she adores him!' Imogen gushed. 'He came over to pick me up last week and we told her where he worked and how funny it was, the whole mistake about the Barrister, Barista thing!'

'Very funny! Barista!' Mateus laughed. 'Me a lawyer! Of course, I'm not studying law.'

'No. Quite.' Bo replied earnestly.

Mateus stopped laughing. 'I came here to study medicine!'

'Medicine.' Bo struggled not to look surprised.

'He's going to be a doctor!' Imogen was exultant. 'He didn't even mention it until our third date!'

Imogen shot a meaningful look at Bo. 'It went down very well!'

Bo smiled. 'I'm sure it did. A doctor, how lovely? Which particular branch of medicine, Mateus?'

'Neurology.'

'A brain surgeon Bo!' Imogen could hardly contain herself.

Mateus nodded sincerely. 'Imogen's mother is a very charming woman.'

'She's taking Mateus to the tennis club next week.' Imogen explained. 'He used to play for the Brazilian junior team.'

'Good God!' Bo looked wistful. 'Where were all the Brazilian brain surgeons when I was in my twenties! And you make a damn fine cappuccino I'll bet!'

He nodded. 'Damn fine actually!' Mateus replied in a mock English accent.

Seeing them talking, Davina blew a kiss and shouted over from the other side of the pool. 'Do make sure Mateus has a drink Imo!'

Imogen and Mateus wandered off and Bo spotted Lois emerging from the tent.

'Well!' She could tell Lois had news. 'I've just been introduced to Talia's husband. You know, Marcus Grossman.'

'Oh right.' Bo waited for Lois to elaborate.

'He's feckin ancient!'

'There's nothing wrong with an age gap Lois!' She thought about Ben.

'No I grant you, but this is an extreme age gap. He's old enough to be her granddad. I mean, can you imagine what he looks like naked!' Lois was making gagging noises.

'Oh stop it Lois!' Bo laughed. 'He's got a Tudor Moat and 600 acres!'

'Revolting! What some of these women are willing to do for a nice kitchen!' Lois shook her head in disgust.

Bo laughed. 'There's always a price to pay Lois.'

'Well, I couldn't do it. If they offered me Windsor bloody Castle! The poor woman must have to get paralytic drunk!'

Lois looked over her shoulder. 'MY GOD IN HEAVEN!'

'What is it now!' Bo wasn't sure she could take much more drama.

'It's him!' Lois whispered loudly.

'Who?'

'Don't turn round, it's SEXY VET aka YOUNG FARMER. He's just at the entrance to the marquee. Davina must have invited him.'

'Oh right. Him.' Bo tried to sound nonchalant.

'Oh God, he's coming over! He's headed straight for us!' She thought Lois might explode.

Bo took a few deep breaths and gulped down the rest of her White Russian.

He was right behind them. She exhaled deeply and turned round. He smiled when he saw her, but before he could reach her, Talia Grossman intercepted him with her vice like grip. Claudia stood behind her looking unusually shy. 'Ben, Ben Hardy, do you remember me? Talia Grossman. You used to look after Marcus' hunters.' Talia flashed her most beguiling smile. 'Now you must meet my friend Claudia Floyd Roberts. She's divorced and she works with Gelada Baboons!'

'Hello Claudia.' He shook her hand. 'Hi Talia. You'll have to forgive me, but there's someone I need to see.' The small crowd of women parted and he walked through them and straight over to Bo. He was wearing a pale blue shirt and jeans and she couldn't take her eyes off him.

'Hello.' He grinned.

'I'll make myself scarce.' Lois sloped off making a thumbs up sign behind him.

They stood a little awkwardly. Bo struggled to think of something to say. 'I didn't know it was a white party, as you can see.'

'No. At least it was easy to find you.' They paused again.

'So you've been very busy.'

'Very.'

'Far too busy to go out for a drink.'

'Yes.' She played nervously with the empty glass in her hands. 'You know I'm old enough to be your mother.'

'What!' He laughed. 'Did you mean to say that out loud?'

'Not really.' Her lips twitched, trying to contain the rising hysteria.

He looked amused. 'How old do you think I am?'

'I don't know. 28?'

'28! I'm flattered. I'm 36.'

'36!' She must have looked astounded because he started to laugh again.

'And you're what 38?'

'Yes, no, 42, well 43 actually.'

He laughed. 'So not old enough to be my mother then.'

'Apparently not.'

Silence. He was flirting with her, definitely flirting. She was flattered, but angry at the same time. She wondered how far he would go, given the chance. She imagined Neil flirting with Mandy, having a similar banter. How old are you now Mandy? 24! Haven't you changed. All grown up! Bastard!

'So which one's your wife?' *Why did she say that.*

'What?' He looked stunned.

'Do you not bring her with you, when you're out flirting?'

'My wife?' His expression had changed completely.

'Yes.'

He looked at the ground. 'My wife isn't here because she died of cancer three years ago.'

Silence.

He put down his glass. 'I don't actually know why I'm here. I think I should probably go.' He turned and walked off.

'Fuck.' She closed her eyes to try to blot out the horror.

Lois, who had been hovering, was back in an instant. 'So, how did that go? Do we have a date?'

'Not exactly Lois.'

'What happened.'

'His wife Lois. You know I said I thought he was a cheating bastard?'

'Yes and I said he's probably divorced and you should just ask him.'

'Well I did. I said 'Where's your wife when you're out flirting. And he said 'she died of cancer three years ago.'

Fuck!

'Yes fuck.'

15

Fallen Angel

It was Thursday morning and Bo lay in bed. It had been several days now but she still couldn't think about the white party without wincing in shame. Why had she automatically assumed the worst? Something to do with the state of her own marriage no doubt. She would send him an apology, think of something to say later.

There were no appointments in London until early next week. It was a beautiful Spring morning and she opened the bedroom window. The garden was awash with daffodils and she could hear a woodpecker tapping away in the chestnut tree. She thought about how her life had changed in the space of a few months. She had separated from her husband, left her job, forged a new media career, signed up with a high street retailer as the face of a fashion range. She had £265,430 in the bank, her house was spotless, her cupboard full of designer clothes. She even had a French manicure on her toe nails.

She thought about Liam and what all this could mean for him. He could study anywhere he wanted now, he was bright enough, maybe in the States. And she could buy him a car. He would be upset about his Dad and mortified by both his parents, understandably, but she hoped in time he would be pleased for her. It must have been obvious that Neil and Bo hadn't been happy for a long time. He would be back in the summer, at least he had been away when all of this hit the news.

She thought about the conversation with Ben. She should just pick up the phone and apologise.

She went downstairs and made herself a cappuccino with her new coffee machine, a free gift from last week's photoshoot. She should definitely phone him, but what if she said the wrong thing, which was highly likely. Safer to send a text and leave it at that, cowardly but safe.

I should call u to apologise but too embarrassed SO SORRY someone said u were married & I didn't think please forgive my stupid comments Bo

She changed it around, tried to make it shorter, more casual. What did it matter anyway. The main thing was that he knew she was sorry. She pressed send before she could change her mind. There, done.

Snickers and Toby jumped onto her lap as she sipped her coffee and flicked through a mail order sofa catalogue. She would probably never bump into him again and could put the whole mortifying episode behind her. She checked her phone for a response. Nothing.

A builder was coming this afternoon to quote for the outbuilding. It could easily be converted with an open plan kitchen diner and bedroom. It felt good to be on her own and able to make things happen. The doorbell rang and she sighed. Angelica had a key but she never liked to let herself in.

Bo stood up to unlock the door. She opened it and what she saw made her let out a scream.

There must have been more than fifty people jostling for space in her garden and more further down the lane. There were journalists, cameras, microphones, cars and vans parked the entire length of the road. When they saw her they surged forward en masse towards the door.

'Bernadette! Why did you take the baby Bernadette? Have you got anything to say to the mother?' She slammed the door and with trembling hands, slid the chain across. She turned her back and leant against the door for support. Dear Lord, so here it was then, her come uppance. No escaping it after all. She must try to stay calm, try to focus. Where were her mobile phones? She walked quickly through the house, locking windows and pulling curtains across. Her hands were shaking so much that she could hardly open up her laptop and type in the name. **Bernadette Maloney**.

Bernadette the baby snatcher! We reveal the shocking truth about Britain's favourite housewife.

She scrolled down. There were literally hundreds of stories. It didn't end.

Shock celebrity exposé. Housewife heroine Bernadette Maloney has been revealed as a baby thief. We can reveal that the woman caught on CCTV cameras 21 years ago walking out of a Liverpool hospital with a newborn baby in her rucksack is none other than 'Angel in a Onesie', Bernadette Maloney.

The housewife whose meteoric rise to fame has seen her rubbing shoulders with TV stars has become a favourite agony aunt for thousands. Her overnight success story began spectacularly with the cliff top rescue of a Wiltshire teenager, but we can reveal that 21 years ago the same Bernadette Maloney was in the news for a very different reason.

On an April morning in 1995, she walked into St Saviour's maternity hospital, Liverpool, abducted a new born baby and walked out of the hospital unchallenged. They were missing for a week before police, tipped off by a landlady, eventually tracked them down to a B&B in a remote village in Wales. Maloney was arrested and the baby returned to her traumatized mother. Due to her mental state, Maloney's family pleaded diminished responsibility and she was given a suspended sentence.

There was a picture of the landlady with a quote 'I was suspicious because she was confused when I asked her things about the baby. She didn't seem to have a push chair or pram or anything with her.'

And there was the grainy CCTV picture of Bo, a still taken from the hospital camera footage. The burgundy hoodie and blue rucksack, just visible as she walked out of the revolving doors.

Lynda Jarvis, mother of the baby says 'She put me through a living hell. I'm stunned that it's the same Bernadette. I can't believe she's the woman who took my baby.'

Bernadette broke my heart. Real life fraud of the overnight heroine who captured Britain's hearts.

She felt a wave of nausea as she started to comprehend the full scale of what was happening to her. She ran to the bathroom and lent over the sink, taking deep breaths as pin prick beads of sweat broke out on her cold pale forehead. 'Dear God, please help me!' She pleaded into the mirror.

She could hear the Betsy mobile ringing in the bedroom and ran back to answer it. Please God, maybe Betsy would have a plan.

'Hello Betsy.' Her voice was weak.

'Are you joking? Are you actually fucking joking? Do you have any idea how angry I am?'

'I can understand how you feel Betsy.'

'I don't think you realise quite how stupid you are?'

'I do.'

'Do you remember our conversation, the bit in the contract where I asked if there was anything about you I should know that might affect our plans?'

Betsy paused as if gathering herself for the next attack.

'Well I'll tell you this much Bo,' she spoke slowly in a white hot rage. 'All contracts are over, null and void: Levene Associates, the clothing range, homeware endorsements, sponsorships, regular radio slot, everything, all over DO YOU UNDERSTAND?'

'Yes I do.'

There was silence at the other end of the phone, but Betsy hadn't quite finished.

'How did you think you could get away with it Bo? Did you not think for one second you'd be found out?'

'I suppose I mean, I hoped it was in the past.' She paused. 'And that I might be forgiven.'

'Forgiven? For kidnapping a new born baby? Are you familiar with the British tabloid press? They're after your blood Bo. I've spent the entire morning taking press calls. The retail deal is off, I'll forward you the email they sent me this morning, it's very clear. This has severely damaged my relationship with them and we'll be lucky if the homewares director doesn't come after us for damage to the brand. This could cost me a fortune in legal costs, let alone time it will take me to rebuild my name. How do you think my other clients will feel about being represented by the Baby snatcher's agent? Hmm?'

'I didn't think.' The door bell was ringing insistently now and the phone rang non-stop downstairs. They were shouting through the letterbox.

'No you bloody didn't, did you. I've spent twenty years building up this company. And I happen to be brilliant at my job Bo. I could have dealt with anything, adultery, shoplifting, a serious drug habit, but this! You ABDUCTED A BABY?'

'Yes I did.' Bo tried to think straight through the panic. 'What should I do now Betsy?'

'Do? In case you hadn't noticed, you're no longer my responsibility. There's nothing you can do, except maybe get yourself a lawyer. Good bye Bo.'

And that was it, a click and then silence. As she dropped the phone on the bed, Bo looked at the pale reflection in the full length mirror looking back at her. 'So you thought you could have your life back did you, thought you could have it all?'

She hadn't cried yet, no point, she would save that for later. She felt stupid now in her cream satin pyjamas and pulled on jeans and a jumper instead.

The other mobile rang. It was Lois.

'Lois, thank God!'

'OH MY GOD BO! Have you seen the papers?'

'Please don't say I told you so Lois. It's started. There's hundreds of them in the garden and more arriving every minute? They're sticking cameras through the letterbox.'

'Oh God, OK my darling. You've got to stay strong. I'll get the 6 o'clock flight to Heathrow. I should be with you by ten. You just need to hang on my darling.'

'Thank you Lois.' Her bottom lip began to tremble.

'Now listen to me Bo. They can't come into your house. This will all go away eventually. It'll be yesterday's news before you know it. You've got £250,000 in the bank. And you've still got Liam and your health.'

At the thought of Liam, Bo choked back tears.

'Where is he, do you know?'

'He should be in Myanmar by now, then back to Thailand. I don't know what I'll say to him?'

'We'll see if we can get hold of him tonight. He'll understand Bo, he's a bright boy.'

Lois was practical again. 'Have you locked all the doors and windows.

'I've done that.'

'And have you got any duct tape for the letter box.'

'Yes.' Bo's voice was a whisper. 'You were right Lois, what was I thinking. It's happening all over again. Did I think there would be no retribution? This time they're going to make me pay.'

'Don't talk like that Bo. You just need to sit tight. We'll go away somewhere. Until all this blows over.'

Lois rang off and she saw a text on her mobile.

Forgiven, I over reacted, u can buy me a drink next Friday I'll pick u up at 7

She didn't reply. He obviously hadn't switched on his TV yet.

The Betsy mobile rang again but she didn't recognize the number.

'Hello.'

'Hi Bernadette it's Vishal! I couldn't get you on your landline, it's constantly busy. It's 3 o'clock in the morning here, but I've got a window in my schedule. How are you fixed for some coaching?'

She wasn't sure what to say. 'Look Vishal…'

'Now don't go blocking me Bernadette! So, let's get started with some controlled breathing. And in… and out.'

I'm not hearing your breathing Bernadette.' Bo was gulping the air.

'How centred are we feeling right now?'

'Not centred Vishal.'

'Ok we can deal with that. Are you ready to empty your mind? Let's concentrate on your breathing and find your safe, peaceful place.'

'Look Vishal, I've been exposed for kidnapping a baby by the British press, there are about a hundred paparazzi camped outside my house and Betsy has terminated my contract.'

There was a pause and she wondered if he had taken all of this on board.

'OK. Well this is awkward Bernadette. I'm really only coaching you as a favour to Betsy, she's promoting my book and DVD in the UK. I'm guessing I should really catch up with her right now?'

Bo didn't answer.

'OK, so keep up with the exercises and hey, good luck with it.'

He rang off.

She put the mobile on the bed and went downstairs to look for duct tape. She could take the phone off the hook but there was nothing she could do about the door bell. The noise of people shouting outside seemed to be getting louder and they kept on ringing the bell, taking it in turns. Maybe they thought she would eventually be driven mad and come outside. At least she had had the kitchen window fixed. As she rooted around in the kitchen drawers, there was the sound of the front door opening. How on earth? She had double locked it. Blind panic. She ran to the hallway, to do what, she wasn't sure.

Davina and Angelica stood in the entrance. Davina in her huge bug eye sunglasses and Angelica carrying a mop and bucket. 'It's OK Bernadette. We've got a plan.' Bo gave Davina a squeeze, trying hard not to weep. Davina looked a bit awkward as she extracted herself. She took off her sunglasses.

'Right, pull yourself together. This is the plan. I'm going to come round and get you in 15 minutes. Pack a bag, we'll make it look like you're going somewhere.'

Seeing Bo's confused expression, Davina waved her sunglasses dismissively and carried on. 'I know what I'm doing Bo, I have several very high profile celebrity friends. The Royals spend half their time driving around in their friend's car boots.'

'Sorry, what?'

'I will drive you in your car to my tennis club, where I've already left my car. We'll do the switch there and then I will drive you back to my house hidden under a blanket in the boot. Meanwhile Angelica will pretend to be cleaning and will let slip to the press, while she's doing the outside windows, that you've fled to Ireland.' Angelica nodded. 'We can keep an eye on them from my house and you can pop home when they've all given up and gone home, OK?' Davina was a little breathless and clearly pleased with the plan.

Bo wondered if she had read the news. 'Don't you care what I did?'

'I expect you had your reasons. Now go and pack a bag and I'll be back for you shortly. And put some make up on.'

Davina slipped her sunglasses back on and strode out and down the path, accompanied by the noise of shouting press. 'Is she in there?' 'What state is she in?' Davina flicked her blonde hair and turned round to face the waiting press.

'She is obviously shocked by the attention, but as calm and composed as she could be, under the circumstances.'

They started chasing her down the drive. 'Is she going to say sorry to the mother?' Davina turned round and smiled politely. 'Thank you. There will be no further comment for the media today.'

Bo watched from behind a curtain. What was Davina doing? It looked like she was holding a press conference.

Looking at her watch, it was 1 o'clock already. She went upstairs, changed into her jeans and started to pack a weekend bag. It might not be a very convincing plan, but it was a plan nonetheless. Her hands were still shaking as she picked out pants, socks and a bra. It didn't matter what she packed she knew that, but she still went to the bathroom to fetch her toiletry bag like she was really going away. She was moving about like a robot on autopilot. Just keep breathing Bo, just keep going, yesterday's news.

She looked at her mobile and decided she really should deal with Ben.

I did something a while back which is about to appear all over the press. Don't want to drag you into this. Not a good idea to meet. Sorry Bo

She pressed send.

Angelica shouted up the stairs. 'You OK, Mrs Spicer. You in whole heap of shit, yeah? I make you tea OK?'

'Thanks Angelica.' She shouted back as she hastily applied bronzer to her sweating cheeks.

The front door slammed. 'Ghastly people!' Davina was back, bang on time and this time carrying an umbrella in spite of the sunshine. 'They really are the dregs of society. Right, give me your keys. We're going to walk calmly to the car. They haven't blocked it in, but it's only a matter of time. Do you want to put a hat on or something? What about a hood?'

'I've got a hoodie, but I'm not wearing it.' She stared at the floor.

'Oh, no I see your point.' Davina looked a little awkward.

'Well put some make up on and a nice coat. This picture's going to be in every paper by tomorrow morning.' Bo wondered how Davina could be so composed, but then this wasn't happening to her.

She did as Davina said and passed her the car keys. As Angelica prepared to hold open the door, Davina's squeezed her arm reassuringly. 'Right here we go, Bo, follow right behind me. Don't smile, it'll look too flippant, but not too serious either. Just try to look normal.'

'Normal.' In any other situation, Bo would have laughed. The door opened and she was almost knocked backwards by the noise and surge of photographers. Davina had told her not to listen to the questions.

'Aren't you ashamed of yourself?' 'Did you not think you'd be found out?'

Keep walking down the path. She followed exactly in Davina's footsteps, looking down, not listening, trying to zone out. A couple of journalists were jostling to get closer and nearly knocked her over.

'Walk faster!' Davina shouted back to her. They cut off her route and she was blocked from the car. Someone spat and it landed on her sleeve. 'Dear God!'

A man grabbed her arm and barred her way. 'The mother said you're a satanic bitch! She wishes you were in prison or dead! What do you say to her?' The man's angry face was an inch from hers. 'What!' Her horrorstruck expression was exactly what they wanted as the cameras flashed away. Davina pushed through the crowd. 'Get out of my way, this is obstruction. You've got your shot. You won't be getting anything else.' She jabbed her umbrella at the crowd and pulled Bo towards the car. 'That's it now, off you go!' Davina held the car door open for Bo and raced round to the driver's side. The baying crowd now completely encircled them, cameras held aloft over heads to get one last shot as Davina switched on the engine and pulled away.

There was a screech of wheels as Davina revved the engine and turned out into the lane, leaving a cloud of dust behind them.

She looked sideways at Bo. 'Alright?'

'I'm OK.' Bo nodded.

As they reached the bottom of the lane, the wholesome neighbours were powerwalking past. The ruddy faced wife saw Bo through the window. She pulled a face that looked like she was sucking a lemon and slowly shook her head.

'Oh do shut up!' Davina beeped the horn and ruddy faced woman leapt out of the way.

One resourceful photographer had leapt on a motorbike and tried to follow them but Davina swung the car at the last minute into a small lane and they watched him shoot past and miss them completely.'

'OK then, change of plan.' Davina was triumphant. 'We'll have to take the long way.' She was determined that they wouldn't be followed and it was half an hour before they finally pulled into the tennis club car park.

She parked up next to the waiting Range Rover and opened it for Bo. 'Right, stay there and try not to be seen. I'm just going to give them your registration number so we can leave your car here overnight.'

Bo watched her disappear into the Tennis Club reception and marveled at her. She really was a force of nature. Without Davina, she knew she would still be huddled on the floor of her bedroom, clutching her knees. A smart looking group of women in tennis gear walked past but they didn't look at her twice. Not the sort of women who read the tabloids, she imagined.

Bo reached for her phone. No more messages from Lois. Ben had replied.

Interesting...not a serial killer? anything else fine, c u on Friday

She would have to put him off. Another text from Mel.

Baloney! wots goin on? U ok? Don't look at social media OK? Some sick peeps out there ☹

She huddled down further into Davina's cashmere throw. There were 7 messages from Katy Partridge.

Davina returned with a cup of tea. 'There you are. Drink that, there's a cup holder if you open the glove compartment.' She started the engine and smiled at Bo. 'I think we'll take the scenic route.'

To her relief, Davina didn't suggest that she get in the boot, but she slid down in her seat with the cashmere drawn over her head as they rounded the corner back into the lane.

They both fell silent as they approached the entrance to her driveway, but they needn't have worried. It was empty, not a single motorbike, photographer or journalist. Davina was triumphant. 'There you see, it worked!' Even so, she made Angelica check the whole house, the garden, apple store and the shed before declaring it safe for Bo to return.

As she let herself in and Davina turned to go, Bo stopped her. 'Davina, I don't know what to say. That was the kindest thing.'

'Not at all.' Davina smiled. 'I rather enjoyed it. I'll pop over tomorrow and see how you are.'

Bo shut the door. The house was dark and silent, with all the curtains closed. She went up to her bedroom and switched on the TV.

The story everyone's talking about today is of course Bernadette Maloney. The shock news that the housewife heroine who saved the life of a teenage girl earlier this year, is the same woman who stole a newborn baby from a Liverpool maternity hospital 21 years ago. Our reporter was at the scene this morning...

Bo's mouth dropped open. 'He's in my bloody garden!'

Thanks Helen, yes there are extraordinary scenes here at Bernadette's Wiltshire home, as we try to piece together what really happened all those years ago. What drove this woman, this celebrity, a real life British heroine that the public really took to their hearts, to kidnap another woman's baby...

They were back in the studio again. *Of course, it's all come crashing down around her now Mike. But were you able to see any signs of remorse, did she seem surprised at all to be exposed? What's been her reaction?*

We just don't know Helen. She emerged from her house at about 11.45 this morning and as yet, there's been no statement to the press. We understand from a neighbour that she has gone into hiding.

They already had the footage of her jostled and grim faced as she stumbled towards the car and drove off.

'Bastards!' She switched off the TV. They were talking about her like they knew her. Trampling on her flower beds, walking around her garden like they owned it.

She sat on the bed and picked up her iPad. Don't look at social media Mel had said. Don't do it! She couldn't help herself. Surely it couldn't get any worse. #bernadettebabythief was trending on twitter.

#maloneychildabduction #foundout #babysnatcher #lyingbitch, she deserves to die a slow death for what she did, I'd happily string her up

No mate, a can of petrol and a match would sort her out

'Dear God', she mouthed as she scrolled through the comments. She should have listened to Mel. Her hands had stopped shaking but now she felt physically sick. There were people out there talking about her death, wanting to kill her, many of them volunteering. How these people loved a public shaming. The excitement of finding a new witch to duck had prompted an online frenzy.

She must try to stay calm. The story would run its course, one day this would all go away. She could cope with the world hating her. Wasn't it better this way? Out in the open, instead of the terrible waiting, hiding, the unspoken shame she had carried for 21 years, the little comments from Neil always there to remind her. But there was Liam to think about. How was he going to cope with all of this? It wasn't just her stigma anymore. She googled the time in Myanmar.

The time now in Rangoon is 19.11. Six hours ahead. She knew she should call him now but she wanted to wait until Lois arrived.

She started when the Betsy mobile rang. She hesitated but picked it up.

'Look Bo, I've just had a tabloid on the phone.'

Bo didn't answer.

'They're offering a very large sum of money for your side of the story. *Bernadette, my story* the exclusive. I mean you kidnapped a baby. Broke a mother's heart. I don't know how I can spin this, maybe get you and the mother face to face for the first time. It's going to be near on impossible to win any public sympathy, but I've got a contact at the Mirror I can talk to. I'm thinking if we start a bidding war, we could do very well out of this indeed.'

'No.' She closed her eyes as she spoke into the phone. 'I'm not selling my story.'

'Think about it Bo. They're talking about £120,000 and that's just the starting bid. This is your last blast, your only chance to win back some public sympathy. Do you want to live with this for the rest of your life?'

Bo smiled wryly, 'I've lived with it for 21 years.'

'And have you thought about money? You won't be getting your job back.' Bo held the phone away from her ear. She could almost hear Betsy's brain working.

'Listen Betsy. I'm not doing an interview. I've got my son to think about.'

'Well it's your son you should be thinking of. If I were you...' Bo pressed the button and put the phone down.

Exhaling deeply, she switched on the TV again to try to distract herself, being careful to steer clear of the 1 o clock news. There was the lifestyle programme she had been on just recently herself. They were interviewing an American psychologist on the sofa. The interviewer was animated.

'So can we ever pinpoint a cause?'

'Not necessarily, it could stem from all kinds of disorders. We have a much higher incidence of these cases in the States. And because of advances in our understanding of DNA of course we can now trace the child back to their birth parents. There have been several cases recently in the States where a child has been reunited years later, having spent their entire childhood away from their biological family.'

The interviewer nodded. 'And do these abductions have anything in common?'

Well, one of the common factors is the woman, the abductor, fabricating a pregnancy in order to dupe her own family and then bringing the baby home as if it's her own. Infant abduction is usually meticulously planned. Often times the partner has pleaded complete ignorance.'

'So, do we think in this case, that Bernadette Maloney could have faked her own pregnancy prior to kidnapping the child?'

'No!' Bo stood in front of the TV, her face white with shock.

'It's certainly a possibility and would have made sense in terms of how she planned to keep the child, but of course she was apprehended before she could do that.'

'Dr Kerry Adonis thank you for joining us.' She turned to the camera. 'And we'll keep you updated on that story as more details emerge. Let's look at the weather…'

'More details…' How naïve to have thought it would all be over so quickly. In the absence of facts, there would be speculation which would run and run. She thought about Liam and a mental image of his smiling face and beautiful kind eyes. She switched off the TV and lay back on the sofa, at last giving in to the tears.

It was 10 o'clock by the time Lois's taxi slipped into the driveway. She let herself into the house and found Bo asleep, fully clothed on the sofa.

'Come on darling. Let's run a bath. I bet you haven't eaten anything have you?'

Bo opened her eyes. 'Lois! Thank you for coming. What time is it? I need to call Liam.'

'It's just gone 10.'

'I must have fallen asleep. Oh no, it'll be 4 o'clock in the morning in Myanmar.'

'Send him a message to get in touch.'

Bo tapped out a message on WhatsApp and showed it to Lois.

Give me a call Liam. Everyone's fine. Just need to let you know about a few things that have been going on. Nothing serious. Love you Mum x

Lois nodded.

Bo looked up at her. 'Have you seen what they're saying about faking my own pregnancy?'

'I was hoping you hadn't seen that but it's all over the place. Listen love, I spoke to Davina. I don't think they're going to leave you alone for a bit. I'm going to take you over there to stay for a few days until this all blows over.'

16

Davina sat opposite Lois, flicking through the Sunday supplements, putting aside the ones that mentioned Bo so that they could hide them before she got up. Davina refused to read the tabloids, which she left to Lois and concentrated instead on the broadsheets.

Camilla Prestwick – 'Modern Life' The Culture supplement

It has been nearly a week since the public shaming of Bernadette Spicer or Bernadette Maloney as we now know her. She has not spoken to the press nor issued any statement since the revelations last week shocked her fans. Seldom has there been such a meteoric rise to fame and equally dramatic fall from grace. But what does this tell us about the modern phenomenon of instant celebrity and the insatiable public appetite for heroes and villains.

We still don't know why she took the baby girl or what happened to the child afterwards. We do know that she was given a non custodial sentence and went on to live a relatively low key family life, giving birth to her own child not long after the scandal and marrying her college sweetheart Neil Spicer. Her story would have been unlikely to come to light, had it not been for a freak accident during last January's torrential storms and the extraordinary footage of Bernadette risking her own life to save a teenage girl, refusing to be winched to safety until the girl was rescued by the helicopter crew. The story has captured the public's imagination like no other, perhaps because it has all the elements of swashbuckling fable, but in this case the super hero and the hooded villain are one and the same...

They had told the press that she had fled to Ireland, prompting a flurry of headlines 'Bernadette on the run' 'Babysnatcher tracked down to Irish hide out'. Which meant that several press were now camped out on Lois' front drive in Kilkenny, much to the entertainment of her teenage sons and irritation of her husband Patrick.

But Bo was in fact only 500 yards from her own front door, meaning Lois and Davina could come and go as they pleased, feeding the cats, fetching her things, checking her messages. The press who at first would surround them, barking questions and holding their cameras into the open front door, had almost given up. They had even managed a couple of outings with Bo hidden under a blanket in the back seat, a trip to see the Bluebells in a nearby wood and a more daring daytime visit to the multiplex cinema in Brinton. By now Bo was desperate to go home, but Lois and Davina insisted that she wait until there were no journalists left outside her house.

As Davina flicked through the pages she was relieved to find at least one broadsheet with no mention of the story. She nearly spilled her mug of coffee as Lois screamed across the table.

THAT LYING FECKIN GOB SHITE OF A MAN!!!!!

Bo was standing in the doorway in a dressing gown. 'What is it Lois?'

'Neil, that's what it is!' Lois was scrolling through the article on her iPad, 'the little creep you married when you weren't in your right mind.'

Bo came and sat down. 'I know you never liked him Lois, but he's still Liam's Dad.'

'Never liked him?' Lois snorted. 'The man's the most piss poor excuse for a human being that ever walked the planet. And you can just thank the Lord that Liam is a carbon copy of you, that's for sure.'

'He's not all bad.'

'Alright well you'd better save your lofty compassion till you've heard this. Because, your charming, soon to be ex-husband has gone and sold his story to the Sunday Mirror.'

'What!'

'Yes. And I quote...' Bo and Davina came and looked over her shoulder.

'My private hell, an exclusive interview with the husband of baby snatcher Bernadette Maloney.' Lois scrolled down the article, picking phrases out, her voice raised for the most offensive bits. 'I stood by her!'

'Oh my God listen to this! *I persuaded the judge to give her a suspended sentence.* Gobshite! It was your Dad that did that Bo, the lying bastard!'

'She has a history of mental illness and her behaviour was becoming increasingly erratic.'

'Give me that!' Bo grabbed the iPad.

Lois continued her rant. 'Is he having a feckin' laugh! Stood by you? Entrapment more like! Bloody lying bloody Judas!'

Bo began to read out loud. 'Neil has now found happiness with new partner Amanda Edwards.' There was even a picture of them outside the front door of Mandy's executive home next to a convertible Mazda. Bo was silent for a moment before she read the last paragraph. 'And they are expecting their first baby in December.'

'Neil, having a baby?' Bo looked dumbfounded.

Lois shook her head. 'And he's letting his family know in a tabloid newspaper. Nice one Neil!'

Bo put the iPad down. 'God, couldn't he have just told me first. I really need to speak to Liam.'

'Yes.' Lois nodded. 'I know but he's obviously in the middle of nowhere.'

'It's been three days Lois. I can't bear it, what the hell's happened to him?'

'At least if he's not picking up his phone, he probably hasn't seen any news. I'll put the kettle on.'

It would be just after 2pm in Myanmar. Bo found her phone. 'I'll try him again.' She took a deep breath and dialed the number.

'Hello, hello Liam?'

'Mum!'

'Liam!' She exhaled deeply. 'Oh thank God. Are you OK?'

'Yeah of course. I'm in Yagon, it's incredible Mum, you'd love it. We rented mopeds and went to the Bagan Temples at dawn yesterday to see the sunrise. It was awesome.'

'Wow that sounds amazing. Did you not get my message?'

'Your message? Oh yeah. You said it wasn't urgent. And we're doing the Inle Lake trip tomorrow. Myanmar is incredible, totally unspoilt. You and Dad have got to come out here.'

'Liam have you seen any UK news out there?'

Davina left the room and Lois put a cup of tea in front of her. She gave a thumbs up sign and closed the door quietly behind her.

'To be honest Mum I haven't looked at the news since I left Thailand, I've been so busy. Why what's been happening.'

'So you've not seen anything about what I've been up to?'

'I saw the pictures of you and Auntie Lois on Facebook at that TV party. Looked like you were having fun! Did she win a competition?'

'No she didn't. Listen Liam, I need to have a longer chat with you. Can you get onto Skype?'

'You sound a bit odd Mum. Are you OK?'

'Absolutely fine, nothing at all to worry about, but I do need to have a bit of a chat. There are some things I need to tell you that I should have told you before. It could take a while and if we talk on the mobile, we'll both be bankrupt.'

'OK. I'm a 5 minute walk from an internet café. I'll call you in 10.'

'OK Liam. Love you.'

'Love you too Mum.'

17

After four days, the media frenzy had died down. There were only two photographers outside the cottage and she persuaded Davina and Lois that it was safe to go home. Every time she went outside to get in the car they chased her and photographed her, sticking the camera in her face, shouting obscenities to try to make her cry. She said nothing, her face impassive. It couldn't last forever. Surely there were only a certain number of shots they could print of the babysnatcher leaving her house before the public lost interest and moved onto the next scandal.

It was Friday, she looked through the gap in the curtain and for the first time since the story broke, there were no photographers in the drive, all was quiet.

She had no intention of going for a drink with Ben, but for some reason, mainly Lois, she hadn't got round to cancelling.

There might not be any press out there now but the thought of them chasing Ben's Defender down the lane and printing pictures of the two of them was too much to bear. She felt a wave of shame at the thought and wondered if she should phone him now to cancel. In any case he probably wouldn't turn up. His last text was before the story hit the papers, so he might just decide she wasn't worth it, or maybe he'd turn up out of curiosity. She felt sick in any case.

She looked up his number and typed a text.

Probably not a good idea to see you, too many press, another time, Bo

She had texted him at 5, no answer.

Lois was round at Davina's watching a film, they were both adamant that this would do her good.

So now she didn't know if he would turn up or not, but had to get ready just in case. She checked her phone. No response to her text. Clothes were strewn all over the bed and half of the bedroom floor. She definitely couldn't look like she had tried too hard. In the end she chose jeans, wedge heels and a white shirt, a designer label freebie, nipped in slightly at the waist. She checked her reflection, make up subtle, hair blow dryed. If he was coming he would be here in half an hour. Still no photographers in the lane.

It was 23 years since she had last been on a date. What on earth was she supposed to say. 'So how long have you been a vet?' She mouthed it in the mirror and felt ridiculous. For feck's sake! This was tragic and wrong and likely to end in further shame. And where could they go where she wouldn't be stared at and photographed or worse. He probably wouldn't turn up anyway. She checked her phone again.

Twenty minutes to go. She still felt sick. But what was the harm? A few drinks, a bit of conversation. The poor man's wife had died of cancer for goodness sake. He would be glad of a night out. Keep it light hearted.

She ran through a mental checklist. Brushed teeth, hidden dirty laundry basket, emptied cat litter, squirted pine fresh in the downstairs loo. What if he smelt her minty breath and thought she was expecting a snog. My God, how did people do this! He wouldn't come anyway.

The door bell rang. My God it's him. He's 15 minutes early!

Don't rush. Slow, deep breaths. She walked sedately down the stairs, checked her teeth in the hall mirror and assumed a breezy, confident smile before opening the door.

'Neil!'

'I've left her Bo. Can you ever forgive me?'

'What!' He stood, dejected on the doorstep, overnight bag in one hand and a bouquet of flowers from the BP garage in the other.

'I didn't think it would be right to let myself in.'

'No.' She opened the door. Breezy expression instantly wiped from her face. 'You'd better come in.' He dropped his bag on the kitchen table.

'Do you want a cup of tea?' She couldn't think of anything else to say.

'I'll have something stronger. Have we got any red wine?' She nodded and pulled a bottle out of the wine rack. He was wearing quite a tight fitting black shirt, which was not his usual look at all. She rummaged around in the drawer for the bottle opener, trying to think what on earth to do. 'Look Neil, it's not a good time. We do need to talk, about what we're going to do and everything, but not right now...'

'She lost the baby Bo.'

'God, I'm so sorry Neil.'

'That's kind of you to say, Bo.' She noticed his hands were shaking slightly and she poured him a glass of wine.

'And I didn't mean to let you know about the baby in a newspaper Bo, honestly. Mandy told them when we were interviewed. It wasn't planned. I didn't say half the stuff in that article. They twist your words.'

'I know.' Her heart was pounding. 'Look Neil, you can't just come waltzing back without warning and expect everything to be fine.'

'I know Bo. It's going to take time for you to trust me again, but I'm willing to give it all I've got. You've been through hell and my place is here with you Bo, protecting you. All this, Mandy and the baby, it made me realise what I'd actually already got with you and Liam.' She thought he was going to cry. 'I know it's not going to be easy for you to get over this. I'll sleep in the spare room for a bit.'

'Neil, no.' She shook her head.

He didn't appear to hear her. 'She's so critical Bo! Every night, it was pilates or down the gym, dinner parties with her friends, she wanted me to learn a language! I haven't been here for you when you needed me but I'm back now. I still love you, you know.' He stood up, reached over the table and grabbed her hand. She pushed it away and the wine glass tipped forwards and soaked the front of her white shirt.'

'Oh shit! Neil. Look what you've done!' She was almost shouting.

The door bell rang. Neil didn't notice the look of horror on her face. He poured himself another glass of wine. 'Are you going to get that?'

'Yes.'

She walked to the front door feeling like a condemned man. It wasn't too late. She could just grab her hand bag and run.

'Hi Ben!'

'Hi!' He was smiling completely normal, as if nothing had changed and she could barely look him in the eye.

'Are you ready to go?' He looked down at the red wine all over the front of her shirt.

'Oh.' She blushed. Neil wandered into the hall, wine glass in hand. 'Are you going to introduce us?'

'Sure. Neil this is Ben, Ben Neil.' She wanted to scream or faint or something.

'Hi.' Neil offered a hand to Ben, 'I'm Neil, her husband.' Bo looked at the floor.

Ben shook his hand. 'I see.' *Why didn't she scream, 'No you don't see!'* The three of them stood in silence. What could she say to make it right. She couldn't find the words. She saw his car and was tempted to run into it and lock the door.

Neil stepped in front of her. 'If you don't mind, it's a private time, what we're going through, we need to be left alone to work things out.'

Ben broke the silence. 'Well I expect you have things to talk about.'

'We do.' Neil put an arm around her. 'But we'll be fine.'

Neil shut the door and she watched him walk back to his car. 'Who was he?'

'Nobody.' He didn't register her stricken face.

'Come on love, let's order a takeaway, there's footie on at 8.' He went back into the kitchen.

'I'm not hungry.' She stood rooted to the spot, looking at herself in the mirror.

Bo started at the sound of a key in the front door. 'Lois!'

'Hello! I just came back to get some crisps. She hasn't got a single decent snack in that house! Unless you call soy beans a snack! What are you still doing here? Sexy Vet's a bit late isn't he?'

Bo followed her through to the kitchen and waited for the inevitable outburst.

'Neil Spicer!' Lois' jaw dropped. 'What the feck are you doing here?'

'This is my house Lois.' Neil bristled. 'Why shouldn't I be here?'

'And where's Ben?' Lois looked accusingly at them both.

'Who's Ben?' Neil shrugged.

'He's been and gone.' Bo looked at the floor.

'What do you mean he's been and gone?' Lois was practically growling.

'He arrived, Neil explained that he was my husband, so he left us to talk.'

'What the feck!' Lois was spitting. 'You've screwed it up again then have you Neil?'

'Screwed what up?'

'You know damn well Neil! Suited you to come home did it? Has she chucked you out already?'

'Don't you talk to me like that in my own house! You bossy, bloody cow!'

They were snarling at each other, lips curled. Lois was bearing down on him. She was almost the same height. 'Every time she has a chance at happiness, in walks Neil Spicer to feck it up!'

'Why don't you get lost Lois! All I've ever tried to do is protect her.' His voice was quiet and menacing. 'You always did over stay your welcome.'

'I'm not going anywhere Neil.'

'Bo and I are giving it another go. She needs me. Pack your bags Lois!'

'You're what?' Lois looked incredulously at Bo. 'Is that right?'

Bo didn't answer.

Lois looked furious and launched into another attack. 'The trouble with you Neil, is that you never get anything by honest means. You were never going to get the best looking girl at College so you trapped her. She goes and gets a top job in London, so what do you do? You get her pregnant again. You never let her move on from the past, fulfill her potential. You and her mother, you've been controlling her, messing with her head her whole life, because you can't stand the fact that she's OUT OF YOUR FECKIN LEAGUE!'

'You're the only thing that's driven us apart, with your constant sniping, putting ideas in her head.'

'I've driven you apart?!' Lois snorted. 'You shagged the bloody babysitter, you pathetic, desperate excuse for a man!'

'And you're jealous and bitter Lois.'

She gasped, temporarily lost for words. He pressed on. 'You want her all to yourself. You always have. You'd rather she was dependent on you than me!'

Lois stood open mouthed.

'What do you know about our relationship anyway, you stupid, arrogant cow! Poor, bloody henpecked Patrick!' He was sneering now. 'We might have a chance if you could keep your interfering, opinionated bloody nose out of our marriage!'

Lois came back at him, inflamed by the mention of Patrick. 'Lovely article in the Mirror by the way Neil, very heartfelt. What was it you said 'I stood by her!' 'She had a history of mental illness!' Not before she met you, you Gobshite!'

'Fuck off Lois!' They were squaring up by the kitchen island. He looked like he might hit her.

'How's Mandy by the way?' Lois piped up. Bo made faces to try to stop her, but Lois was relentless, taunting him. 'How's your NEW family, Neil?'

Lois had recovered herself. She turned to face him and spoke slowly and deliberately. 'She doesn't want to get back with you Neil. Face it!'

Lois hadn't noticed that Neil had started to cry, but Bo had. He sat at the kitchen table, his shoulders convulsed with weeping.

She looked at him, the tears cascading off his face, such a familiar face.

'Lois!' Bo looked at her wearily. 'It's probably best to leave us alone for a bit.'

She nodded, a little shame faced. 'Suit yourself, but really! Davina and I were watching Thelma and Louise, if you want to come over.' Lois picked up a Doritos multi-pack and let herself out.

Bo put her arms around Neil, it was an automatic response. She hadn't held him this close for a long time.

'I'm sorry Bo, I'm so sorry. Please forgive me. I'm begging you, can you ever try to forgive me.'

She rocked him back and forth like a child as he wept on her shoulder. 'Of course I can.' He was her family after all, him and Liam. She glanced over his shoulder at the photo of Liam on the noticeboard. When all the rest of it came crashing down, they were all she really had.

18

But if we turn penitently to Him, He enables us to bear our punishment with a meek and docile heart.
— Elizabeth Gaskell

She sat at the dressing table, playing with the wedding ring on her finger. They had been back together for 3 months. There hadn't been a cross word, Neil had been nothing but kind and attentive, almost overly so. He referred to her time in the limelight as 'all that fuss' and the name Mandy Edwards was never mentioned. They stepped politely around each other like awkward strangers. He was a good man, no doubt more than she deserved. She heard him coming up the stairs.

'Oh there you are. I couldn't find you.'

She turned round and smiled.

'Well I'm off. I won't be late, I'll only have one drink after the match.'

'Ok, have fun, don't get into any fights.'

He laughed. 'I won't. I forgot to tell you, I spoke to Liam on my way home.'

'How is he?'

'Great, all the better now he knows we're back together.'

'What! Oh. You told him. I was going to wait.'

'Why wait. He was stoked Bo, really happy. You could tell he was relieved.'

'You should have asked me first.'

He sat on the bed and took her hand. 'Look, I know it's going to take time Bo. For you to trust me again, there's no hurry, I'm your husband. Liam and me, we're your family and we love you. I just want to protect you, you know. Always have in my own stupid way.'

She nodded.

'We've been through this before and we'll do it again.' He squeezed her hand. 'Stay in and chill out.' As if she had a choice.

'Are you going to watch a bit of Netflix? There's a bottle of wine in the fridge.' She knew she was drinking too much at the moment, but he didn't seem to mind.

'Do you want me to shut the downstairs curtains before I go?'

'Yes please.'

A car horn sounded in the drive. 'There's my lift.'

The front door slammed after him and she was left alone for another day. She looked in the mirror, ashamed of her self pity. Why couldn't she just accept her lot. She was married to a good man, with a wonderful son, a lovely home, financially secure. Just give it time, she told herself. All this would blow over, the hate campaign, the isolation. She tried to think of a time when she had been madly attracted to Neil, perhaps there had never been a time, unless she'd had an awful lot to drink.

She had even been to the doctor. He said it was very natural at her age to feel unattracted to your husband.

Your hormones are probably all over the place. Just give it time.

She noticed Neil had started wearing his wedding ring again. He was being very kind, you couldn't fault him on that, nicer than he'd been for years, bringing her flowers and presents. She couldn't help noticing that he took more pride in his appearance and Mandy had certainly given him a taste for expensive clothes. He was spending quite a lot of money, an Armani suit and a Rolex watch, new speakers and last week a VIP season ticket. He was talking about a new car, which was ironic given that hers was parked in the garage with a slashed tyre and 'BITCH' daubed in red paint across the windscreen. It wasn't worth driving into Brinton any more, with all the comments and people staring and a snapped off wing mirror, but last week someone had come into their driveway at night armed with a knife to slash her tyre. She told herself it was probably just young kids, but she hadn't been out since.

Neil warned her not to look online and she never intended to seek out the trolls and vicious comments, but sometimes she was food shopping online and found herself straying onto Twitter or Facebook. The CCTV shot of her coming out of the hospital door with the baby had gone viral, 12 million views. And there were over 26,000 comments.

'Disgusting bitch' 'Why the fuck is she still walking free…rot in hell' 'If I were that baby's mother I'd have topped her' 'Fucking hypocrite offering advice!' 'Women like her deserve what's coming to them'.

It was easy to feel like a prisoner in your own home, under house arrest. And she knew she had allowed herself to become like this, a recluse, reluctant to go out, drive the car, meet anyone. And Neil didn't push her to try. 'All I want to do is keep you safe Bo.' Her world now revolved around his coming and going, the main focus of her day, his arrival home. She had become an OCD cleaner. Hoovering and dusting daily, wiping down the skirting boards, disinfecting the cat trays. She always had dinner ready for him at 7, nothing too adventurous, meat and two veg, for a man who thought that Chilli was exotic.

They did go to the cinema most Saturday nights, at least she could wear a hat and hide in the darkness, but restaurants were not worth the bother, they couldn't resist the chance to take her picture and last time an older, quite respectable looking woman had actually spat. The trouble was, her face had become too well known.

Davina popped round every few days and updated her on the tennis club gossip. Not surprisingly Lois had stayed away since the bust up with Neil. She could feel her disappointment from afar.

And then there were the stupid, day to day things, inconveniences really, like the dog shit on the door step, the bins emptied all over the driveway almost every week and her favourite rose bushes, dug up and flung across the lane.

A few weeks ago, a radio programme had phoned up, wanting to do an interview about social media shaming. Neil took the call and turned it down flat. 'I think that's enough fame for one lifetime don't you Bo.' Neil could be strong in a crisis. He was one of those types that is very convinced of his own opinions but insecure underneath it and took criticism very personally. She tended not to question his decisions.

She spent the afternoon tidying Liam's room and emptying out old clothes. She would get Neil to take them to the charity shop. There were trousers from six years ago when he still needed elastic and buttons to hold them up, dinosaur slippers, two pairs of pyjamas with mice and gruffalos on. She sniffed them and felt tears well up for the innocence of a time that was past, the school runs and nativity plays before all of this came back to haunt her. It would be alright if she could just hang on, it would get better. She wouldn't always be glancing furtively out of the window as soon as darkness fell, looking for a movement in the driveway, wondering when Neil would return.

She put a chicken in the oven and peeled some potatoes in an effort to keep off the wine for a bit longer. At 7 she opened the bottle and had finished most of it by 8. By 9 she gave up and started picking at the chicken. She had run out of Gardeners' World episodes to watch, when finally she heard his key in the door.

He tripped slightly as he came into the kitchen. 'Neil it's quarter to 11.'

'And? Is there a curfew?'

'No, it's just that you know I'm stuck here on my own. You could have said, that's all, I made roast chicken.'

'I'll have it tomorrow. I had a burger at the match.'

He wasn't really drunk but just enough to do that thing where you over pronounce your words and talk too loudly. He opened a bottle of beer from the fridge.

'Listen I've been thinking Bo. It's time I moved back into our bedroom.'

'No.' She tried to hide the look of horror on her face. 'At least, not yet.'

He went silent for a while as if taking this in and then slipped from the stool onto the floor, struggling to get up on one knee in front of her.

'What are you doing. For God's sake Neil, get up!' It was almost funny watching him trying to balance and focus at the same time.

'Bernadette Spicer, you and I are going on a second honeymoon.' He pulled some papers out of his jacket pocket. It's all booked, I've got the tickets. It'll be a new start, somewhere no one knows who you are.'

She couldn't help but laugh.

He thrust the tickets at her. 'Here, look. We'll spend some time together before Liam gets back, away from all this crap and we'll be man and wife again.'

She took the tickets. 'Croatia!'

'You always said you wanted to go there.'

'Yes, but I didn't think you were bothered.'

'Well I am now. I just want to make you happy Bo. Just you and me. Five days in Dubrovnik, then five days at a spa hotel by the beach.'

'You hate beaches Neil!' She was laughing again. 'I didn't think you'd even heard of Dubrovnik.'

He shrugged. 'It'll be our second honeymoon Bo. Twenty one years later.' He was slurring slightly but his eyes glistened. 'We'll get some sun and after that we'll come back and I'll move back in to our bedroom. Happy anniversary Bo!'

'Happy anniversary.' She smiled and raised her glass. She was completely nonplussed. This was the most surprising thing he had done in twenty one years of marriage.

'Twenty one years!' She shook her head. 'It's hard to believe isn't it. Do you know what Monday is?'

He shook his head.

'It's Cathy's birthday. Her 21st on Monday.'

'How do you expect me to remember that?'

'I'm going to go up to Liverpool to see her.' She braced herself for the response.

'For God Sake's Bo, can't you just let it rest. You always get in a state for weeks after. How are you going to get there anyway? You can't drive your car.'

'I'll get the train.'

'You'll be recognized. It's not safe.'

I don't care, I'm going.' She paused. 'Come with me then.'

'No. I can't take a day off work.' He downed the rest of his beer.

'Well I'm going anyway. I'll get the train and if it gets late I'll stay up in Liverpool with Uncle Pete.'

'Suit yourself.' He didn't seem to be in the mood for a fight. 'I'm tired, I'm going to bed.'

19

'Forgive us our trespasses...'

Her heart was beating faster than usual as she checked the contents of her handbag for the fifth time. Keys, mobile, purse, cats fed, don't forget the bins. She checked herself in the hallway mirror, dressed in black from head to toe. For someone who had once wanted to travel the world she was certainly making a big deal about a day trip to Liverpool. The taxi was waiting in the lane and she felt a small thrill of escape as she shut the front door behind her and dragged the bins out to the front of the gate.

The train was virtually empty and she tucked herself into the window seat at the back of the carriage and pulled out the paper she had picked up at the station. The four hour train trip went quickly and it was lunchtime by the time the taxi pulled up on the corner of Gladstone Road, outside the florist she visited once a year. She chose a small bunch of roses that reminded her of raspberry ripple ice cream and six white lilies. Walking down the familiar street, past St Francis' Catholic High School, where she herself had been one of the girls now chattering on the steps, then on past the nuns' retirement home and left into the church yard. It was empty and as usual she went first to her parents' grave.

Thomas Joseph Maloney, Beloved Father & Grandfather, May he rest in peace. She had designed his headstone, dark grey marble with gold letters. She laid three lilies at the foot of the headstone. 'Love you Daddy.' She whispered and stepped back from the grave.

Cathleen Elizabeth Maloney 'Lord make me an instrument of your peace.' This was her mother's choice of epitaph and she was always struck by the irony. She closed her eyes and tried to think generous thoughts. 'Rest is peace Mum.' She placed the remaining three lilies on the grave and picked up the bunch of cream and pink roses.

Cathleen's grave was at the furthest edge of the graveyard, at the base of a yew hedge. There was a bench right in front of it. She was pleased to see the vase was still where she had left it next to the headstone and she took the water bottle out of her handbag, filled it and started to arrange the roses. 'Happy birthday darling girl.'

Cathleen Mairead Spicer 'Little angel, loved forever.' She had never been happy with the headstone, the nuns had suggested it, but then no words could capture it, so what did it matter. The rain had stopped and she sat down on the bench and unbuttoned her coat. She hadn't noticed the old lady walking up the path and jumped slightly when she sat down next to her.

'Hello Bernadette. I thought I'd find you here.'

So many years had passed, it took her a minute to make out those familiar piercing blue eyes. 'Sister Marianne!' The old lady nodded and smiled. Bo kissed her warmly on the cheek. 'How are you Sister?'

'I saw you from my window. Up there.' She pointed. 'I've seen you before but I never managed to get down here in time. I'm not as quick on my feet as I used to be.'

'I tried to see you, you know, last year. They said you were too ill, that you wouldn't be able to recognize me.'

'Ah yes. Well they don't like me talking to people about the past, you see. They're not bad people, but I suppose they think the Catholic church has had enough criticism, without me blathering on about things that can't be undone.'

She saw Bo's expression and changed the subject. 'And what about you. How have you been Bernadette? You used to be quite the rebel, a real force of nature, such a beautiful girl.' She chuckled. 'Ah yes, it wasn't always easy trying to teach you Latin. I always wondered what happened to you, what sort of life you had, you know after all that trouble. Did you manage to move on?'

Bo paused for a while, struggling to control her voice. 'Not really.'

'Oh dear. But you went off to India didn't you?'

'Yes, but that was before University. I taught in a school for a year.'

'Such an exciting life ahead of you.' Sister Marianne saw her distress and stopped. 'Did you ever talk to anyone? Did anyone hear your confession.'

'No.'

'It might have helped.'

Bo played with her wedding ring. 'I don't think so.'

Sister Marianne persisted. 'It's a healing process.'

'I don't see that.'

'The ritual of contrition, disclosure and penance, it can be a tremendous comfort.'

'I'm sorry sister but as far as I'm concerned it's all about sin and shame and guilt and punishment. In my hour of need, that's all I got from the church.'

Sister Marianne shook her head. 'It's not the church that's the problem, it's the people in it. You've neglected your faith.'

'Yes, I have. You know my mother tried to force me to confess while I lay in my hospital bed. 'The Wages of Sin is death', she said. Her favourite phrase. 'Cathy died for your sins.''

'What a load of rubbish!' Bo was taken aback by the force of the old lady's response. 'Your mother, God rest her sinful soul, was full of pious nonsense.'

Seeing Bo's surprise, she carried on. 'But you know it was fed to her by that wicked man Father Delaney. How he escaped prison I'll never know. They just hushed the whole thing up and moved him on.'

'What do you mean.'

'Your mother and Father Delaney. You must have known they were sleeping together.'

'No!'

'Well then I'm sorry, but maybe it'll help you to forgive your mother. She was under the influence of a very manipulative man. He preyed on vulnerable women.'

'My mother, vulnerable?' It wasn't the first word Bo would have picked.

'Because of her drinking, you know, she was a very unhappy woman. And he picked on many others in the congregation, some of them very young indeed.'

'My God.' Bo tried to take all this in. 'Do you think my father knew?'

'Everyone knew.'

They sat in silence for a while.

'My father always said the disgrace I brought on the family made her ill.'

'I expect it was easier for him to think that. The drinking and the cigarettes would have had more to do with it.' Sister Marianne had always been very matter of fact. 'It was very sad in any case. Do you live nearby?'

'No, we moved south years ago.'

'So, you've come up have you, to visit the graves?'

'Yes.'

'And you come every year don't you.'

'Yes. On her birthday, she would have been 21 today.'

'My goodness, would she really.' Sister Marianne turned to her with those bright blue eyes she remembered so well, now milky with age. You could never get anything past her. 'You haven't let her go yet have you Bernadette?' It wasn't really a question.

'No.'

'Shall we say a little prayer.'

'Alright.' It had started to rain very lightly.

They bowed their heads. 'Heavenly Father…'

'SISTER MARIANNE!' A tall nun came jogging up the path towards them. 'What are you doing out here all on your own? You didn't tell anyone where you were going.'

'Oh, here we go. The guards have tracked me down.' Bo looked concerned but Sister Marianne laughed. 'It's alright. I'm not on my own, Sister Helen, this is Bernadette.'

The nun's expression changed. 'I know who she is.' She avoided eye contact. 'Come along Sister Marianne! It's about to pour down.'

As she was led away Sister Marianne turned back to Bo. 'Don't throw your life away Bernadette. You know, it is not you who needs to seek forgiveness.'

Bo watched their progress up the path until they turned the corner, through the graveyard gate and out of sight.

She sat on the bench staring ahead, twisting her wedding ring round and round, oblivious to the rain or anything around her. An hour or more passed as voices long since dead drifted in and out of her head. The rain grew heavier and coursed down her face. Her black coat was damp and she only noticed the cold and started to shiver when the phone buzzed in her pocket. A text from Neil.

U staying in Liverpool? I'm out with the boys tonight

There was a notification on Facebook. She wasn't going to look.

It's Barry Perkins' birthday! Tell him you're thinking about him.

For fuck's sake! She saw the time on her phone and sighed. 4.22. She'd missed two trains. There was a bus stop outside the school which went to the station, if she hurried she might just make the 5.15. She stood over the grave. 'Good bye my little love', touching her fingers to her lips, she turned around and walked quickly up the path to the entrance gate.

She had made it with seconds to spare and as the train rattled on through the dark landscape, she stared out of the window, her frowning expression staring back at her unblinking. She was only just absorbing the revelation of her mother and Father Delaney and whether or not the recollections of an old lady could be relied upon. But already the events of the past and every decision she had made since were shifting in her mind, recalibrating, in light of this disclosure. She had been struggling for a long time, she knew it, weighed down as it turned out, by the judgement of hypocrites.

Something occurred to her and she reached for her phone and dialed Lois' number.

'Bo?' Lois answered immediately.

'Hello Lois.' She hesitated for a second, before whispering into the phone. 'Lois, did you know that my mother was sleeping with Father Delaney?'

There was silence at the end of the line.

'My God, you knew and you didn't tell me?'

She heard Lois sigh. 'I didn't like to, your poor father. Some things are best left in the past Bo. I didn't see how it would have helped, that's all.'

'That's all!'

'What difference would it have made Bo?'

'It would have made a difference.'

'She was jealous of you Bo.'

'Jealous?'

'Yes, my Dad always said she was a bitter woman. There you were all beauty and brains, going off to University, leading the exciting life she felt she was denied. She was never happy with your poor father. She married the wrong man.' There was a pause at the other end. 'Just like you.'

'For pity's sake Lois! You never miss an opportunity to criticize him. He's been really good to me these past few months, I couldn't fault him.'

'I'm sorry love, I know it's not what you want to hear but I can't stand the man. The only impressive thing about him is his sperm count.'

'Lois.' Bo groaned. It was the same old refrain and once she was off, you couldn't stem the flow.

'And all of this means he's got you incarcerated, can't you see it? Stuck at home at his beck and call, right where he wants you.'

'Lois listen to me!' She spoke very deliberately. 'I'm not stuck at home. I told you he's taking me on a second honeymoon to Croatia, I've always said I wanted to go and he remembered and booked the tickets, all his idea.'

'I know, you said.' Bo could hear her tone change. It was not like Lois to hold anything back.

'What Lois?'

'Do me a favour Bo, why don't you ask Neil where the last of the England World Cup qualifiers is taking place.'

'What do you mean?'

'Just ask him. Patrick told me. He can't even make a romantic gesture without thinking entirely of himself.'

She rang off and looked at the time. Another 2 hours to go. Rooting around in the bottom of her bag for a packet of tic-tacs, she pulled out a scrunched up bit of paper. She opened it up. 'Mandy Edwards is screwing your husband.' There is was, the note that started it all. She had thought she had thrown it away. The spot light above her head picked out the words and her expression changed as she noticed something she had not seen before. 'My God.' She mouthed and slipped the note back into her bag.

By the time the train pulled into Brinton, Bo had googled the entire England World Cup qualifying match schedule. It was 9.45pm and she was glad he would still be out when she got home.

It was dark and pouring with rain as she made her way across the bridge and into the station car park, her coat still damp and her black hair dripping. A battered Defender pulled up beside her and the driver wound down the window. It was Ben.

'You look like you've been to a funeral. Do you need a lift home?'

'No, I'm absolutely fine thanks.' She kept walking, rain pouring off her face.

'Where's your car?' She didn't answer, conscious that she was going to look foolish once she reached the taxi rank.

'It's out of action, I'm getting a taxi.'

He drove alongside her. 'Oh for God's sake get in, it's pouring and I'm going right past your door.'

She kept walking. 'Really I'm fine.'

'Just get in Bo.'

She realized she had no choice and reluctantly walked round the car.

He leant over and pushed open the passenger door. 'Where's your car anyway, have the police finally taken you off the road?'

'It needs some work done.' She did up her seat belt. 'Thank you.'

'Are you alright? You look terrible.'

'It's been a long day.'

There was hardly any traffic and they sped up the A road towards the Lower Hinton turn off. He looked sideways and took in her smudged mascara and damp coat. 'Do you need to go straight home or would you like a drink first?'

Without thinking she looked at him and replied. 'I'd bloody love a drink actually.' She felt a sudden urge to down a glass of something very strong. 'I don't tend to go out in public much these days.' He noticed the strain in her voice.

'What, because a few people might stare at you.'

'A bit more than that. Last time I went out for dinner, a woman actually spat.'

'Oh OK. Well I know a very dark pub. And if anyone spits, I'll punch them.'

She laughed. 'OK.'

They drove up a single track to a small pub she had never been to before. He was right, it was very dimly lit, with just a couple of farmers sitting at the bar. There was a wood burner in the corner with a seat either side and he led her over to it. She took off her coat and hung it on the back of the seat to dry. He ordered a pint and she had a large glass of red wine, which she had to try hard not to gulp.

'So, what's been happening to you?'

She raised her eyebrows. 'Don't you read the news?'

'Yes. Hard to escape the story.'

'You remember Betsy?'

'I'm hardly likely to forget, I remember the dog mostly.'

She smiled. 'Well unfortunately she did a very good job, turning me into a minor celebrity. Everyone's favourite household heroine, or not, as it turned out. So now everywhere I go, I'm stared at, sworn at, photographed, or spat at. It gets wearing so you don't bother.'

He shrugged. 'Just tell them to fuck off.' She laughed at the ease of his solution.

'I know I should and I've tried not to get paranoid. I was starting to calm down about the whole thing, but then the other day it shifted up a gear. Someone has started coming into our drive at night. Last week they slashed my tyre and wrote 'bitch' on my windscreen in red paint. It freaked me out a bit.'

'Ah, hence the car being out of action.' He studied her face. 'It can't be good for you, being a recluse. What does your husband say?'

'He thinks it's best if I stay out of public places for a while.'

Ben raised his eyebrows. 'Really?' He looked over at the bar. 'Well let's see how famous you really are.' He took her empty glass and went up to the bar. 'Evening Frank.' He greeted one of the farmers on the bar stool. 'I'll buy you both a pint if either of you can tell me who that woman is sitting over there?'

'It's not my ex wife is it?'

'No don't worry Frank. Nigel? Any idea?'

'Let me put my glasses on.' He peered over at her. 'Is she in Holby City?'

'Nope.'

'She's a cracker whoever she is. News reader?'

'No.'

He brought over her drink. 'You see, not everyone knows who you are. So, if you're not going out in public, what were you doing on a packed train tonight?'

'I went to Liverpool.'

'What for?'

'To visit a grave. It turned out to be quite a day. I received absolution from a nun I hadn't seen for 21 years.' She took a long glug from her glass of wine and noticed there wasn't much left.

'Do you want to talk about it?'

'No I don't.' She played with the glass in her hand.

'Absolution? For what?'

'Mortal sin.' She gave a wry laugh.

'Catholic shite?'

She nodded. 'Well you haven't got a faith I suppose.'

'No, I haven't.'

'Who do you pray to?'

'I don't.'

She shook her head. 'I don't believe you. Everyone prays.'

He started to laugh.

'What's the matter with you?'

'I was just thinking. I've met you what? Four or five times?'

She shrugged. 'Something like that.'

'The first time you blockaded the road with your car, the second time you got into a fight on the Speed Awareness Course, the third time?'

She filled in for him. 'You nearly drowned in liquid shit.'

'That's right, but you were prepared to wade in after me, so I'll let that one go. And the fourth, let me think, you accused me of cheating on my wife.'

She gasped at the memory. It was so bad she started to giggle.

He carried on. 'No hang on, the fifth time, I came to pick you up and your husband, who hadn't previously been mentioned, was standing at the door.' He shook his head. 'I should probably steer well clear of you.'

'Probably.' She held his gaze and they stared at each other.

He broke the silence. 'So, you took back the husband who slept with the babysitter.'

'Not exactly.' She thought about Neil, waiting at home for her and took a large swig of her wine. 'Anyway, how do you know that?'

'I googled you.'

'Oh.' She cringed at the thought of what else he had read.

'And how's it going with the husband?'

She shrugged. 'He's been kind.' And then after a pause. 'It's my fate.'

'Bullshit.'

'It's complicated.'

'Obviously.'

She looked at him. 'I wonder what will happen the sixth time.' Maybe it was the wine. She knew she was being provocative, but she was happier than she'd been for a very long time and she didn't really care.

'I wonder.'

He took the empty glass from her hand. 'My trouble is, I don't seem to be able to stay away from you. Do you want another one?'

'God yes. Are you trying to get me drunk?'

'Yes.'

'Why?'

'So that you forget about your fate.' She couldn't tell if he was serious but it made her breathless. She smiled and watched him go up to the bar. By now she was feeling a warm glow of excitement. Why shouldn't she be allowed to feel like this, for once in her life.

He came back with her wine. She looked over at the bar. 'Do you think they sell cigarettes?'

'You're not having a cigarette.'

'Why not, I hardly ever smoke.'

'I'm a vet, it's not good for you.'

She pulled a face, laughing. 'I know, but I'm not a Spaniel.'

He smiled and brushed a damp strand of hair away from her cheek. 'You can't have a cigarette because I'm about to kiss you.'

The rush of yearning through her whole body was instant and she could only just whisper. "What about my husband?'

'I don't give a fuck about your husband.' He stood up and pulled her towards him, drawing her against his chest. His mouth was gentle at first, but they were soon kissing with such intense desire, that both farmers stopped talking and turned to stare. When she opened her eyes, both his hands were still holding her head, his fingers entwined in her hair.

He kept hold of her, staring at her, oblivious to anyone else. 'I thought so.'

'Thought what?' She answered breathlessly, shocked by what she had just done.

'I thought it would be like that. Shall we go?'

'Yes.'

He took her by the hand and led her out of the pub.

'Where are we going?'

'My house.'

She struggled to keep up as he gripped her arm and whisked her along the dark corridor and out to the car park.

He drove so fast, the battered Defender lurched around the potted lanes and she clutched the seat to stay upright. Seeing her grip the seat he slowed down for a second. 'I'm sorry, it's just something always seems to get in the way.' He looked at her. 'You can escape now if you want. I should drive you home.'

She stared straight ahead. 'No, don't.'

With that, he accelerated so hard she was thrown back in the seat. Would she be doing this if she was sober? She pictured Neil's face and tried to block it out. If she could just be allowed this one time. She caught her reflection in the car window. *I may never feel this way again and I will not feel guilty.*

They didn't speak again until the car pulled up outside an old converted barn.

The lights came on in the drive as they got out of the car. A dog barked and she shivered in anticipation as he opened the front door.

They were only just over the threshold and he pushed her up against the hallway wall and kissed her again in the darkness. He pulled away for a second and looked at her, running his hand under her hair. 'You are so beautiful.' He whispered in the darkness, his hand sliding inside her shirt and all the way up her back.

For a fleeting moment she had time to think. *I am in a barn in the middle of nowhere with a man I hardly know.* She felt him reach round to unzip the back of her top. *And I know exactly what is going to happen next.*

With a shaking hand, she tentatively opened a few of the buttons on his shirt. He pulled it impatiently over his head and threw it on the floor. She could hardly breathe as his bare chest pressed against hers as he kissed her neck and down towards her breasts.

My husband is at home waiting for me.

He lifted her against the wall, her legs wrapped around him and carried her up the stairs and down a dark corridor.

If I can just have this, just this one night, I promise to accept my fate.

He pushed open a door and lowered her down onto the bed in front of him. Running his eyes along the length of her half naked body, he kicked shut the bedroom door behind them.

20

It was still dark when she woke up and it took her a few seconds to work out where she was. *Shit!* She could hear his breathing, sleeping soundly beside her. Her head was thumping, an intense pain in both temples, nausea and a parched mouth. However much wine had she drunk last night. She closed her eyes and exhaled deeply. *So you got your bit of passion. Go home to your husband with the memory of last night stored away safely until you die*

The room was almost completely black but there was a shaft of light under the door. She could just make out his naked profile and her clothes strewn on the floor. She slid tentatively out of the bed, lifted the clothes off the floor and slipped quietly out of the room and down the corridor. She found her top discarded at the top of the stairs. The bathroom door was open and she flicked the light switch and quickly pulled on her clothes.

She stared at her bloodshot eyes and smudged eye make up in the mirror. So, this was infidelity. She had wanted to feel genuine desire, complete abandon and she had, but now she just felt hungover, old and a bit ashamed. For the first time in over twenty years, she had been unfaithful to her husband, the father of her child. After all those years, in one reckless act, she had broken her vow. She looked down at her shaking hands. My God and she had done it while wearing her wedding ring.

There was no glass so she leant down and drank straight from the tap, gulping the water before splashing it on her face. She reached up to open the bathroom cabinet to see if there was anything to take her make up off, but stopped herself, wondering if she was rifling through a dead woman's things.

She sighed deeply. *Bernadette Spicer, what have you done?* The sun wasn't up yet and she guessed it was about 5.30. She tried to count the glasses of wine. She'd only had three, maybe four, five, why did she feel so terrible. But they were very large glasses. But no cigarettes, that was a good thing. *A good thing! You slept with a man, who is not your husband and you're proud of yourself that you didn't smoke!*

She wanted so much to be at home, how much would she pay to turn back the clock. Well Lois would be pleased at least! She mustn't tell a soul, not even Lois. And now she was sitting here, fully dressed on a bathroom stool, in a remote barn, wondering whether to wait here for what could be several hours or go back into the bedroom, but that would mean getting undressed. She could call a taxi if she could find her handbag, which might look a bit dramatic and she didn't even know where she was. She couldn't very well get back into the bed fully dressed. And she was hardly likely to go back to sleep.

She looked in the mirror again. A forty three year old woman on a one night stand, stuck in a bathroom, too embarrassed to go back into the bedroom. This was ridiculous. She would go back in and lie on top of the bed with her clothes on. It seemed like a reasonable solution. She opened the bathroom door which creaked loudly. It was just starting to get light outside, but the corridor was still pitch black and she felt her way along the wall. She couldn't remember which was the bedroom, she was fairly sure it was the second one. She opened the door and in the growing light, she could see she was in the wrong room. It looked like a bedroom but was obviously a very large store room, packed full of clothing and photographs and other paraphernalia, a guitar, ski boots, dresses and jackets, rows of women's shoes, a wedding dress on a hanger and pictures everywhere, she squinted and looked at them, Ben and his wife skiing, on a beach, on horseback. She picked up the framed photo next to her, a smiling bride and groom. She realized the room smelt of perfume.

The door clicked behind her. 'What are you doing?'

She swung round, startled as if caught in the act, clutching the wedding frame to her chest as Ben stood looking at her in the doorway. 'I'm sorry, I was trying to find the bedroom.' She clumsily tried to replace the photo frame on the shelf but couldn't get it to stand up properly.

'Just leave it.' He sounded angry. 'My wife's things.'

'Yes, I'm sorry.'

She followed him back up the corridor and it felt like a lifetime away from the passionate scenes of the night before.

'Would you mind driving me home? I should be getting back.'

'Sure. The kitchen's at the bottom of the stairs, help yourself to coffee.' He looked like he might say something else, but headed back towards the bedroom. 'I'll get dressed.'

Moments later the Defender bounced along the narrow potholed lanes and she clutched her handbag to her, wishing the journey could be shorter. They both stared straight ahead. She wondered if this could be anymore awkward if they were seventeen.

He was the first to speak. 'Listen, I…it probably wasn't such a good idea to..'

'No.'

Silence again. She felt she should say something at least. 'Well we're adults aren't we, not teenagers, so it's all fine.'

'Sure.' They both decided to leave it at that and there was silence for the rest of the journey until the car turned the corner into her lane. She thought about Neil, he wouldn't be up yet. 'Do you mind dropping me here. I'll walk the rest of the way.'

'Are you sure?'

'Yes, thank you.'

As she opened the door there was no 'I'll call you' or any pretence, they were adults after all.

She didn't look back but heard the car turning in the lane and heading off. What must she look like, stumbling along the lane in the half light. Thank God no one could see her. She walked round the bend towards the cottage, wondering if that was the most mortifying morning she had ever experienced.

As she rounded the bend, she froze with fear. Someone was in their driveway, picking up their bins and throwing the contents, literally hurling them over the drive, kicking cans and bottles to scatter them further, tipping the contents far and wide.

She stood unseen, watching, eyes wide open, her heart racing, hardly able to take it in. Finally, when he had finished with the bins, she watched as he pulled up a couple of her newly planted lavender bushes, ripped them apart and tossed them nonchalantly into the drive, hardly looking back as he kicked a bottle across the drive. He was holding a can of spray paint now, poised in front of the door, ready to start. But suddenly, as if he sensed her presence, he turned around to see her standing there watching him.'

'Bo!'

'Neil, what are you doing?'

He stood rooted to the spot. 'I thought you were staying in Liverpool.'

She stared at him. 'You did all of this? The rose bushes?' He didn't answer. 'The car, Neil?'

He looked at the ground. 'Don't overreact Bo. I'll clear it up.'

'You slashed the car tyre?'

'I thought you'd leave me. It was for your own good. We're meant to be together you and me.'

She shook her head. 'Not like this Neil.'

He looked at her imploringly. 'Liam will be home soon, we'll be a family again.'

'You wanted me to be scared.'

'No Bo, I wanted to keep you safe.'

'Safe? You manipulated me, you've always manipulated me.'

'To protect you, for your own good Bo.' He sounded like he was going to cry.

'By slashing my tyre, painting 'bitch' on my car, making me frightened to go out.'

'There are people out there that would string you up Bo.'

'I'll take the risk. It's over Neil. I'm not living like this anymore.'

He stood like a broken man.

She pitied him but it did nothing to weaken her resolve. 'I promise I will never tell our son or anyone else what you have done, but I want you to go Neil, pack your bags and move out. It's over, do you understand.'

Shaking his head, he started to follow her into the house.

She turned round to face him. 'No. You can clear up all this shit first.'

When he hesitated, she looked him in the eye. 'And Neil?'

'Yes.'

'Next time you want to write a shoddy little anonymous note, to tell me that you're sleeping with someone else?'

He looked dumbstruck.

'Yes Neil. Next time, don't use my fucking glitter pen.'

She found her key, let herself into the house and slammed the door.

21

If you wait long enough the sun will eventually come out.
— **Lois Shaunessy**

She was exhausted and just wanted to sleep but first she
ran a bath and wiped the smudged makeup off her face.
Lying in the bath she thought about Sister Marianne's
words. 'It is not you who needs to seek forgiveness.'
Catholic shite as Ben would say. Ben. What did he know
anyhow. A man who says he doesn't pray. What an
unbelievable mess she had made. She closed her eyes and
ducked her head under the water. She thought about her
mother and Father Delaney and the guilt she had carried
for so long.

The Sacrament of Penance. She wondered if it would
have helped after all, if she had just gone along with them
and confessed to Father Delaney. The thought made her
feel sick, asking forgiveness from that vile man. Contrition,
confession and penance, well she might not have gone
through with the confession but she had certainly done
her time on contrition and penance. She reached for a bar
of soap and ran it round her ring finger. Her hand was

calloused either side of the ring and she eased it off and left it on the side of the bath.

She waited for Neil to go and eventually heard the front door slam and his car engine start. She felt nothing this time, nothing but relief. Dragging herself out of the luke warm water, she pulled on her dressing gown and walked into the bedroom. She bent down and pulled out the box from under the bed and lifted it onto the duvet. There was a white knitted cardigan, a pale yellow babygro, the tiny pink hospital ID band and a small fur rabbit that Bo had bought for her. There were also two envelopes, one containing the death certificate and the other, a letter addressed to Bo at the flat in Allerton.

No one else had ever read it and when Lois referred to 'that bloody letter' she had always assumed it was from Bo's mother. It wasn't, it was from her father. It was written in his carefully scripted handwriting but with a much less steady hand than usual. She took it out of the envelope, a single sheet of paper, grown yellow with time.

Bernadette

I know you have been trying to speak to me on the phone. I don't have anything to say to you at the moment so I thought I would write you a letter. Your mother's passing has hit me very hard. She was an extraordinary woman, beautiful, devout, frail. All I ever wanted was to make her happy and in that I know I failed. What you did brought shame on this family Bernadette and in the end, I think it was too much for her. I don't believe it would do any of us any good to have you parading yourself at the funeral. Father Delaney and the nuns will be there to support me. I hope Neil and the baby are keeping well, I would like to meet the little boy one day. Perhaps in time we can talk about forgiveness but for now, confess your sins as your mother had wanted and pray for her soul.

Dad

She closed her eyes and waited for the tears to come, but this time they didn't. Poor Dad, whatever he knew or pretended not to know, he was a loyal man. He never did meet Liam. She slipped the envelope into her pocket and went downstairs. At the back of the kitchen drawer where she hid her cigarettes, she found a lighter, took the envelope over to the sink and lit the corner. As the flames crept across the paper, she dropped it into the sink and watched until all that was left were a few blackened ashes. 'Sorry Dad.' She ran the tap and the ashes swirled around and disappeared down the plughole.

Her mobile phone was on the kitchen table and she picked it up and searched through her contacts. There it was, Katy Partridge. She hesitated for a moment, not because she doubted her decision, more because of what it would set in motion. She took a deep breath and called the number. Katy picked up straight away.

'Katy? It's Bo Spicer. Have you got a moment?'

'Sure!' Katy could hardly contain the excitement in her voice.

'You know you wanted to know all about rock bottom? Well here we are then.'

Katy waited at the end of the line. Bo carried on. 'I'm going to give you a bit of an opportunity, an exclusive. Hopefully we'll both come out of it a little better off. OK?'

'Right?'

'So this is what's going to happen.' Bo paused as she tried to assume a Betsy-like resolve. 'You will get the exclusive

TV interview, my side of the story. In exchange, I want £120,000 and you can get whatever fee you are able to add to that because no one else is going to interview me, only you.'

'OK, but I've never done national TV Bo.' Katy sounded breathless. 'I'm pretty sure I can get you that for a really straight forward newspaper or magazine exclusive, but I don't know if they'd accept me as the interviewer on national TV.'

'Well here's your chance.' She sounded more self-assured than she felt. 'No more tabloids Katy, I've seen what they've written about me and Neil's interview. I want it on TV, an interview with you or not at all.'

Katy was silent. Bo carried on. 'I know it's a lot of money, but I've already been offered £120,000 by one newspaper, so I know it's not out of the question.'

Katy paused. 'Look Bo, can you give me a bit of time to make some phone calls and come back to you.'

'Of course. But I'll need an answer by tomorrow morning.' Bo made that bit up. She hadn't thought about timescales, but she knew if she was going to do this it would need to be quick.

Two hours later, Katy phoned back. 'OK. I think we've got a deal. ITV want it! They might run it as part of the Jonny Barton show on Thursday night or as a standalone interview earlier in the evening. But they definitely want to do it!' She was practically squealing.

Bo swallowed hard. 'Well, good.'

Katy continued in a slightly more business-like tone. 'So, we'll need to get the interview recorded the morning of the show. Can you be in London first thing on Thursday? And they want an agreement signed immediately so that they can start to promote it. They'll send a courier with the paperwork.'

When Bo rang off she immediately called Lois, it went to her voicemail.

'Lois, look I'm sorry I never listen to you and by that I mean most of my adult life. I've chucked Neil out and I'm being interviewed on the Jonny Barton Show on Thursday night. I'll pay for your flight, but do you think you could get over here?'

22

Lois was pulling faces and mouthing 'Jonny Barton!' as Bo struggled to hear what Katy was saying over the phone.

'Yes, that's fine Katy. Just text me the time and address for tomorrow.'

Lois interjected. 'And we'll need to see the questions. She's not to go mentioning rock bottom all the time.'

Bo nodded. 'And Katy, this is a big break for you, so in exchange, you need to email me the questions so that I can veto any I don't like OK?'

'Fair enough!' Katy rang off.

Lois looked at her. 'Are you sure you want to do this?'

'Quite sure.'

Then we'd better decide the important stuff like WHAT THE HELL YOU'RE GOING TO WEAR!'

They both started to laugh, which turned into a sort of nervous hysteria. When they stopped laughing Bo looked pleadingly at Lois. 'Is it too early for a glass of wine?'

'Not at all, extreme circumstances.'

As they piled rejected clothes on the bed and swigged the best part of a bottle of Pinot Grigio, the mobile rang and they both stared as Betsy's name appeared. Bo looked at Lois. 'What shall I do?'

'I don't know, answer it I suppose.'

Bo picked it up.

'How bloody dare you!'

'Hi Betsy!' Bo tried to sound composed.

'How bloody dare you go behind my back. Do you not think I know everyone at ITV?'

'And that bloody little upstart Katy Partridge. If you think she won't stitch you up, you're very much mistaken. Have you negotiated any editorial control?'

'Sorry?'

'I thought not!' She's going to stitch you up like a kipper. And make no mistake Bernadette, I will be coming after you for every penny of my 20% commission.'

'Well you can't have it Betsy, because if you cast your mind back.' And by now Bo was having that 'out of body' sensation. 'You sacked me.'

'No I didn't. I offered you an interview. It was my idea to get you the exclusive for God's sake. I fed you the idea and suddenly you think you don't need an agent, like you're some kind of media guru. Is Lois with you? I bet this was her idea!'

By now Betsy's voice was booming across the bedroom on speakerphone and Lois, who had drunk more than her fair share of the bottle, was bent double trying not to laugh.

'Well thank you for the vote of confidence Betsy. I am in fact capable of making a decision without Lois.' Lois was shaking her head. 'And you did sack me. You only called me back because you thought you could make some money out of a tabloid interview. And I don't remember you being too picky about the quality of the journalism. I've negotiated £120,000 and it's TV, so at least I'll have a chance to control what I say.'

'Control!' She thought Betsy was going to explode. 'You think you're going to have CONTROL! And you negotiated £120,000 did you, for prime time TV. I could have got you five times that YOU STUPID WOMAN.'

Lois was now pulling silly faces and Bo knew she had to curtail the conversation.

'Sorry Betsy, I've really got to go!'

'20% Bernadette, or I'll instruct my lawyers to take you to the cleaners.'

'Good bye Betsy.'

It was well past midnight and discarded takeaway cartons lay scattered on the table next to a second bottle of Pinot Grigio. The two women poured over Katy's emailed questions. Bo had signed the ITV agreement the day before, which had arrived by bike courier. They were now scrutinizing every one of Katy's proposed questions. They had rewritten almost half the questions. To be fair, she had avoided direct references to 'rock bottom' but to Lois' disgust, she had snuck in 'do you think you were at your lowest ebb.' Lois shrieked and scored it out.

Bo yawned, 'Come on Lois, we need to get some sleep.'

'You're right, we can finish this in the car tomorrow, it's coming to pick us up at 10am.'

'Well we'd better get off to bed then.'

She woke at 6.30 with a mild hangover but the absolute conviction that today would be the day that it would come to an end. They had picked out some black trousers and a pale blue shirt, not too showy not too drab. She was sitting at the kitchen table eating toast with a tea towel tied round her neck when a car pulled up in the drive.

'What?' She looked out of the window at a shiny black Mercedes and then at Lois.

It was Lewis ringing the doorbell. Lois smiled. 'I know isn't he an utter gent!'

'How did he know?'

'Betsy was in his car when she was ranting at you. He texted me last night. He said it would be a privilege to drive us to the studio!'

'Oh that's so kind!' She felt a lump in her throat and went out to greet him. 'This is very kind Lewis, thank you.' She resisted the urge to hug him.

'My pleasure.' He smiled. 'We can't have you turning up to ITV in a mini cab now can we?'

'Certainly not!' She laughed. 'Can I get you a cup of tea and some toast?'

'No thank you, Mrs Lewis made me a thermos. I'll be waiting in the car.'

Bo went back inside to get her things. 'There's a lot of kindness out there Lois, as well as all the nutters. Betsy would sack him if she found out.'

'I know.'

The letterbox flapped open with a theatrical 'yooohooo!'

'Davina?' Bo opened the door. 'I just heard on the radio. You're doing a TV interview!'

Bo was shocked. 'They're promoting it on the radio!' It was in the contract, but she had imagined a couple of mentions in the ad break.

'It's everywhere Bo!' Davina was a little breathless. 'TV, radio, front page of the Daily Mail, I even saw it on Facebook this morning! Bernadette My Story, tonight at 7pm.'

For the first time, Bo felt a little sick. Lois looked at her watch. 'We'd better go.'

Davina stood in the doorway. 'I'm coming with you!'

'What!' Lois rolled her eyes.

'You are not going without me.' Davina stood firm.

Bo smiled. 'Of course not Davina.' They walked to the waiting car and Lewis got out.

'Have you room for another one Lewis.' Bo laughed.

'I expect so.' He smiled and held the door open.

23

If you tell the truth you don't have to remember anything.
Mark Twain

They were shown into a dressing room as soon as they arrived. Katy was already there, sitting in front of the mirror applying her trademark lipstick, while an assistant fixed her bouncy blonde do with spray.

She clapped her hands when she saw them come in. 'Well done! Excellent! The studio's booked in 20 minutes, so we've got plenty of time to run through the questions.'

Plenty of time! Bo looked at her, with her red lips and her school prefect bravado. Underneath it they were probably just as nervous as each other.

Lois got straight to the point. 'Right. Where do you want to go through these?' She waved the printed questions at Katy, who could see the numerous crossings out and scribbles. There was barely a question that hadn't been rehashed in Lois's familiar scrawl.

Katy smiled reassuringly. 'The director's approved the questions Lois. We have to stick to the script.'

'Hang on a second. You said we could give you feedback

on the questions Katy!'

'Yes I did, but I can't change them 20 minutes before the interview Lois!' Katy spoke between gritted teeth.'

Davina stepped between them. 'Look, we've only got a short time. If she doesn't like a question, she can just stay silent surely? And then you'll have to edit that bit out, yes?'

The make up artist arrived and Bo was shown to a seat. The conversation continued above her head.

Katy turned to Davina. 'That's right. All I'm doing is keeping the flow going. Bo remains absolutely in control of the interview. My job is just to prompt her when necessary.'

Lois snorted in disbelief. Bo could see that this was going nowhere. 'Look Katy. I will tell you everything you want to know, I just don't want it twisted OK. Just the truth.'

'Of course Bo.'

'I'm not stupid, I know what kind of interview you need, but no schmaltz, do you understand. And you're not to mention Liam.'

'Fine.'

Davina butted in. 'And no camera shots of her fidgeting hands or panning to her feet shuffling or that kind of rubbish. I've seen what you do.' Davina was Lois' height in her wedge heels and the two women towered over Katy.

'Of course not. But once we start it's very important that the camera keeps running, just answer the questions, keep the flow going. Most of it will be edited out afterwards anyway.'

'Would you ladies like to come with me.' An assistant with an ear piece tried to usher Davina and Lois out of the dressing room.

'You can watch the interview on a screen next door.' Katy explained. 'There's coffee and croissants.'

Lois stood firm with Davina nodding by her side. 'We're not going anywhere, why can't we come with her?'

'It's a closed set Lois.' Katy kept her cool. 'The director wouldn't allow it.'

Lois' eyes narrowed. 'This is a mega opportunity she's given you Katy Partridge! Don't you forget to have a bit of decency in your cold journalist heart.'

Katy nodded as Lois was steered towards the door. 'And if you even mention rock bottom I'll be through that door like a gazelle, do you understand me?'

Once they had finished her make up and sprayed her hair, Bo and Katy were led down the corridor by the assistant producer. They were shown into a small studio. It was empty apart from two big black leather chairs on a stage, a lighting rig already set up and a cameraman waiting for them. It was incredibly bright and reminded Bo of an operating theatre. The producer showed them to their seats. As they started to check the camera angles and move the chairs, the director appeared out of the darkness.

'Hi! Bernadette! I'm Dan.' They shook hands. He was in his early forties and wore a flowery shirt, black rimmed glasses and converse trainers. It was a media look that Bo had started to recognize, that and the extreme enthusiasm. He seemed nice though.

'Nervous?' He smiled.

'No, yes, only a little.'

He squatted down next to Katy who was clearly in awe. Bo couldn't quite make out the muttered last minute advice. Was she not supposed to hear? As he walked away, he gave Bernadette a thumbs up and winked. *A winker!* She only just managed to suppress a giggle. She mustn't laugh, it would be like laughing at a funeral. They started the count down. This was it then.

Three, two, one…

'Bernadette Maloney. Most of Britain now knows you as the 'Angel in a Onesie', the housewife heroine who saved the life of a teenage girl so dramatically on our TV screens. But this is the story of another Bernadette Maloney. And for the first time since the story broke, this is the truth from Bernadette herself.' Katy's eyes narrowed as she talked directly into the camera.

'Because on the afternoon of March 14th 1995, you walked into St Saviour's Maternity Hospital on the outskirts of Liverpool and kidnapped another woman's new born baby.' Bo was so taken aback by Katy's practiced poise that she forgot she was supposed to respond. Katy raised her eyebrows to prompt a reaction.

'That's right.'

'Police arrested you a week later in a bed & breakfast in Wales and the baby was returned safely to her mother.'

Bo nodded.

And you received a suspended sentence based on a plea of diminished responsibility.

'Yes.'

'But those CCTV images of you taking the baby. That's not quite the beginning of the story is it, Bernadette?'

'No.'

Katy narrowed her eyes. 'Why don't we rewind a little. Take us back to a year before those events Bernadette. Tell us how you met your husband Neil.' The scarlet lips smiled in studied sincerity.

'I was studying Modern History at Liverpool University. He was doing a business course at what used to be the Poly.'

'And I believe he was quite persistent.' *That was definitely off script.*

Bo frowned and said nothing.

'According to your friends you were the college beauty and he was punching well above his weight.' Katy wasn't even attempting to follow the agreed questions.

'Well I don't know about that.' Bo tried not to think about Lois pacing furiously next door.

Don't panic. Just tell the truth Bernadette.

'So you were young, beautiful and clever, with the offer of a well paid job waiting for you in London, is that right?' *Bloody Katy, bloody Partridge!*

'I had a job offer yes, in a big advertising agency.'

'But you never took the job, did you?'

'No, I didn't.'

'Bernadette Maloney, you're your own worst enemy.' She could hear Lois' gently mocking voice all those years ago as if it was just this morning. 'So what do you do, when you catch your boyfriend snogging someone else at the Graduation Ball? You drink six tequilas and go and sleep with that irritating little gobshite from the Poly, that's been after you for two years.'

And so it would have remained, a shoddy one night stand and the first time she had ever been blind drunk, or 'paralytic' as Lois liked to put it. But six weeks later she was looking at a pregnancy test kit and the two blue lines were unmistakable.

Her friend had said she should get rid of it. Don't tell anyone, just slip off, I'll come with you. But it was never an option, because looking at those two blue lines filled her with horror but another, stranger feeling kept coming to the surface. She was going to have a baby. It was one of life's miracles after all.

'Why not?' Bo looked at Katy's questioning expression. 'Sorry?'

'Why did you not take up the job?'

'I was pregnant Katy.'

'And was that a problem?'

'A problem? You try telling your strict Catholic parents that you're pregnant by a man you hardly even know.'

That was when her mother had started to get ill, the shame of it all was too much. Her mother was a fervent Catholic, definitely more so since Father Delaney, the new priest had arrived.

They had been so proud, Bernadette, the only member of the family who ever went to University. She had never seen her father cry before. The only saving grace was that Neil was Catholic.

Neil wanted to get married right away. But there was no way she was going to marry him, no matter how much pressure from both sets of parents. Lois was the only one who agreed with her.

'And Neil wanted to get married before the baby was born.'

'Yes.' Bo almost forgot where she was. 'I wasn't having any of it, but I did move in with him. He had a job in sales and we found a two bed flat in Allerton. My mother was appalled, they were all desperate for a wedding.' *Neil was really great actually. He painted the baby's bedroom pale green with little flowers and animals all over. He made one of those mobiles with birds and hung it over the cot. It was beautiful. He's very creative, Neil.*

'I grew very fond of him over the coming months. And there was the shared excitement of it all, counting down the days. He came to every antenatal appointment. It wasn't a difficult pregnancy, I breezed through it actually, but then I was so young.'

She remembered sitting in a coffee shop with Neil on a Saturday when she felt the first kick, like a little butterfly inside her. She would never forget that.

'And it was a little girl, 7lbs 4 oz. We called her Cathleen Mairead, after my mother   She was beautiful, long black eyelashes and those perfectly formed little lips you just want to kiss and just a wisp of black fluffy hair. Her little fingers wrapped round mine. I had never felt such love. I wanted to wake her up, she was so quiet. But nobody said anything you see. I think they thought I'd realized, but I hadn't. So one of the nurses had to say to me. 'Bernadette love, she's not going to wake up.' The poor woman that had to tell me. They said it was because of problems with the placenta, I hadn't been feeding her properly. And then they took her away.'

'She was dead when she was born Bernadette.' The older nurse was more direct. 'She's not dead! Bring her back to me!'

'I thought they were lying you see. I was hysterical, I was shouting and screaming. She was warm, how did they know she was dead. I swear I felt the grip of her fingers around mine. The nurse in charge said it was better if I didn't see her.'

There was a pause and even Katy Partridge remained respectfully silent.

'And you never saw Cathleen again?'

'No.'

She remembered her parents coming into the room. They had been waiting outside, waiting to hear the good news. Neil was crying.

Nobody knew what to say. They shuffled around awkwardly and when they left the room she heard her mother's voice in the corridor.

'This is God's doing. By the grace of God' she said, 'It's just as well.'

By the grace of God, it's just as well. She would never forget those words.

She heard her father. 'For God's sake Cath, keep your voice down.'

And there was a lot more her mother had said when the priest arrived.

'The Wages of Sin is Death, isn't that right Father Delaney.' She slurred slightly as she spoke. 'She died for your sin, to save you from damnation. Confess your mortal sin before God Bernadette, confess your wickedness to Father Delaney.'

'Get out! Both of you, just fucking GET OUT!'

"The Wages of Sin is Death.' That's what they told me, that it was my fault.'

Katy frowned. 'And you believed them?'

Bo stared out into the darkness. 'Yes I did.'

She turned back to Katy. 'Cathy would have been 21 last week.'

Katy didn't react, she wasn't expecting that and looked down hastily at her notes to find the next question. 'Doctors who have looked at your case have suggested that you were suffering from a severe form of post-partum depression, possibly even psychosis.'

'Is that what they call it.'

'Do you accept that you were suffering from a mental illness?

'Of course.' Bo frowned. 'You don't go walking into a hospital and steal another woman's baby if you're in your right mind, do you?' She shook her head. 'It's a very strange thing, to go from being pregnant to not being pregnant, without a baby to show for it. It's a terrible thing.' Her voice trailed off.

'Did you ever get a proper diagnosis?' Katy was sticking doggedly to the script.

Bo shook her head.

'According to a doctor who gave evidence at your trial, there is a huge shift in hormones that affects brain chemistry. The judge took that into account when he sentenced you.'

Bo didn't appear to be listening. 'Your body doesn't catch on. They give you pills to stop the milk, but the loss is so deep.'

'The doctor said and I quote from the court records, that the 'shift in hormones', coupled with the severe depression experienced from neo-natal death triggered a psychotic episode.'

Bo didn't seem to respond.

'Were you offered counselling Bernadette?'

'I don't remember. They tried to make me speak to the priest.'

Bo looked like she was far away and Katy struggled to get back on script. The director said something into her ear piece.

'Your own baby died and you went to the hospital to steal someone else's.'

'No!' Bo seemed to rouse. 'It wasn't like that at all. I went to the hospital to try and find her.'

'You thought she was still alive?'

'I didn't know. I was in a bad state.'

'It's been suggested you were delusional. What I mean is, did you think the baby you abducted was your own?'

'I honestly don't know. I've thought about it, as you can imagine. At the time, I wasn't aware that she was anyone else's, but I'm not sure if I thought she was Cathy.'

'So you're saying you didn't set out that day to steal a baby.'

'I didn't go to the hospital to take a baby, no. But then I saw her lying there in her cot, alongside the other babies. She had that little wisp of dark hair.'

'Surely you knew you'd be caught?'

'All I wanted was some time on my own with her. But yes, I knew they would take her away again.'

She remembered the smell of the hospital like it was yesterday. Going home was the worst bit, packing her bag and going home without Cathy. Walking along the corridor, supported by Neil, up in the lift and out of the revolving doors to the waiting car. It was a lovely sunny day and she stared straight ahead, with her bag on her lap as Neil put the ticket into the machine to lift the car park barrier.

'And you weren't offered any other support?' Katy's voice pulled her back again.

'They gave me tranquilisers to help me sleep, but I flushed them down the toilet at the hospital.'

Katy leant forward. 'Why did you do that?'

Bo looked her in the eye. 'Because I didn't want my senses dimmed in case I forgot, any tiny detail of her face or hands.' Seeing that Katy didn't understand she carried on. 'I knew I wouldn't have a photograph you see, no one would talk about her, I would only have my memory to rely on.'

'We'll have another one,' Neil had said. It was a stupid thing to say and made her want to shout, but she knew he didn't know how else to comfort her.

'How long after did you go back to the hospital?'

'They gave Neil a couple of days off, but he had to go back to work. I was relieved if I'm honest, to be on my own. I couldn't fit into my own clothes, so I put on my maternity jeans and his hoodie. I decided to go to the hospital, to try to find her.' Bo looked at her hands. She realized how it sounded, now that she said it out loud.

'I couldn't bear to cut the hospital identity band from my wrist, so I was still wearing it when I went back.'

She knew where to go. If she could just avoid the horrible nurse and find the young, kind one, she might be able to tell her what happened to Cathy. Neil had talked about arranging a funeral, like he was just going to accept everything they had said. She couldn't remember the exact way it happened, but she did remember the line of plastic cots and staring desperately at the faces of the tiny babies inside. And there she was, with her wisp of hair. And when she lifted her out of her cot and kissed her head, her little hand wrapped itself around Bo's finger. A nurse smiled as she walked past her and Bo smiled back.

Katy's voice snapped her back to the studio. 'Can we turn for a moment to the mother of the baby you stole, a woman who missed out on the first week of her child's life. What do you think she was going through, to know that her newborn baby had been kidnapped by a potentially psychotic woman?'

Bo shook her head. 'Just terrible. I could say that I cannot imagine the pain I caused her, but I can imagine, which makes it harder to bear.'

'And do you ask her forgiveness now?'

'No. I wouldn't expect it.' Katy didn't even react, just straight on to the next question.

'It's been reported that she's called you Satanic. What do you say to that?'

Bo looked resigned. 'She can call me anything she likes.' She noticed a camera panning onto her hands.

Katy paused for a while for dramatic effect.

'And you went on to marry Neil. Tell us how that came about.'

'When the police came to find me, Neil and my cousin were with them and Sister Marianne from our local church. They took the baby away and I was heavily sedated. I don't remember much about the next few weeks. I don't even really remember Cathleen's funeral, isn't that a terrible thing? Her own mother can't recall the details of her burial. Sister Marianne and the other nuns organized the funeral. I just remember it was a dark wood coffin and I would never have chosen that for her.'

Katy looked unmoved and carried on. 'You avoided a prison sentence?'

'Yes, based on a plea of diminished responsibility, because of the state I was in.'

'And six months later you were pregnant again.' This was not what they had agreed. Bo struggled not to look shocked.

'Yes I was, and Neil and I got married in Liverpool shortly before the baby was due.'

He had been amazingly supportive during all of this; 'devoted' her parents had said, 'controlling' was what Lois called it. Her mother said she didn't deserve him. It was Lois' opinion that Neil took advantage of the situation, to tie her down. It wasn't as simple as that. They'd had their laughs over the years, struggled together, built a family.

'And you gave birth to Liam?' Bo's eyes widened. This was way off limits and Katy knew it. *Say nothing.*

There was a long silence. Bo didn't reply and Katy finally gave up.

'Do you blame the medical profession? Do you think how you were treated led to you taking the child?' Off script again and this one sounded like she was chasing her next headline. Bo wondered how Lois was taking this. *Keep your head.*

'I don't blame anyone. Maybe if I'd had more time with Cathy, if she hadn't been taken away so quickly I might have come to terms with it better than I did, reacted differently, who knows.' *Maybe if my own mother and Father Delaney hadn't preyed on my grief.*

'So, flip forward 20 years and you find yourself clinging to a cliff edge in torrential rain. You became an overnight sensation when you saved the life of Melinda Johnson; an instant celebrity and the UK's favourite agony aunt.'

Bo nodded, relieved to move on.

Katy shook her head in disbelief. 'But surely you realized you'd be found out, the more famous you became?'

At least this one was in the script. 'I had no idea how it would turn out. I thought it would all be over in a few days.'

'But it wasn't and the British public really warmed to you.' Sincere look again from Katy. Bo thought about some of the troll messages she had read, the threats.

Katy pressed on. 'People seemed to trust you. Do you think that what you've gone through has helped you to understand other people's problems?'

'I'm not sure about that.' Bo paused. 'I certainly think you shouldn't go around wagging your finger at people if you don't know what they've been through. Most people are living with some kind of burden.' It felt like the worst was over, like Katy had relaxed her grip.

'And you and Neil are still together, happily married in spite of everything?'

'No Katy, as you know, we are not.' She held Katy's gaze, hoping she could sense her contempt.

'You've separated?' *Mock surprise.*

'Yes.'

'And what do you say to people watching now, who might accuse you of enjoying your celebrity status. Of using this to try to extend your 15 minutes of fame.' Bo was genuinely taken aback by this one and the camera zoomed in on her startled expression. She tried to keep her head. *Don't panic, say what you think.*

She looked across at Katy. 'I never asked to be famous. I didn't go looking for it, it just happened to me. And I've seen such cruel things written by people who don't know what they're talking about. I just wanted to give people the facts if they care to listen and then go away.'

Katy nodded, apparently satisfied. 'You're donating your entire fee for this interview to charity.'

'That's right.'

'Split between PRETERM, a charity supporting bereaved parents of stillborn children and the Post Natal Depression Support Centre.'

She nodded.

There was a pause and Bo wondered what cynical twist Katy might be planning.

'And do you hope that other women won't have to suffer as you did?' She looked ridiculously intense.

'Of course.'

'And what are your hopes personally Bernadette? For the future?'

Bo paused for a moment. 'Just to be able to move on.'

Katy nodded and there was a dramatic pause as she looked earnestly at the camera for her final words.

'And that was the extraordinary, exclusive story of Bernadette Maloney, a saint and a sinner, the angel in a onesie, her dramatic rise to fame and equally dramatic fall from grace.' Bo wasn't expecting the summing up and was slightly startled when Katy, who had been addressing the camera, turned to look at her again. 'Bernadette Maloney thank you for sharing your story with us tonight.'

Bo nodded and the camera seemed to stay on her for a very long time. Was that it? There was complete silence in the studio until Dan the director jogged towards them clapping his hands.

'Bravo!'

The assistant producer came over and unclipped her mike. Dan was all fired up again, like they'd just created some work of art. 'Just wonderful Bernadette, straight from the heart.' He shook his head. 'So natural!'

They walked back up the corridor, Bo a few paces behind Katy and Dan who were gushing with excitement. Bo braced herself for Lois' reaction. And what on earth would Davina make of all this?

As they walked ahead, Bo heard Dan and Katy talking, 'That was TV gold Katy. How on earth did you persuade her to give you the scoop?'

She didn't hear the rest, as Lois emerged from a side door behind her, arms waving in indignation. 'So much for sisterhood! The little cow!'

Bo couldn't help laughing. 'Was it that bad?'

'No it was fine, but she stitched you up. It was great Bo.

I mean it was right and proper, in spite of her attempts. How do you feel?'

'I feel good actually. It's done isn't it.'

Lois smiled broadly. 'It certainly is, the mother of all confessions!'

Davina walked up and gave Bo a hug. She looked slightly red eyed. 'Well, I think there's only one thing to do in a situation like this.'

They both looked at her. 'Let's go and get absolutely pissed!' It was very un-Davina like and Bo and Lois laughed.

'I'm a member of a club in Knightsbridge. I'll get us a rooftop table for lunch.'

'Thanks Davina.' Bo smiled and realized how desperate she was to get out of this strange place.

Katy came up to say goodbye. Bo could see Lois poised to attack and shook her head to stop her. There was no point now.

Katy was typically upbeat and gushing. 'You know Bo, I spoke to Melinda yesterday. She's going out with that awful boy again. I don't think he's very nice. I think she said he'd slapped her. The silly girl was talking about moving in with him. Still, what can you do.'

None of them replied.

Katy pulled a face. 'These girls, they make their own bed!'

24

If you are humble nothing will touch you, neither praise nor disgrace, because you know what you are.
Mother Teresa

They stood outside the studio entrance, wondering what to do next. Davina put on her sunglasses and reapplied lip gloss. 'Is Lewis coming?'

Lois shook her head. 'No. He'll pick us up later. He had to work for Betsy all day. We'll have to make our own way back into Central London. I think we're just round the corner from Ealing High Street.'

Bo was keen to get away from the studio. 'Come on, let's just walk and see if we can find a bus or something.'

As they crossed a green, towards the main road, Bo spotted a bus with Hammersmith on the front. 'Quick, if we run we can get this one.'

Lois got there first and managed to hold the bus, while Davina struggled to jog in her nude patent heels.

Bo took some money out of her handbag and Lois rolled her eyes. 'You just tap your card Bo. God how long have you lived in the country!'

They found some seats near the back. Davina looked genuinely excited. 'Well this is fun! I haven't been on a bus for years!' Lois and Bo exchanged a glance.

Two women sitting at the front started staring and whispering. It was obvious they were looking at Bo. Their faces were contorted with malice as they mumbled inaudible insults. Lois put a hand on Bo's arm. Bo smiled at her. 'It's fine really.'

The bus pulled up at Chiswick High Street and another woman stood up to get off. She had a small child in tow and as she carefully helped her down the step, she looked up and shouted down the bus. 'She's the baby thief, that woman at the back! Bernadette, she stole a woman's new born baby.'

Every head turned to look at her. Lips pursed and heads shaking. An old man with a stick muttered, 'shameful'.

One of the two women at the front turned very deliberately round to look at Bo and mouthed, 'you make me sick'.

Lois, who was sitting next to the aisle could take no more. She leapt to her feet. 'No, you make me sick actually! The lot of you! Sitting there with your pious little faces. Judging other people you know nothing about. I bet you've all got some dirty laundry haven't you.'

Oh God. Bo put her head in her hands,

The old man started to tut. Lois was affronted. She pointed her finger at him. 'Let him who is without sin cast the first stone.' He looked quite shocked.

She warmed to her theme. 'John's Gospel Chapter 8, verse 7. '*So when they continued questioning him, he lifted up himself, and said unto them, He that is without sin among you, let him first cast a stone at her.*' There was something of the

Martin Luther King about Lois as her voice boomed down the aisle. The whole bus was mesmerized.

The bell rang and she was interrupted by a recorded voice. 'This is Hammersmith, Hammersmith your final stop. Please leave the bus and take all your personal belongings with you.'

Even as they queued and the passengers stepped off the bus, Lois continued to berate them. 'Watch ITV tonight at 7! Then maybe you won't be quite so bloody self-righteous!'

'Lois!' By now Bo couldn't stop herself giggling. 'It was sounding fantastic until you did the ITV plug!'

Davina nodded. 'I must say Lois, your knowledge of the New Testament is very impressive.'

'The benefits of a good Catholic education Davina.' Lois reached for her tissues and dabbed her upper lip. 'Right, we can get the Piccadilly line from here straight to Knightsbridge.'

Davina pulled a face. 'Let's get a taxi shall we?' They all nodded.

'There's one!' Davina was off like a shot, waving her sunglasses at a passing black cab. 'Taxi!'

The driver lowered the window and Bo winced as she spotted a copy of the Mirror on the seat next to him. The front page was entirely taken up with the hospital CCTV picture of her dressed in a hoodie, 'Babysnatcher to tell all in dramatic TV confession'. Davina was already sitting in the taxi and as Bo bent her head to get in, the driver spoke through the intercom. 'It's you, isn't it? Bernadette Maloney?' She nodded. 'Get out! Go on, hop it. All of you. I'm not having that bitch in my cab!' He drove off and they stood on the curb staring after him.

Bo looked at the others apologetically. 'Look, this is turning into a nightmare. You go off and have a nice dinner.

I'm a bit tired anyway, I might just take myself off home on the train.'

'No, you bloody well won't!' Davina was steadfast. 'They won't all recognize you. It's only in the tabloids, we just need to find a slightly better class of cab driver. Taxi!' She was off again, waving a Hermes scarf at passing taxis.

She was right. The second cab driver was a sixty year old Sikh and clearly didn't have a clue who she was. They pulled up on Sloane Street shortly afterwards, right outside the entrance to Davina's club. Lois recognized the row of designer shops from their last visit. 'Girls, it's Bellagamo! Just one little look!'

Bo sighed. 'There won't be any more freebies Lois. And there's nothing in there that you and I can afford.' Lois looked at them both pleadingly.

'Oh, come on then.' Davina led the way. 'The table's not free for half an hour anyway.'

The store was buzzing with upmarket shoppers. A mother and daughter were trying on shoes; the daughter sulking, surrounded by a dozen rejected pairs. There was a general impression of opulence, scarves, designer hand bags and expensive perfume; self-assured women who looked like they'd dressed up to come out shopping. A couple of Japanese women flicked through a rail of silk dresses. Lois was immediately drawn to a bejeweled pair of wedge sandals. She removed them from the display and held them aloft. 'Bo! Look at these! Have you ever seen anything so perfect!'

Bo worked her way half-heartedly along a rail of trousers. There was nothing under £800. She noticed that none of the other women even looked at the price. There was a display of wallets and trinkets by the till that caught her eye, a fluffy keyring for £180.

The sales assistant came up and she smiled at her, hoping it wasn't obvious she wouldn't be buying anything.

The woman simpered a little without actually speaking as if she was struggling to find the words. 'I'm awfully sorry but I'm going to have to ask you and your friends to leave.'

Bo could hardly make out what she was saying. Did they stand out that much? Davina was certainly dressed for the part and she and Lois were looking pretty smart too?

'I don't understand.'

Lois was over in a shot. The sales assistant continued to smile as she whispered. 'It's not me. It's just that we've had complaints from other customers. And we...'

'Complaints about what?' Lois interrupted loudly.

'Well, you know. Your friend. Who she is.' Her voice trailed off and she gave a little embarrassed cough.

'Well why didn't you show a bit of backbone and tell them to feck off then!'

'Lois!'

'I'm afraid I can't do that Madam. Some of them are very valued customers.'

Davina emerged from behind a mannequin, plainly enraged. 'Valued customers! Dear girl, I've spent more money in this shop than you earn in a year. My friends and I are just off to my club in Sloane Street, where we'll be dining with my very dear friend Vanessa Staniforth-Cummings.' The sales assistant looked blank, as did Lois and Bo.

'Vanessa is Fashion Editor of the Evening Standard!' Davina explained with utmost disdain. 'And I shall be telling her exactly what I think of your shoddy customer service and your rather naff, gold window display.' Davina turned to exit and the others followed. As she opened the door she turned back and addressed the whole shop loudly. 'Let's just hope the Saudis like your ghastly handbags. To be honest, everything in this shop's a little bit too footballers' wives for me.'

Bo and Lois struggled to keep up with Davina as she strode up Sloane Street. Lois, slightly out of breath, caught up with her. 'Are we really having dinner with Vanessa Staniforth Whatsit?'

'No, but she is a very close friend, you met her at my party. And I shall be having words with her, that much is true!'

Davina pressed a buzzer and spoke into the intercom, 'Davina Edgerton Davis.' The heavy doors immediately swung open and they were ushered in.

A young man in a black suit and walkie talkie showed them up the stairs. Davina marched ahead. 'Now, I think I explained on the phone, we need a quiet space, where we won't be gawped at or approached by other members.' She was loving this.

'Of course Madam, we have the corner area reserved for you.'

Lois trailed behind with Bo. 'Isn't she fab!'

Bo pulled a face. 'She's sounding a bit like Betsy though.'

'Not at all, Davina has a kind heart, I'm not sure Betsy even has one.' They both nodded.

They were shown through an archway to a rooftop restaurant. Bo and Lois' mouths dropped open. It was a hidden oasis of green grass, gravel pathways and olive trees, right in the middle of London. Mini orange and lemon trees were dotted around linen covered tables and glamorous looking people in white jeans and sun glasses sipped Rosé under cream umbrellas. There was the sound of hushed conversation and muted laughter. A few people stared and Bo noticed some of them stop talking to look up as they walked past.

'This was a mistake Lois, they're all gawping at us.'

'They're only checking us out to see if we're famous. That's what these people do.'

They took their seats and Davina ordered a bottle of Rosé. The manager came over and gave them the menus. 'How lovely to see you again Mrs Edgerton-Davis.'

'Thank you, Graham.'

Davina looked very much at home. 'Can I be an awful pain and have the Sea Bass without the shrimp butter and spring veg instead of the new potatoes.'

'Of course.'

Lois and Bo exchanged a look.

'Madam?' He looked at Lois.

'I'll have the double baked cheese soufflé and then the pork belly please.'

Davina took off her sunglasses. 'No Lois. It's too much.'

'I'm sorry Davina?' Lois looked at her in mock disbelief.

'The cheese and then the pork belly. Too fatty, not good for you.'

'I can assure you Davina, I know perfectly well what's good for me and when I've finished, I shall be having the baked Alaska.' Lois held her gaze.

Davina shook her head and looked down at the menu. Bo ordered the cheese soufflé and then the Sea Bass. She was relieved when the bottle of Rosé arrived and caused a distraction. Davina swirled it around theatrically in her glass before tasting it. Lois was clearly disappointed by the size of the measure. She downed it in one as if to prove the point and reached for the bottle in the ice bucket.

Davina could contain herself no longer. 'No no Lois, that's your water glass.'

'I don't feckin care if it's my tea cup Davina. It's a drinking vessel is it not?'

Bo realized that they had not had any lunch. Blood sugar levels were low. 'It's a funny thing with 'feck' isn't it?' She tried distraction. 'I mean, why is 'feck' more acceptable than 'fuck'?'

Lois shrugged her shoulders. Bo carried on. 'Did you hear what Katy said about Melinda? Do you think it would be interfering if we tried to do something about it?'

'Like what?' Davina looked animated.

'I don't really know, but between us, we must be able to think of something.'

'I'm in!' Lois raised her glass.

'Me too!' Davina lifted hers.

Bo smiled. 'Well then, let's drink to 'Saving Melinda."

'Saving Melinda!' They clinked glasses.

'And did you hear what that snotty little cow Katy said about 'these girls making their own bed'. Self-righteous little madam! What would she know about life. She's just damn lucky she hasn't been dealt any harsh blows that's all.'

'Quite.' Bo noticed that Davina was nodding vigorously. Lois waved the empty bottle in the direction of the waiter.

'My God, it's 6.30! Half an hour to go before you're on air, Bo!' Lois reached for her phone. 'It's absolutely everywhere! They've even released excerpts on Youtube. Look at this! It's the bit where you picked up the baby and the nurse smiled at you and you smiled back.'

Davina made a face at Lois. The waitress arrived with the starters. 'Salad leaves?'

'Here, thank you.' Davina took another swig from her wine glass. 'And Sexy Vet who used to be Young Farmer, what's happened to him?'

Bo shrugged. 'Nothing much.'

'Nothing much? You've gone a little bit red Bo. Let's see then.' Lois swiped her phone from the table. You always were a crap liar. 'Oh hello!' Lois was exultant. 'She's even got him saved as 'Sexy Vet' in her contacts. You know he can see that don't you!'

'What! No, he can't! Lois stop it! No that's completely screwed unfortunately.'

'I suppose the whole 'accusing him of cheating on his dead wife' thing didn't help.'

'No that was unfortunate.'

I shouldn't think he'll ever speak to you again Bo.

'Probably not.' She paused. 'I did sleep with him though.'

'What!' Davina and Lois nearly spat out their drinks. By now they were well into the second bottle.

'Yes.' Bo was enjoying the moment. 'I bumped into him at the train station on my way back from Liverpool.'

Lois was indignant. 'And why did you not tell me any of this before?'

'Because I'm not exactly proud. A drunken one night stand. Incredibly awkward. And then the next day I stumbled into the wrong room at his house and violated a shrine to his late wife. It smelt of her perfume. He caught me clutching their wedding photo.'

'What the fuck!'

'Exactly.'

Lois shook her head. 'You're a dark horse Bernadette Maloney.' She paused briefly. 'Was the sex good though?'

Bo said nothing but smiled.

'Yessss!' Lois slammed the table with her hand and made the glasses shake.

'Lucky cow!' Davina poured herself some more wine.

Bo sipped hers slowly. 'It was stupid anyway. And it just made me feel incredibly sordid the next day.'

Lois was slurring slightly. 'If you were a man you wouldn't even think about it.'

Bo stared into the middle distance. 'I just wanted to remember what it felt like to be kissed by someone that made my knees go weak, is that so wrong?'

Lois and Davina both sighed.

Davina shook her head. 'I don't think I can even remember that.'

Lois snorted. 'Paddy hasn't kissed me for years, not properly you know. A slap on the arse as I empty the dishwasher, that's as close to romance as I get.'

'Lois!' Bo flipped her with her napkin. 'Patrick's a wonderful man, he adores you and you know it.'

Lois went to the loo and when she came back to the table she nearly tripped up in her excitement. 'OH MY GOD! They've got the interview on in the kitchen and all the staff are watching it!'

'Just as well we've already got our food then.' Bo tried to look more nonchalant than she felt.

Lois looked surprised. 'Don't you want to watch it?'

'No! Let's just finish up and go shall we.'

Davina was struggling to keep her eyes focused. She raised her glass as if to propose a toast. 'Well at least your husband isn't fucking a Thai lady boy!'

Lois nearly choked. 'I beg your pardon!'

'Yes! There you have it!' Davina was slurring quite badly. 'Now we're all in confession mode!'

'No!' Bo's mouth dropped open.

'Yes! Why do you think we came back from the Far East? Because my husband couldn't keep his hands off the locals, that's why!'

'Jesus Christ!' Bo mouthed.

'I came home one day to find him in bed with a Thai boy. Angelica's brother in fact. So just count your blessings it was only the baby sitter Neil was shagging!'

Lois put her hand over Davina's. 'For the love of God, you poor woman!'

Bo was still shaking her head. 'Angelica's brother! So you know Angelica's not from the Philippines then.'

'Of course she's fucking not!' Davina's head started to loll around. 'I wasn't born Davina you know! Changed my name from Donna. I do love telling Talia Grossman I was born on an estate, at least that's true.'

'Blimey.' Bo exchanged a glance with Lois. 'We should probably get the bill.' She waved her hand in the air, but there was no one around. 'I'll go up and ask for it.'

She walked through the terrace and waited at reception. There was no one there. The manager and a small group of waiting staff emerged from the kitchen. When they saw her, they looked like naughty children caught in the act.

'I just wanted the bill please?'

The manager recovered himself. 'Yes of course Madam. I'll bring it to the table.'

Bo walked back across the roof terrace, conscious of every eye on her. Lois was trying to make Davina drink a glass of water, but most of it was going down her shirt.

'God, Bo, I blame myself, she's bladdered!'

'I'm not surprised. She's not used to drinking! She told me she only ever has one gin and tonic on a Friday night.'

'Oh feck!'

Davina's eyes rolled around and she swayed forward slurring. 'Patpong! He fucking LOVED it there with his FUCKING Lady Boys.' She slumped back again.

'Lois, I don't think she can walk.'

A waitress came up to the table. 'Ms Shaunnessy?'

Lois looked guilty. 'Yes.'

'Your driver is waiting outside, whenever you're ready.'

Bo hoped she hadn't noticed the state of Davina, now slumped forwards over her uneaten Sea Bass. 'Thanks. We're just waiting for the bill actually.'

The waitress looked awkward. 'Actually, I think the manager is coming over to talk to you about that.'

Lois and Bo looked at each other as the waitress walked away. 'Oh my God Bo. What's he going to say?'

They braced themselves for a scene, both women looking at Davina and wondering how they were going to lift her out of the restaurant.

'Bangkok girls? I should say so!' Davina was cackling quite loudly now.

Bo frowned. 'We can't let her make a show of herself. She'd die of shame if she was thrown out of her own club.'

Lois sobered up quickly. 'Bo, if I get Davina out of here, can you deal with the bill?'

Bo nodded, 'Of course, I'll put it on my card.' She lowered her voice. 'But how are you going to get her out without everyone noticing she's piss drunk?'

'Pass me your phone. Hello Lewis? It's Lois here. I think we might need a bit of a hand getting Davina into the car.'

Lois waved her hand in the air to call the waitress over. 'I'm going to need a couple of strong young men to help me.' Lois spoke under her breath, 'My friend here is having a severe allergic reaction. I don't want to cause a scene, but I think someone must be eating a walnut salad on another table. She's very sensitive, that's all it takes.'

'Oh my God.' The waitress rushed off to summon two young waiters.

Lois was commanding, 'Quickly, that's it, I just need her supported down the stairs. Our driver has an epi-pen in the car.'

Lois strode across the roof terrace her voice raised. 'Nut allergy coming through!' Davina was hastily lifted out of her seat and borne swiftly through the restaurant. Lois turned and addressed the other tables. 'Anaphylactic shock! There's a nut somewhere around here. She pointed accusingly. Guests were looking guiltily into their salads. 'She'll be fine. Just need to get her to the car.'

Bo was left staring after them. Alone now at the table she reached into her handbag for her wallet. This was going to be expensive. The Rosé was £28 a bottle. The manager came rushing up to the table

She looked up and tried to assume a confident smile. 'So sorry, if I could just have the bill?'

'There is no bill Madam.'

'Oh, does it go on her account? It's just that I don't want my friend to have to pay for all of us, so if you don't mind I'll settle up.'

'There is no bill, we just watched the interview Madam.'

'What! Oh God.' She started to flush.

'The kitchen staff and I would like you to accept dinner as a small gesture of admiration if you like.'

She didn't speak, but stared at him in disbelief.

'You are brave Ms Maloney and honest. Shall I help you on with your coat.'

'Yes, thank you. Thank you very much.'

'I hope your friend makes a speedy recovery.'

'Oh yes, I'm sure she'll be fine tomorrow.'

25

Thirty pieces of silver...

Lois was over the road with Davina who was still feeling the after effects of the night before. Davina had come over for breakfast. Her hair was disheveled and enormous sunglasses couldn't disguise bloodshot eyes and pallid cheeks. She waved away a bacon sandwich, clearly fighting nausea, while Lois read out the newspaper headlines.

'Forgiving Bernadette! *Last night, the nation watched agog...Bernadette Maloney's no holds barred interview strikes a chord with the British public...Heartfelt confession turns the tide...Bernadette Maloney, once again the nation's sweetheart.*

'Listen to this Bo! '*Donations to the charity PRETERM have reached £2 million as a huge wave of public sympathy follows TV confession...Viewing figures hit an estimated 9.5 million. 9.5 million!*'

Every tabloid, Sunday supplement and gossip column had covered the story. She was exonerated. It seemed the nation had decided to offer her a pardon after all. She still didn't dare look at social media.

'It's over Bo! You confessed all and in spite of that little vixen's attempts to screw it up, they could see it was genuine. They're on your side Bo!' Lois clearly expected her to be more relieved, excited, unburdened. She wasn't sure how she felt about the sudden adulation.

The red light on the answer phone blinked insistently. Bo sighed as she played back the messages.

Bo it's Betsy! Here me out! We're talking long term now darling, a career in the media, clothing ranges, advice columns, not written by you obviously, regular slots on TV panels, Loose Women, the sky's the limit. You cannot pass this up because of your personal feelings towards me! Bo, pick up the phone! Message left at 9.54am

Bo! It's Betsy. Look, it's always business with me darling, I don't do feelings. What happened before, don't take it so personally. I just didn't think I could offer you any more help. Message left at 10.06am

Bo, pick up the phone, I've had two high street retailers on the phone. I presume you haven't got your old job back? Look, let's not be naïve here, Neil will want his share of the house which will mean selling it and what are you going to do for money? Call me! Message left at 10. 21am.

Davina had recovered sufficiently to take Lois to the tennis club. Lois was decked out, head to toe in Davina's designer tennis whites. She was looking quite pleased with herself as they both drove off in their sunglasses. Bo had a meeting with a builder so she left them to it.

She wandered through the old apple trees, cup of tea in hand, picking her way between tall clumps of nettles and brambles. Neil had never liked this house, he had always preferred a new build, but this was the one concession he had allowed her when they moved here for his job. At least the state of the place meant that they could afford it. It could be lovely, but they'd never really got round to doing it up. Bo loved its tumbledown walls, old apple trees and scruffy charm. The builder had left and promised to send her a quote. There was much sucking in of air and shaking his head as he surveyed the damp old apple store, which presumably meant she should brace herself for a sky high quote. It was sunny and warm and she sat on the old orchard wall, closed her eyes and felt the warmth on her face. Liam would be home in exactly two weeks. Just 14 days until she picked him up from the airport. She had started to cross off the days on the kitchen calendar. She was planning to spring clean the house, maybe paint his bedroom, tidy up the garden, plant up some containers.

A slight movement at the bottom of the garden and the click of the gate made her open her eyes. A woman walked into the garden and up the path. It wasn't unusual, it was easy to miss the front of the house. The woman must have been in her early fifties, grey hair and a worried expression made her look slightly older. She was hesitant as she approached and Bo noticed she couldn't look her in the eye.

'It's Bernadette isn't it?'

'Yes?'

'Bernadette Maloney?'

Bo nodded.

'I'm Linda Jarvis.'

Bo didn't register at first. Jarvis. Why did that name sound familiar.

'You might not know my name, but you took my baby. A long time ago now. I'm the mother of the baby.'

Bo could feel the colour drain from her face. *Why has she come here? She's going to stab me. I am going to die and I will never see Liam again.*

Seeing her expression, the older woman explained. 'I just wanted to meet you, that's all. To see you face to face, put it to rest.'

Bo's hand was shaking and she spilled some of her tea. 'You saw the interview?'

'Yes I did.'

They stood awkwardly for a moment. 'You'd better come in.'

The woman followed her through the garden door and into the kitchen. 'What a lovely cottage.'

'Thank you.' Bo replied. 'Would you like some tea?'

Bo pulled out a chair for her and they both sat down. She didn't appear to want to say anything. Bo filled the silence. 'I am sorry you know, so sorry.' Bo looked at the floor. 'I hope that came across in the interview. I was mad with grief. I don't think I knew what I was doing.' The woman looked at her and didn't reply.

'It changed the course of my life. I'm sure it changed yours too.' Bo added hurriedly.

'Yes it did, I had terrible problems, adjusting.'

'Yes.'

'It was a few years before I could let her go anywhere with anyone else. I had very bad panic attacks. And then when the second baby came, I suffered severe post-natal depression. The doctor said it was most likely a reaction to what happened before.'

'Oh God!'

'The marriage broke down.'

'Jesus!'

'And the strangest thing. I was one of your biggest fans, followed your advice blog, read all the articles about you. I really liked what you said about women being too hard on themselves, all of that. So strange, to find out that it was you! That you were the evil woman in the hoodie.' She gave a little laugh.

I'm definitely going to die. There will be a pool of blood on the kitchen floor.

Bo stood up to put the kettle on. She glimpsed the oven glove on the island. If she tried to stab her, maybe she could intercept the knife with the oven glove. As she came back to sit down she moved it onto the table.

The woman carried on. 'I thought I'd got over it, put it in the past. And then all of this hit the headlines.'

'I know.' Bo shook her head. 'It was all completely out of the blue, all this madness. The cliff, Melinda, the accidental hero bit, the fame. I didn't invite it, but once you have TV cameras and journalists camped outside your house, well, it took on a life of its own.'

'Did you not think they'd find out who you were?'

There it was again 'who I am'. It made Bo's voice shake. 'No, yes. I suppose I didn't expect any of the fuss and media stuff to last more than a week, but as it snowballed, yes, I was more and more anxious.'

'You've done alright though by the looks of things. Is your husband not home?' Bo felt sick.

'No. He left.'

'Oh yes, I read that.' The woman looked around the room. She seemed fixated on the calendar, where Bo had circled the 24th with 'LIAM'S HOME!!!!' written in big bold letters and each day crossed off for the last month.

'You might have already heard me say this, but when I took your baby.' She couldn't explain but she felt compelled to try. The woman turned and looked at her impassively. 'I'm not sure if I knew she wasn't mine, but I certainly didn't think she was anyone else's. Does that make any sense at all?' She knew it probably didn't.

The woman stared straight ahead.

'I've thought about what I did to you almost every day for twenty one years. You must have gone out of your mind.' Bo's voice caught.

The woman nodded.

'She was safe, you know that, as safe as if she'd been my own. I promise you, I never meant her any harm.'

With no warning, a single tear rolled down the woman's cheek. Bo wanted to comfort her but she knew it wouldn't be welcome.

'You've been a shadowy figure you see, all these years. That picture of you, the evil woman in the hoodie, kidnapping my baby. I just wanted to come and see what you were really like. Find out if you were a normal human being.'

'I understand. You wanted to slay the monster.' *My God, why did she say that?*

'I couldn't understand you see, how anyone could possibly be so evil, to take a new born baby away from its mother. I thought you must be some kind of monster, but then I saw the interview. I didn't realise you see, that you'd lost your baby, that you were suffering, you know.'

'No.' Bo looked at the floor. 'I don't expect you to forgive me but does it help at least, to know about the circumstances?'

The woman nodded her acknowledgement. 'She's 21 now, my daughter.'

'I know she is.' Bo looked away. There was a long silence. She looked up at the calendar. 'My son, Liam, he's been away travelling. He gets back in two weeks.'

'No!' The woman looked horrified suddenly. She put her finger up to her lips and shook her head manically.

Bo flinched. She was gesticulating urgently, but Bo couldn't make out what she was trying to say. Had she gone too far, assuming an understanding, that they could chat easily about their children like newly acquainted mothers?

The woman spotted something. She stood up suddenly and strode across the kitchen floor, she was behaving so strangely and now only inches away from the knife block.

Bo braced herself, but instead, she picked up a pad of post it notes next to the phone, scribbled something hurriedly and came back to the table, slapping the scrawled note on the table in front of Bo.

I'm taped up. Everything recorded for the paper. Keep the kids out of it.

She looked apologetically at Bo and lifted her jacket slightly to reveal a wire taped to her hip. Bo exhaled deeply, consumed by relief. Of course. She hadn't come here of her own accord. They looked at each other and Bo smiled before taking the pen and writing another note.

Thank you

The woman looked surprised. Bo wrote again.

Thank you for telling me. Keep talking!

Bo gestured for her to say something but she looked confused and didn't reply.

'Well, I'd better get you that cup of tea then?'

She boiled the kettle again and they scribbled furiously while the noise covered their silence.

How much are they paying you?
£10,000 for this, £15,000 more for a picture
Picture?
2 photographers waiting outside the front door

Bo raised her eyebrows. She couldn't help thinking that Betsy could have got her more.

'Sugar Linda?'

'No thank you. And I never said you were Satanic by the way. I just wanted you to know that. They put words in your mouth.'

'They do.' Bo brought the mugs over. They sipped their tea politely. It was hard to improvise. After a long silence, Bo wrote a note and passed it to her.

Ready to face the cameras?

Linda looked confused and picked up the pen.

You'll do it?

Bo nodded. The least she could do was get this woman her money.

'How did you get here Linda?'

'Train to Brinton and then a taxi.'

'Do you need me to call you one.'

'No I'll be fine, I'm getting a lift.'

'Of course.' Bo gestured towards the door. 'Shall we?'

Linda nodded. They stood in the hallway a moment, both reluctant to open the door. Linda put her hand on Bo's. 'Good bye Bernadette. It was good to meet you. I wish you well.'

Bo smiled. 'Thank you.'

She opened the door and the two women stood awkwardly next to each other as the photographers stopped chatting and rushed towards them.

26

Have you completely lost your marbles? So you give away £120K to charity, fair enough, everyone loves you for that, blah blah. But now you've gone and given away the scoop of the century AND the photoshoot for absolutely BLOODY NOTHING! We could have got six figures minimum. Listen, I know for a fact you haven't got enough money to survive without your husband, so WHAT THE HELL are you doing? You NEED ME Bernadette! **Message left at 6.36pm.**

'No I don't Betsy.'

Bo walked over to the phone. **Message deleted.**

She took a bottle of wine out of the fridge and a glass off the sideboard. The sun was still warm as she walked through the garden gate and headed up the track towards Devil's Chimney. Lois had turned down her offer of a walk and was going round to Davina's. It was a beautiful evening and she was grateful for the chance to be alone after the events of the last few weeks.

The chalk track was dry and dusty and the hillside covered in grass and buttercups. How different to the last time she had made her way up here. After 10 minutes she rounded the final bend, not quite so breathless as last time. She stood and took in the view, the vast expanse of the Wiltshire Downs rolling out in front of her. The ledge where they had sat had tumbled down and shattered at the base of the cliff, leaving a sheer rock face fenced off from walkers. She was glad you could no longer go to the edge. There was a bench a little way back from the rock. She sat down and poured herself a glass.

The gentle green and yellow landscape bathed in evening sunlight was so far removed from that night in January, it was hard to believe what had actually taken place. She realized as she looked around that for the first time in a very long time, she felt calm, no anxiety, just a certainty that whatever happened next, she would be able to manage. She didn't blame Neil. After all, wasn't it her choice to become so fearful, so reliant on others. 'Such an exciting life ahead of you', Sister Marianne had said. She exhaled deeply and took a swig of wine. Well it wasn't over yet.

She thought about Mel and the boyfriend. She was probably fine but she would go and see her tomorrow, just to make sure.

There was a movement behind her and she looked up.

'Ben!'

'I came round to see you. Lois said you'd come up here.'

'It's the best place to see the sun set.'

'It's beautiful.' He sat down beside her. 'I just thought I'd check if you needed airlifting off.'

'Thanks.' She couldn't help smirking.

'You're not planning on jumping then?'

'No. I just came up here for some peace and a glass of wine. It's been a busy few days.

'Yes. I saw the interview.'

'Oh shit, really? For some reason, I didn't think you'd watch it.'

'Of course I did. Especially the bit about you not being with your husband anymore.'

'Yes, what a stitch up. I wasn't expecting them to announce that on national TV, anything to boost the ratings.'

'Is it true?'

'Yes. I think you could tell I wasn't exactly acting like the devoted wife.'

'No.' He looked around at the view. 'So you finally kicked him out?'

'He left and we've agreed to separate.'

'I'm not going to say I'm sorry.'

She didn't know what to say. They sat for a bit, just looking at the setting sun.

He broke the silence. 'I am sorry about the other night though.'

'It wasn't ideal was it.'

'No.'

'I say the other night,' he sounded like he was struggling to find the words. 'It was really just the morning that was the problem.'

'Yes.'

'So you don't regret the bit before the next morning.'

'No. From what I can remember.'

'It was just when you sobered up, that the problems started.'

'Exactly.' She laughed. 'I don't regret sleeping with you if that's what you're saying.'

He smiled. 'Good.' They were silent again.

He looked around, taking in the jagged clifftop. 'I'm surprised there isn't a plaque. Where exactly did you fall from?'

'It's not there anymore, the ledge we were sitting on gave way under us.'

'It was incredible, what you did. You didn't let her go.'

'Oh my God, don't you start! You sound like Katy bloody Partridge.'

'Seriously. You saved her life.'

'Shut up!'

'Sorry.'

She tried distraction. 'Would you like a glass of wine?'

'Why not.' She filled up the glass and handed it to him.

'The night I picked you up from the station, you'd been to visit your daughter's grave?'

'Yes. It was the anniversary.'

'I had no idea. I'm sorry.'

'Well why would you. And I'm sorry I barged into the room with all your wife's things.' Now that she had mentioned her she felt bold enough to carry on. 'Do you mind me asking what happened?'

'We'd been married for about two years, together for years before that. We were trying for a baby. It wasn't working out, so they offered to do some tests. When they scanned her they found she had ovarian cancer.'

'Bloody hell.'

'She died two years later.' He sounded matter of fact but she knew he was anything but.

She didn't know what to say. He broke the silence. 'It's hard knowing what to do with your memories.'

She nodded. 'It is. You don't ever want to forget.'

'No. But you have to be allowed to move on.'

'Well I'm not really the best example of that.' She turned to look at him. 'Do you really not pray?'

'I was lying.'

She smiled. 'I thought so.'

The sun had dipped behind the hills.

He sat back and stretched out his legs. 'So what are you going to do with your life Bo Maloney? Now that you're young, free and single?'

'I'm not sure about the 'young' bit, but free and single sounds very good.'

'Is that right?'

'Yes it is. One night stands are a bit shoddy in your forties.'

'I wouldn't know.'

She laughed. 'I expect you'll find out soon enough. Anyway shall we go before it gets dark and they send the helicopter for us?' They got up from the bench and started to walk down the hill.

'Seriously though.' She looked at him intently. 'I am looking forward to being completely self-reliant. You see everyone thinks I need them and I don't.' As she said it, she tripped on a large stone and stumbled forwards. He instinctively reached out and caught her before she fell.

'What?' He was smirking.

'Don't say anything.'

'I wasn't going to.'

They walked down the path in silence towards the house.

27

She opened her eyes. The sun was pouring in through the half closed curtains straight into her face. She squinted as she looked around the room, taking in the discarded clothes on the floor, an empty glass of wine by the bed.

There was a gentle, rhythmic breathing next to her. Instinctively she clutched the duvet to her. *Sexy Vet is in my bedroom, lying on my Egyptian cotton fitted sheets.* It took a considerable physical effort to stop the giggle from bursting forth.

She looked sideways without moving her head. There he was, naked apart from his watch. In her bed. His brown back a couple of inches away from her face. She could smell the soapy sandalwood of his aftershave. *Oh my God.* At least he was still asleep.

I've done it again. I've slept with him. It's fine. I'm not a child anymore, not some breathless 20 year old, wondering where it's going from here. Would it be awkward again when he wakes up? Well at least she wasn't clutching his wedding photo.

The hand that was draped over the sheet, suddenly moved. The whole brown torso flipped over and the other hand snaked purposefully across her breasts and pulled her towards him.

He smiled. 'Good morning.'

'Hi.' Thank God he couldn't read her mind.

'Bit less awkward than last time?'

'I think so.'

'Good.' He looked at his watch. 'I'd better get going, I'm working at 11.'

She glanced sideways and saw his watch. *10.30! Shit!*'

He looked amused. 'What's the hurry?'

'I'm supposed to be somewhere at 10.'

There was a familiar ring from the other side of the room. 'Oh God, that'll be Lois. Where's my phone? I've got no clothes on.'

'Hold on, I'll get it.' He leapt unselfconsciously across the room and she had to look away.

'It should be in the pocket of my black jeans.' He found it and handed it to her.

There were two phone messages and a text from Lois.

Bernadette Maloney get your clothes on, we're waiting in Davina's drive! OPERATION MELINDA!!!

'I've got to go. We're planning to save Melinda.'

He shrugged his shoulders. 'What from?'

'Herself mainly.'

She hurriedly texted back. **Sorry! I'll be there in 10 mins!**

He pulled on his jeans and came round to her side of the bed. He was laughing. 'Does it feel less sordid now that it's a two night stand?'

She sat up, still clutching the duvet to her. 'A little.'

'Of course now you've got to get out of bed with no clothes on which will be embarrassing.'

'No, because you're going to pass me my dressing gown from the back of the door.'

He laughed as he passed it to her. She walked down the stairs in front of him and found the front door key in her handbag to let him out.

Standing in the doorway as he got in his car, she wondered what to say. He hadn't kissed her or said good bye but strode off without a backward glance. Still, she didn't think she should shut the door before he had gone. Was one of them supposed to say something? God, this was awkward. She rather hoped her wholesome neighbours would walk past and see her waving off her younger lover. He started the engine and she turned to go back into the house.

He wound down the window. 'Come round tonight and I'll order curry.'

'Curry!' She was so surprised it came out like a screech.

'Yes. Do you not eat curry? Is it not sophisticated enough for someone of your age?'

'No.' She turned round and gave him a withering look. 'Curry would be good.' And before he could wind up the window. 'Chicken biryani, pilau rice, one Peshwari Naan and Tarka Dahl.'

'Good.' He looked impressed. 'And wine? Presumably you'll need wine to sleep with me again.'

'Yes.' She smiled. 'Plenty of it.'

'I'll get a case.'

'I'll see you later then.' She tried to sound breezy and nonchalant.

He nodded. 'I'll pick you up at 8.' As he wound up the window she was desperate for him to drive away so that he couldn't see the stupid grin on her face.

He beeped as he accelerated off and his car disappeared round the corner in a swirl of dust.

Before she could go back inside, Lois appeared like an apparition, striding through the dust cloud and up the drive towards her.

'Bernadette Maloney! We've been sitting waiting for you for half an hour, while you've been shagging James Herriot there!'

'Sorry Lois! Just give me five minutes and I'll come over.' Lois raised her eyebrows. Bo held up her hand. 'Seriously Lois, five minutes!'

Lois smiled and walked away. 'Dirty cow!' She shouted over her shoulder. 'I'm surprised you can walk!'

Fifteen minutes later, they were hurtling down a dual carriageway in Davina's Range Rover. They had decided that Davina was the better driver, in case they needed to get away quickly. In spite of much longwinded debate, Operation Melinda lacked any kind of coherent plan. There was instead a vague idea that they would check out if she was OK and if the Dave person was a genuine problem.

'Do we know where we're going? Romney Leys isn't it?'

Davina wore her bug eye sunglasses. 'Yes all sorted, the postcode's in the satnav. I got the address from Katy Partridge.'

'So? How many times?' Lois snorted from the front seat.

'What?' Bo pretended not to know what she meant.

'Put us out of our misery! How many times did you shag James Herriot?'

'No comment.'

'More than once?'

'Of course.'

'More than three times?'

'All I will say is this. More times than the entire last 10 years of my marriage.' They all screeched with laughter.

Lois looked at her in the mirror. 'It won't last you know! Once the passion is spent.' Lois lowered her voice. 'And once he finds out you're old enough to be his mother.'

'I'm not Lois I told you, he's 36.'

'36!'

'Yes. Anyway, I know very well it won't last.' She caught Lois' eye in the mirror. 'But he's asked me over tonight for curry and sex.'

'Curry and sex!' Lois was dumbstruck.

Davina looked slightly disgusted. 'Girls! Can you please pay attention, there's a sign to the left for Romney Leys, but the Satnav is telling me to keep going straight.'

'Keep going straight!' They all agreed.

The satnav led them into a housing estate. It was grey and bleak, with no one around apart from a couple of teenagers in hoodies kicking a beer can across the road. They found the right house number and Davina decided to stay in the car, while Lois and Bo walked up the path to the front door and rang the bell.

It took a long time before anyone answered. Eventually there was a shuffling and a blurred figure appeared through the opaque broken glass. She wore stained trackie pants and a dressing gown and as she opened the door they were hit by a strong smell of alcohol.

'Are you Mrs Johnson?' Bo tried. 'Melinda's mother?'

She took the cigarette out of her mouth. 'Who wants to know?'

'We're friends of hers.' Lois added.

'She an't got no friends.' The woman looked them up and down suspiciously and took another drag.

Bo tried again. 'Could you tell us where to find her.'

The woman was obviously bored of the conversation now and started to close the door. 'She don't live here no more. Moved in with her boyfriend.'

Bo stepped forward, tempted to put her foot in the door. 'Where do they live?'

She waved her cigarette to where they had entered the estate. 'Burton Leys estate, other side of the roundabout.'

'Do you know the street number?' Lois added.

'Haven't got a clue.' She shrugged and shut the door on them.

They stood looking at each other. 'Great, now what do we do?'

'I don't know.' Bo started to walk back to the car. 'Drive round the estate a bit I suppose. Ask if anyone knows her?'

'We'll never find her.' Lois was losing her enthusiasm.

Davina drove round for half an hour, back and forth, down each side street. They came back and asked the two boys kicking the can and then an old lady on the Burton Leys estate if they had seen a tall redheaded teenage girl, but no one had.

Lois caught Bo's anxious face in the mirror. 'We're going to have to leave it Bo. We'll go home and see if we can do a bit more digging.' Davina turned the car round towards the roundabout.

Bo stared helplessly out of the window. 'Hang on! There she is! That's her at the bus stop!' Mel was getting off the bus, shopping bags in hand.

Lois was impatient now. 'Well she looks absolutely fine to me.' She was right. Her hair was bouncing as she walked along in sunglasses and high heels, carrying two enormous shopping bags with her. 'Look at her, Bo! She looks great.'

Bo frowned. 'She's well out of her mother's place that's for sure.'

Davina slowed the car down near the bus stop. 'Let's just say hi, make sure she's OK and get out of here!'

Bo got out of the car. 'Wait there. I just want to talk to her.' She walked up the pavement towards her.

'Mel?'

'Baloney! What are you doing here?' She looked anxiously around.

'How are you? I just wanted to see how you are. Is this where you're living? Can I come in for a bit?'

'No!' Mel looked horrified. 'You shouldn't be here. You'll get me in trouble.'

'What kind of trouble?'

She looked around again, as if they were being followed. 'There's a playground round the back of the building. It's always empty. We can go there for a bit.'

She led Bo down an alley way and into the small playground.

They sat on a park bench. 'Well you look well anyway.' Mel shrugged and as Bo tried to help her lift one of her shopping bags her sunglasses slipped, revealing a large purple shape around her left eye.

Bo sighed. 'He hits you.'

Mel nodded, staring straight ahead. She spoke in a monotone. 'Thanks for coming. It's nice of you but I've got to go. I've got to clean the flat and get his tea ready.'

Bo held onto her arm. 'Why don't you go to the police.'

Mel stared blankly ahead. 'They've been round a couple of times. The neighbours called them one night. The walls are so thin they can hear every word.'

'And what did they do?'

'Nothing, said I could press charges, but I can't. He said he'd kill me and I believe him.'

Bo held her hand. 'Mel. You don't have to live like this.'

Mel snatched her hand away and took out a packet of cigarettes. 'Easy for you to say Baloney.'

'I thought you made some money with the interviews.'

'I did, 5 grand. He took the lot. I don't have my own money.'

'Can't you go home to your mothers?'

Mel lit a cigarette. 'My mum just drinks all day. He brings her vodka and she lets him in so he can bring me back and beat the shit out of me again.' She looked older than her 17 years. 'Listen Baloney, thanks for coming and all. I'd love to stay chatting with you but he's back in 20 minutes and if I'm not there I'll be in trouble all right.'

Bo put a hand on her arm. 'Why don't you come with me?'

Mel shook her head. 'I've got to go now. It'll be alright.'

Bo stood up and shouted. 'No, it won't be alright Mel, IT ISN'T GOING TO BE ALRIGHT. It'll get worse. It always does.'

Mel started to cry, her shoulders heaving.

Bo held onto her shoulders. 'Listen, I'm not leaving you with him. And I'm not leaving unless you come with me, so we're both in the shit now.'

'Why can't you just stay out of it, you'll only make it worse for me.' Melinda shouted at her angrily. 'Just fucking leave me alone!'

Bo shook her head. 'No. You come with me now or I'm staying put.'

Mel could only just speak in between sobs. 'I'm so scared. Last night he dragged me across the floor by my hair.' Bo put her arm around her, the tears had soaked her shirt. 'I thought I was going to die.'

'You're not going to die. You're going to come with me. Go and get some of your things, quickly.'

Melinda nodded, but Bo wasn't so sure. 'I'll come with you to the flat.'

Mel shook her head. 'No, you stay outside, in case he comes back.'

She picked up her shopping and hurried off back down the alley. Bo kicked herself for not following her and finding out which door she went through. She walked round to the front of the building. No sign of her. Why the hell did she tell her to get her things, as if she needed some kind of overnight bag when she was about to have the crap beaten out of her. *For God's sake!* Bo felt utterly sick. She paced around the pavement, Davina and Lois up ahead in the Range Rover saw her and started to turn the car around.

They pulled up alongside her and Lois wound down the window. 'What's happening Bo? Ready to go?'

'No! He beats her, she's scared for her life and he's on his way home any minute.'

'Can't we call the police?'

'They can't do anything unless she presses charges. I don't know which flat she went into.' Bo was breathless. 'She said she'd come with us, but she's not going to. Too scared. And now she's disappeared.' She could feel pains in her chest. 'Shit. I think this is him coming.' She knew it was him.

'Come on Mel! Please! Where the hell are you?'

There was a look about him, even in the distance, an angry way that his limbs moved. As he got closer Bo recognized his face from the pictures on Mel's phone.

'Get in Bo, he might recognize you. I'll try to buy some time.' Lois got out of the car and walked up to him. Davina snorted at the wheel, 'This is completely insane!' Bo heard Lois talking to him. 'I'm looking for the Romney Leys estate, is this it?'

'No.'

'Are you sure, because someone else said this was Romney Leys.'

'This is Burton Leys.' He mumbled and tried to get past, but Lois blocked his way.

'Hold on, let me just get my phone out here and check the address they gave me?' Lois fumbled around in her bag and they did a dance on the pavement as he tried to get past her.

Bo put her hands to her face. Davina was right, this was crazy and utterly pointless. She looked through her fingers and as she studied his face and watched his lips moving, he caught sight of something. His expression changed entirely from sullen to snarling. He was spitting and shouting at someone. She looked round to see what he was looking at. It was Mel, coming out of the building, a small rucksack on her back and a look of such fear on her face that Bo opened the door and screamed at her. 'Get in the car!' Mel started running towards the open door.

'Where d'you think you're going, you fucking slag!' He tried to push past Lois, but she got in the way.

'Get out of my fucking way!' He was screaming, his face purple with rage.

— 311 —

Bo pulled Mel hurriedly into the car and slammed the door. Getting out the other side, she sprinted up the street to where Lois and Dave were now shouting. Davina followed slowly in the Range Rover. Bo waved at her desperately to go. 'Just drive Davina, take her away. Call the police!'

Lois squared up to him. 'And what are you going to do if I don't? Are you going to hit me? Come on then, you cowardly little shit, let's see you hit a woman!'

Just as Bo caught up with them. Thwack! There was a strange crunching noise as Dave's fist met Lois' nose and Bo gasped as a spray of blood covered the front of her shirt. 'I'll fucking kill you. Slags!' Lois went flying backwards. Bo grabbed his fists. He was incredibly strong. *Please God he doesn't have a knife!* She held the fists firmly, but couldn't stop them moving and he swung a punch towards her, hitting her straight in the eye. The only way to avoid the blows was to hold him tightly round the waist, her head pressed to his belly in a strangely tender embrace. A few people came out of their houses to watch the entertainment, but no one moved to help. Two of them held up their phones to film the fight.

Lois was up off the ground. 'You fucker!' She lunged towards him. Bo could see that Davina hadn't driven off and instead, Mel had escaped from the car and was shouting and running towards them. Even with Bo clinging to his middle, he managed to lurch towards Mel. He pushed her backwards and shoved her to the ground, kicking her as she lay on the pavement. 'Bastard!' Bo released herself from his middle and as he continued to kick, she jumped on his back. He swung her round, like some strange bucking bronco party ride, her fingers rammed up his nose. Round and round they went, she could feel herself slipping as he struggled to free himself. All she could think of was to put her hands over his eyes. His arms flailed around, temporarily blinded, trying to make contact with the burden on his back. 'Help us!' She screamed. But no one came, they just stood impassively in their doorways, holding up their phones.

In all the commotion he hadn't noticed Lois who had managed to get behind him. She reached for her upturned handbag and grabbed something from inside, a nylon shopping bag. Struggling to her feet she rammed it firmly over his head, pulling the drawstrings tightly around his neck. He floundered backwards across the pavement shouting abuse and giving the three women just enough time to run screaming to the car. Wheels screeched as Davina accelerated off and they looked backwards to see Dave ripping a Bag for Life off his head and kicking it across the road.

Once they were safely over the roundabout and driving up the dual carriageway, Lois held a bunch of tissues to her nose. 'Well, that was awkward!'

They were all too shell shocked to reply.

Bo sat in the back with Mel. She looked down at her own hands and noticed they had started to shake. 'Alright?'

Mel nodded. 'It just hurts to breathe.'

'I'm not surprised.' Bo pressed her fingers round her face and winced.

'Is everyone OK?' Davina looked sideways. 'Good God Lois, your nose!' It had started to swell and Lois pulled the mirror down to have a look. 'Bloody hell! Well I'll tell you this much Mel, you may not be pressing charges, but I bloody will!'

Mel started to cry. Bo squeezed her hand. 'It's over, you're safe.' She tried to make her smile. 'You've got fighting fairy godmothers.'

'Ugly sisters more like.' Lois snorted through the blood soaked tissues. Davina slowed down and pulled the car up outside Costa Coffee by the side of the train station.

Lois, who had tilted her head back to stop the blood flow, looked round impatiently. 'Why are we stopping Davina? I don't think anyone wants a coffee.'

Davina opened the car door. 'I just want some expert advice. Stay there!'

She was back a moment later, Mateus running out after her in his Costa Coffee uniform. He gently removed the tissues from Lois' face and felt the bridge of her nose. He nodded at Davina. 'It's broken.' Bo waved him off and pointed to Mel. 'I'm fine, it's just the eye. Have a look at her ribs though, she got quite a kicking, says it hurts to breathe.' Mateus pressed her ribs. 'I can't be sure, it feels like two of them might be fractured. You need to go to A&E. Do you want me to come?'

Davina shook her head. 'We'll be fine.' She reached for a packet of wet wipes and started to rub the blood stains off the cream leather seat.

Bo could tell Lois was in a bad way. There was no protest and she hadn't even asked why the Costa Coffee assistant manager was checking her injuries.

When Davina led them into A&E, they were a sorry sight. They limped slowly behind her, Mel bent double, Lois' face smeared with blood, her nose three times its normal size and Bo with a dark purple eye and split lip.

The nurse took down their details. 'If I can have your names and dates of birth, you can take a seat and wait to be called. Have you been in a road accident?'

'No,' Davina replied. 'We've been in a fight.'

28

She sat on Ben's sofa, a bag of frozen peas over her eyes as he dipped poppadoms into the chutney and fed them to her. By now her lip was also swollen so she drank wine through the side of her mouth with a straw.

They had just watched the fight on YouTube for the fourth time. By 9 o'clock it had 1.2 million likes and 460,000 shares. #broncobernadette and #baggedthebastard! were both trending on twitter and Lois had phoned to say that the press were once again camped outside her house.

'It's funny isn't it. I blamed all those people with their phones for being useless, but in the end, it was their filming that led to him being charged.'

'I'm not sure 'funny' is the word I'd have chosen.' Did you not think he could have had a knife? I wish I'd asked how you were planning to save Melinda.'

'Would you have tried to stop us?'

'Probably not. But at least I would have come with you.'

'Well he's been arrested anyway, three counts of GBH, he'll get five years hopefully.' She sucked on the wine straw. 'The best bit was when they breathalyzed Davina.' She sniggered under the bag of peas. 'She was so angry.'

'Did they not believe you?'

'I don't know. But while we were in A&E a nurse showed the police the footage of the fight. It was already all over the internet.'

'And where's Mel now?'

'Staying at Davina's, she broke two ribs.'

'Jesus. Two broken ribs, one broken nose, a black eye and a split lip. Was it worth it?'

'Of course. It worked, she's safe.'

He ran his finger along her bottom lip. 'I thought you were prim when I first met you.'

She winced as he touched her. 'Well now you know, I have a criminal record and I like curries and fighting.'

He lifted off the frozen peas and looked at her eye. 'I'll give you something for the bruising.'

'You're a vet, not a doctor.'

He shrugged. 'Same thing.'

'Is it for labradors?'

'Probably.'

She pressed her finger to her eye. 'Do you think it will have faded by the time Liam gets home.'

'When does he get back?'

'Tuesday.'

'No.'

He went into the kitchen and came back with a tube of strong smelling gel.

Her phone vibrated on the table. She sighed. 'Oh God, I've just got to take this. I've been avoiding her.' She sat up on the sofa.

'Betsy! Yes it's me. I got all your messages thanks.'

She stood up and wandered to the far end of the room. 'No I know. You saw the footage. Really. Did they? No, no I don't intend to pass up every opportunity, not all of them. No, I agree I need an agent.' Her voice rose. 'I'm agreeing with you Betsy!   I actually have a new agent.' There was an explosion of abuse down the phone. 'Well if you let me speak I'll tell you. She's from the Edgerton Davis Agency......Davina Edgerton Davis. Yes. Well you might not have heard of her Betsy but she is very experienced.... well connected..... Only 15% actually and she is more aligned to my way of thinking. No YOU sacked ME and I have the email from you to prove it.....what? I don't think I need a mindfulness coach or diet lunch deliveries. No. I'm sorry. I don't want a yoga trainer. I just need someone who understands what I will and won't do.' There was a further torrent from the other end of the phone. 'This is pointless. Sure OK, you do that! Bye Betsy.'

She exhaled deeply as she put the phone down. 'Sorry about that.'

He was laughing. 'My God. Was that the owner of the unfortunate Bichon Frise?'

'It was.' She sat down again.

'You're going to keep on with the media stuff?'

'Some of it. I'm not going to sell my soul to every shop on the high street like she would, but I need to make a living. I've got things I want to do.' She didn't mention the ex-husband that would need paying off.

He smiled. 'Good for you. Now put your head back for a second and I'll put this stuff on your eye.'

She closed her eyes. 'It smells disgusting. Is it seriously for dogs?'

'Of course it's not.' He was very gentle as he dabbed it round her eyes. 'It's for cows.'

'Do they get many black eyes.' She mumbled.

'Other end actually, when they've given birth.'

'My God, that's disgusting. Is that a new tube? You're not even qualified to treat humans are you?'

'Yes I am actually. I'm very qualified. Now does it hurt anywhere else?'

She kept her eyes shut. 'I don't think so, but I should probably have some more wine to dull the pain.'

Epilogue

Vanity Fair Women of the Year Awards

Bo glanced across the table at Liam in his black dinner jacket. She smiled. He looked very handsome and she could see it wasn't going unnoticed by several young women on an adjacent table. He caught her eye and laughed at her expression. 'Mum!' He came over to her side of the table and crouched down beside her. 'I'm not even joking, I've been offered a modelling contract! This woman just gave me her card.'

She frowned. 'Don't you even think about it Liam Spicer. You're going to be a famous engineer, not a bloody underwear model!'

'Calm down Mum, I was just saying.' He grinned.

Ben sat on her right and whispered into her ear. 'You look stunning.' He kissed the inside of her hand. 'Davina wants to know if she should confirm or deny.'

Bo looked at him. 'What do you think?'

'Don't mind either way.' He shrugged.

'Shall we wait until we get back from India. Three more weeks. As long as Liam and Lois know.'

Patrick and Lois had flown in the day before. 'Do you know', she sounded affronted. 'Patrick won't let Lois come and stay with me again, unless he's there.'

'I don't blame him.'

'Hello darlings!' Davina rushed over to the table, strikingly elegant in emerald lace and satin. 'I've just been schmoozing the Commissioning Editor of BBC Daytime. Gorgeous woman! Loads of opportunities! Quite a few retail brands here tonight and they all want to meet you Bo.'

Bo laughed. 'Well you know what you're doing Davina.' She took a sip of her drink and whispered, 'You know the drill. No diet food, definitely not personal loans, funeral plans or incontinence pads. And no exercise videos, mindfulness, anti-ageing products, hardcore porn, or gambling. Anything else is fine.'

Ben smiled. 'It doesn't leave her much to work with. How about a Playboy centerfold?'

'Why not.' Bo nodded.

Davina rolled her eyes. 'Very funny, now do you have your speech ready in case you win?'

'No, I thought I'd just wing it Davina.'

'Wing it?' She looked appalled.

'Yes. Whatever comes into my head! I should be fine, as long as I've had enough to drink.'

Davina sighed. 'I know you're laughing at me Bernadette, but you know the importance of detailed preparation.'

Bo squeezed her hand. 'I'm joking Davina. I've got the piece of paper in my bag, at least I think I do.'

'Good. And are you absolutely sure you don't want to go to the after parties? That's where all the networking takes place.'

Bo looked apologetic. 'We just wanted to have dinner with friends and family.' She was exhausted. She had finally taken herself off to the doctor this morning. She had been hoping to be prescribed HRT, it had certainly done the trick for Lois and her lack of energy lately was becoming a worry. He had carried out some blood tests and this afternoon had rung her with an entirely different diagnosis. She smiled to herself as she sipped on her drink, which everyone assumed was Prosecco and was in fact ginger ale. Even Ben hadn't noticed. No wonder she had struggled with her zip. She looked at his face and wondered what he would say when he found out. She would tell him after the scan next week.

Ben saw her smiling. 'What are you smirking at?'

'Just thinking about Melinda. She's coming later.' Bo looked up at Davina. 'Did you hear, she got an A* for Art & Design.'

'Very good. Now what do you want me to say to the press?' She looked at them expectantly. 'Confirm or deny?'

They turned to each other for a moment. 'Deny.'

Davina nodded. 'If you say so. Now when you said it had to be an Indian restaurant, I've struggled to find anything decent, but I have managed to book us a table at the most upmarket Indian restaurant I could find, contemporary Kashmiri cuisine.'

Bo smiled. 'Thank you Davina. As long as they do biryani. And poppadoms.'

Davina looked across the room. 'I need to catch up with Katy Partridge. Oh God, Lois has found Monty Don. I might need to intervene.' She walked off towards them.

***

Katy Partridge reapplied a layer of crimson lipstick. An assistant blotted her nose with a tissue and brushed powder over her forehead.

Counting you in Katy!

Three, two, one...

Good evening. This is Katy Partridge reporting live for Celebrity Sunday. We're right here on the red carpet for one of the most glittering events of the year, the Vanity Fair Women of the Year Awards. Stars of stage and screen are out in force tonight to recognize and celebrate some of the most influential women in Great Britain. Looking stunning in floor length black velvet and Asprey diamonds, Bernadette Maloney arrived earlier, flanked by the two men in her life, her son Liam Spicer and boyfriend Benedict Hardy. She is hotly tipped to win an award tonight. Rumours that Bernadette and Benedict are engaged to be married have been strongly denied by her agent...

Printed in Poland
by Amazon Fulfillment
Poland Sp. z o.o., Wrocław

49189441R00190